THE BARBARY MARK

Anne Cleeland

ARTEMIS
—PRESS—

ISBN: 0998595616
ISBN 13: 9780998595610

*For Tammy's mom, who loves a redemption
story; and for all others like her*

CHAPTER ONE

With a fine show of bravado, Nonie lifted her chin to address the ring of stone-faced men who confronted her. "I am not without supporters, you know. They will pay a handsome ransom." Inwardly, she winced, because she shouldn't have said "handsome ransom"—too confusing for non-English speakers. Instead, she amended, "I'm a very valuable prisoner, I assure you."

Their harsh expressions did not change, and she was tempted to lay claim to a noble bloodline, but then decided it wouldn't wash—not with this complexion of hers. The Irish aristocracy would never allow such a wanton mass of freckles to see the light of day, although Tanny had always tried to console Nonie by claiming the freckles were angel's kisses. If this was indeed the case, however, the angels had been ridiculously over-fond, and no amount of cucumber paste had ever made the slightest—*slightest* difference.

A pox on my unfortunate complexion, Nonie thought for the thousandth time; else I could have passed as a baroness, and postponed this reckoning until such time as I could think of a better excuse to spare my miserable hide.

One of the men leaned in to murmur something in Arabic to the Dey—which seemed an ominous development—and so she pulled her thoughts away from cucumber paste, and back to the situation at hand. It would be best to pay attention; matters were grim—or at least, grimmer than her usual.

She stood, bedraggled—and certainly bedeviled—as she tried to avoid looking into the flames of the two fire-trays that illuminated the chamber, one on either side of the dais. Likes the dramatic, she concluded, as she gazed upon the Dey of Algiers, seated on his elaborate peacock chair. The Mughals were a superstitious bunch; perhaps it could be used to her advantage—if she managed to survive the night's events, that was.

The crackling flames illuminated the faces of the men who stood on either side of their leader; ruthless men, who served at the Dey's pleasure, in this particular circle of hell. One appeared to be minor official, and the other—the one who'd spoken to the Dey—was undoubtedly the Agha, who handled the Dey's slave trade. A hard-eyed, dissipated man as befit his trade; and fleshy besides—that type were always wont to bleed overmuch, in her experience. And the tall gentleman who stood behind him would appear to be the famed necromancer—although she couldn't be certain, having little experience with men of that stripe. He was dressed in a dark, long-sleeved *djellaba* and was smoking a thin pipe, looking mysterious and very much the part. Rather handsome, if you liked your men lean, and hawkish. He hadn't spoken, but only observed dispassionately, as the Agha took the lead in questioning her.

"I will give you one last chance to tell me; where did you find these?"

With unmistakable menace, the Agha approached her, lifting a long, double strand of large pearls, which glistened in the flickering firelight. Through their loops, she could see the necromancer, watching her with his unreadable dark gaze, as the smoke from his pipe curled around his head. Thoughtfully, her own gaze rested for a moment on the brooch pinned to the front of his turban, the square, golden cross design embedded with rubies. "The pearls were given to me by the ship's captain—although 'given' is perhaps not the right word; 'lent' is more apt, being as how there was no question but that I would have to give them back."

As she recited the story, she considered her options; she'd never pass muster as a concubine—her hair must look like she'd been pulled through a bush backwards. Instead she'd have to convince them she was too valuable to execute outright, and tell a tale of sunken treasure. "There are plenty more pearls where that came from," she disclosed in an artless manner, pausing to wring the sea water from her skirts. "There was an entire chest, brimful of them."

At this, the Agha glanced over at the Dey with a significant look, and then continued his pacing. "You are English?"

"Good God," Nonie exclaimed, horrified. "Bite your tongue; I am as Irish as the day is long."

"What were you doing on a Dutch merchant ship?"

"Sinking, mostly." She paused, then added fairly, "And drinking a great deal of wine, before that. I confess it has occurred to me that the two events are not unrelated."

"What happened to the captain—and the crew?"

She spread her hands. "I've no idea—and is it fair that they left me to fend for my poor self, I ask you? No, it is not; not a twinge of chivalry amongst them." Indignant, she tossed her head, which was not well-advised; when wet, her fiery hair fell nearly to her waist, but as it dried, it gathered into a tangled mass of thick curls that now sprang from her head as though it had a life of its own—not to mention it was stiff and salty from its recent immersion into the Bay of Algiers.

In a threatening manner, the Agha positioned his face close to hers; so close, that she could see the pulse beating in his throat beneath his chins—not an attractive man at all, small wonder he was compelled to dally with slaves. "Are you acquainted with an English lord named Droughm?"

Nonie blinked. "I'm afraid I am acquainted with no English lords—although my neighbor's cat is indeed named Droom. He is an excellent mouser, and a Hospitaller, besides." She paused, allowing the reference to sink in, as she carefully avoided looking at the necromancer.

But the Agha did not appreciate the change of subject, and leaned in, his beady eyes narrowing. "Where—exactly—did the ship sink?"

"My mother didn't raise a fool," she protested. "I'll first need assurances that you are not going to do me in."

The Dey, who had been watching without comment, now made an impatient gesture toward the necromancer from the depths of his chair. "Enough; find out what she knows."

"Very well," said the tall figure at the back. "Bring her along."

A guard stepped forward to seize Nonie's arm, and she was marched down the marbled hallway in the wake of the retreating necromancer, her trailing skirts leaving a wet mark on the tiled floor. "Are you going to cast a spell on me?" she asked with great interest. "Can you erase my freckles, while you are about it?"

"Silence," cautioned the guard, with a jerk on her arm.

"Good luck, with keeping the likes of me silent," she replied, almost kindly. "Better men than you have tried."

After a few turnings, the necromancer led them through a Moorish arch and into a well-appointed antechamber, where they were met by beautiful young woman, dressed in a silken *kaftan*. With a word, the necromancer dismissed the guard, and then the girl, who seemed rather surprised, but bowed her head and retreated on silent feet, steepling her hands after slanting a quick, covert glance at Nonie.

Watching the graceful girl close the double doors behind her, Nonie offered, "Now look what you've done—she'll think she been thrown over for the likes of me, poor thing."

The necromancer ignored the comment, and then proceeded through a side door, off the antechamber. After hesitating for a moment, Nonie decided that she may as well follow him, and cautiously emerged in what appeared to be a stillroom, featuring shelves stocked with jars and canisters, the scent mildly reminiscent of camphor, mixed with herbs. As he lit the lantern on the mixing table, he asked, "Why are you here?"

She brushed damp, salty curls from her forehead, and regarded him with surprise. "I'd little choice. But perhaps you will tell me why a Hospitaller casts spells for slave traders." Either he didn't realize the significance of the Maltese Cross on his brooch, or he was having a fine joke.

"I do not cast spells," he corrected, his expression impassive, as he turned to face her. "I communicate with the dead."

"Oh—well, that's a rare talent, indeed. And who, exactly, is dead?"

"The Dey's mother."

Nonie allowed her admiration full rein. "Well done; I am beginning to think you are a grifter of the first order."

He made no effort to respond, but instead crossed his arms, as he thoughtfully met her gaze. "I know who you are."

With some amusement, she raised her brows. "I suppose you are to be congratulated, then. Who are you?"

Again, he ignored the question. "I will deliver you safely away from here, but you must not come back. Is that understood?"

"I am not one to take direction well," she confessed. "It's the hair."

He allowed his gaze to encompass the glory of her curly red mane. "You would do better to disguise the hair."

"I was recently fished out of the sea," she defended herself, stung. "What will you?"

With a measured gesture, he turned to pull a vial, and then a canister from the shelves. "I will give you a potion, and when you wake, you will be on an outbound ship."

"I see. And how am I to know you will not try to have your way with me?" Teasing, she allowed a palpable thread of hope to be heard in the words—he was rather attractive, in a sinister and menacing sort of way. I have always been attracted to sinister and menacing, she thought with regret; it is a terrible, terrible failing.

Once again, he ignored the question. He's as close as a clam, she thought, amused. I would very much like to provoke him into saying something unguarded, if for nothing more than the sport of it. As she watched, he measured out a viscous, amber-colored liquid into a small cup, and then was almost startled when he chose to break the silence.

"Where did you come by the pearls?"

She arched a brow. "Lord, everyone is mad on the pearls—they seem to think I've a treasure trove, hidden away in my corset. Why is this?"

He did not lift his gaze from his potion-making, but replied in a mild tone, "You are not wearing a corset."

"Sirrah," she admonished, quirking her mouth in mock disapproval. "Spare my blushes."

He continued his preparations, his long fingers shaking the cup slightly. "It is almost as though you knew you'd be tossed into the sea."

Astonished, she stared at him, her clear green eyes wide. "You cannot think I *hoped* to land in this miserable place, for heaven's sake—at the very least, I would have filched some more pearls, for my troubles."

He glanced up at her. "How did you acquire those?"

"I told you—I was having a fine supper with the captain, when he asked me to model them for him; a gift for his wife, he said." She paused, thinking on it. "I'm rather surprised he had a wife—he certainly did not behave as though he did."

"His name?"

"Captain Spoor, it was. An unintelligible Dutchman with bad teeth—I charmed him, I did."

But the necromancer was not to be charmed in his turn, and remarked with palpable skepticism, "You sailed alone?"

Lord, the man was a one-man Spanish Inquisition. After weighing her options, she confessed, "In truth, I was sailing here on a mission of mercy. A friend has been seized by the Barbary pirates, and is now in desperate need of an extraction. So—as much as I would like to take your potion, and have all my cares erased— alas, I cannot."

Watching her, he shook his head slightly in warning. "This is not the place to attempt heroics."

"No, and my attempted heroics have certainly not gone well thus far—it's a sad case, I am."

Raising a dark brow, he countered, "Come now; you did manage to sink the ship."

She stared at him in surprise. "You flatter me, but I assure you that I am no sinker of ships."

He did not pursue the topic, but instead regarded her for a long moment, his thoughts unreadable. "If I allow you access to the *bagnio,* you must not interfere with me."

"Never for a moment," she readily agreed. "And what is it you are about, aside from chatting up the Dey's dead mother?"

As was his wont, he ignored her question. "If I discover that you have been indiscreet—"

She bowed her head in shame. "I do have a tongue that runs on like a fiddlestick."

He nodded gravely. "Yes. Your hair has much to answer for."

So—she was given a glimpse of humor, and it seemed that the brooch was indeed a fine joke. I rather like him, she thought, her mouth pursed so that she didn't laugh. I shouldn't, but I do. "Are you an American?"

He turned to take the cup between his hands again. "Do you speak Arabic?"

This seemed a non-sequitur, but she gamely attempted to keep up. "I do not."

"What can I tell them, to convince them that you are worth keeping?"

"I cannot raise the dead," she confessed. "However, I can do card tricks."

"These are serious matters." He lifted the cup to the light, reviewing it carefully. "You would do well to be serious." He peered inside, and she thought she could hear a faint, effervescing sound. Frowning, he shook the contents gently, as though impatient.

"I laugh, so that I do not weep." Despite herself, she craned to see what it was he did, and as she leaned in, he released the small vial into the concoction, with the result that there was a sudden hissing sound, and a cloud of mist that rose up into her face. Startled, she looked at him. "You can't be thinking that I'd willingly drink this?"

"Not at all necessary," was his reply.

As a roaring sound rose in her ears, she swayed on her feet, and the last thing she remembered was his arm grasping her waist, so as to break her fall.

CHAPTER TWO

A t least I am in, Nonie consoled herself, rubbing the heels of her hands in her eyes, whilst trying to clear the cobwebs from her poor head. And in one piece—leastways, as far as I can tell. She squinted up toward the small grated window, and wished it weren't quite so high.

Gingerly, she sat up on the narrow canvas cot to contemplate her surroundings and—after taking an assessment—was cautiously relieved. Having heard terrible tales of the *bagnios* where captured slaves were held, she found herself alone in a tiny, dim cell which appeared to be relatively clean—although there was a dark stain on the opposite wall that could not withstand scrutiny.

With a grimace, she contemplated her bare feet, noting that the bedraggled dress had disappeared, and she was clad only in her shift, which still smelt faintly of the sea. As she considered this development, it occurred to her that if the necromancer wished to constrain her to the premises, he'd hit upon an efficient method; an unclad Westerner would be like a jackdaw among the doves, here in the land of the Mughals, and she may as well be shackled to the floor—she certainly could not move about freely.

As if on cue, Nonie heard a noise outside the cell door, and the face plate opened to reveal a pair of unfamiliar female eyes, looking into hers. "Top o' the mornin'," Nonie called out.

The face plate closed, and after the key grated in the lock, the door opened to reveal a slim young woman, who slipped in with a bundle under her arm. "I speak English—some," the woman related in a soft voice. "But I do not know 'top in the mornin'."

"Never you mind, then." Nonie sized up her companion, decided she was harmless, and then tried to rein in her accent as best she could. "I am Sionnan, but my friends call me Nonie. Are you here to rescue me?"

"My name is Fatima—Saba does not speak English." The woman could not quite suppress her satisfaction with this state of affairs.

"Saba is to be pitied, then. What have you there?"

"Clothes." The woman set her bundle down upon the cot, and untied a string to reveal a serviceable *kaftan* and—thankfully—the traditional headdress that covered the hair, complete with a dusky veil that could be pulled across the face, so that only the wearer's eyes were exposed.

Nonie noted that her companion wore the exact same uniform, and decided it must be all the rage for oppressed females who'd little choice in the matter. "Excellent, and I thank you. I will also need sandals, and any spare water you may have—what did you say your name was?"

"Fatima," the woman repeated in her soft voice, as she settled back to sit on her legs. "Saba will come to deliver instructions, and I must translate."

So; I'm to have a keeper, Nonie surmised. The man doesn't trust me an inch, bless him; best to start befriending the watchdog. "You speak excellent English, Fatima; where did you learn?"

"I lived in France," the woman replied serenely. "Before I came here."

Nonie nodded, and decided it would be bad manners to probe into Fatima's life before she was captured by the infamous Barbary pirates, who'd served as the terror of the Mediterranean for hundreds of years. Between the British and the Americans, various attempts had been made to put a stop to the pirates' slave trade, but this corner of Algiers was mainly known for lawlessness and dark deeds—some deeds darker than others.

With gentle insistence, Nonie prompted, "Do you suppose I could have a bit of water?"

"It is coming," Fatima assured her, her soft eyes concerned. "We were waiting for you to wake."

Thus reminded, Nonie observed in a tart tone, "Yes; your master has much to answer for—knocking people out, willy-nilly."

With a stricken expression, Fatima could make no immediate response, and Nonie contemplated the interesting fact that anyone thought this sweet young woman stood any chance at all against the likes of her wily self. Her thoughts were interrupted when once again, the key turned in the lock, and the necromancer's slave girl entered, carrying a basket over her arm. "Ah—this must be Saba. It is a shame we have nowhere for everyone to sit."

Upon closer inspection, Nonie found that her impression from the night before was not mistaken; the newcomer was exotically beautiful, with dark hair that cascaded down her back, and an impressive figure beneath her *kaftan*.

Saba spoke to Fatima in Arabic, and set the basket on the floor. When the cloth was removed, the contents proved to be flatbread, with dates and a very welcome flask of water. As Fatima responded to Saba's questions, Nonie lifted the flask, and drank deeply, hoping the necromancer had hidden no further surprises in the offerings—it hardly mattered; she was as dry as a bone and would have sold her soul for a drop of whiskey, even if it knocked her out again. She then nibbled on the bread and the dates, listening to the two women converse until Fatima made a gesture indicating the need for sandals, and Saba interrupted to make a suggestion. With a nod, Fatima bent to unfasten her own sandals, and hand them over to Nonie. "You are to see if my sandals are acceptable."

They were indeed a good fit, albeit not of the highest quality. "I am sorry, Fatima—it hardly seems fair."

"No—no," the woman explained. "I speak English, so I am to take your place when you are away." Shaking her head with regret she added, "I am not as tall, and my face is not as pale, but there was no one else, so I will stay in the bed, and keep myself covered."

Nonie nodded, processing this surprising revelation. Apparently, the necromancer had wanted to know if she spoke Arabic so as to find a suitable substitute to sit in her cell. Which also meant she was to be allowed out—a relief, all in all; she'd had a twinge of alarm, after the duplicitous mist-in-the-face incident.

Saba made a comment, which Fatima translated. "You must not go anywhere, or say anything, until you have been given instruction."

That will be the day—when I take orders from a necromancer's floozy, thought Nonie with amusement.

"Do you understand?" asked Fatima with some anxiety, when Nonie did not immediately answer.

"Of course, I understand, Fatima—you speak English very well." She leaned in to confide, "I don't think Saba likes me very much—perhaps she is worried I will steal her master away."

Poor Fatima met Nonie's eyes in a frozen panic, and so she hastened to add, "Don't tell her I said it—I was only teasing, Fatima." Not razor-sharp, was our Fatima.

After another remark to Fatima, Saba gracefully rose, tapped a signal on the door, and then departed in a whisper of silken trousers. "I'm to stay here, with you," Fatima explained unnecessarily.

"Well, that's a blow to the back," Nonie remarked in a mild tone, as she carefully balanced on the flimsy cot to examine the window. "How am I to connect with my contact, whilst you are underfoot?"

"Pardon?"

"Although—come to think of it—that may be your very purpose; to thwart me at every turn." She turned around to smile an apology to Fatima. "I'm always talking to myself; pay no attention, Fatima."

"Yes, miss."

"Nonie."

"Nonie." The woman smiled with shy pleasure.

On tiptoe, Nonie returned to the window, and was testing the strength of the bars, when she heard the door open and then close behind her. Without looking at her latest visitor, she remarked, "Lord; the Cat n' Fiddle back home is not as busy as this wretched cell."

"Miss Sionnan Rafferty, I believe."

"Not quite." She craned to peer without much success into the narrow alley below—it was a pity she wasn't a bit taller, or the window a bit lower. "That's how it's spelled, but the Gaelic is pronounced with a 'sh,' which causes no end of confusion. I was named after the goddess of feckless redheads."

"Her friends call her Nonie," Fatima offered tentatively.

"But it's Sionnan, to you," she corrected, and finally threw him a quick glance over her shoulder. "Am I to be coshed-out again?"

With a quiet word, the necromancer excused Fatima, and then stood silently as Nonie continued reviewing the alley below with her back to him—there was not a lot of activity to observe in the heat of the day, but mainly she was intent on ignoring her visitor.

After a few moments of silence, he offered, "There is an Irish prisoner in the *bagnio*—Mr. James O'Hay."

At this, she turned to face him, balancing atop the cot, and portraying no consciousness of the fact she stood barefoot, and in her shift. "All right—you win; I am all attention."

"Is he your object?"

She regarded him thoughtfully, and made no answer.

He crossed his arms, the long black sleeves of the *djellaba* hanging almost to the floor. "Come—you must see I had little choice, if I were to make it believable."

"I suppose I had hoped for a professional courtesy, between us."

His dark eyes held hers. "On the other hand, I was able to report to the Dey that although I could coax no information from you about the pearls, you spoke of a dangerous moon that presaged the shipwreck."

"Oh-ho," she exclaimed, intrigued despite herself. "So, I'm an oracle, am I?"

He bowed his head in acknowledgment.

She had to grudgingly admit that this appeared to be a masterstroke. "Excellent; hopefully, I'll survive long enough to rescue Jamie, before the Dey realizes that it is all a sham."

"Yes; but in return, I will have your promise that you will leave and not return."

"Don't worry, my friend; I won't be able to shake the dust off my sandals fast enough." Cocking her head, she considered him for a moment. "Tell me more about your schemings—which are impressive, I must say, and especially on such short notice. Where will I be going, whilst poor Fatima is slated to take my place?"

"Wherever you'd like."

Suspicious, she contemplated him with a skeptical eye. "And why would the likes of you help the likes of me?'

"Professional courtesy," he responded in a grave tone.

She laughed aloud, unable to resist. Why, I believe I shall have to steal Saba's master, she thought—these still waters appear to run very deep. "Are you Armenian?"

His lips curved into a small smile—apparently, he was also unable to resist. "Is it your intention to go through the alphabet?"

"I am not good at guessing," she admitted. "All other accents sound similarly strange to me."

"I will help you, and I would only ask that you do not interfere with what I do here."

"Perish the thought." She thought about it for a moment, in the musty silence of the cell, with the bright sunlight slanting through the tiny window. "And what—exactly—is it that you do here?"

"You will have an audience with the Dey, soon," he replied in a non-explanation. "Follow my lead, when you do."

"Can I see Jamie, today?"

She detected a trace of sympathy in his eyes, which in turn made her lose her train of thought for a moment—truly, he had lovely eyes. "It would be best to wait a day or two, so that suspicions are not aroused. Can you do this?"

Although it seemed she'd little choice, she could not be easy about the delay. "It's just that Jamie's not one to handle prison very well, and the sooner I can pull him out of this miserable place, the better."

"Of course. It does not appear that he is suffering, from what I have learned."

"Well then; you relieve my mind."

Apparently, he was not fooled by her mild reply. "Patience, please—do not attempt the window, it is a long fall."

Dimpling, she teased, "You will goad me into trying, with such a remark."

He regarded her for a long moment. "Remember that you will be needed to make prophecies."

"Lord; I can hardly wait."

With a final, amused glance, he turned and left.

I believe he fancies me, despite himself, she thought with no small sense of satisfaction, as she leapt lightly to the floor. *And what a stroke of luck, to be styled as the necromancer's assistant; Jamie and I will be home in time for Christmas.*

CHAPTER THREE

After an uneventful evening, the following morning Nonie was informed by Fatima that she was to be moved to new quarters—it seemed that the necromancer was indeed worried she'd attempt an escape out the window. Therefore, it was with a great sense of satisfaction that she was escorted by two taciturn guards through the ancient Kasbah area, into a different building that seemed to be in closer proximity to the Dey's palace.

The room featured a moderate-sized arched window, and a fire grate, although why anyone would willingly start a fire was beyond her—it was like living on the sun in this miserable place, and she'd never complain about chilly London again. There was also a dressing screen, and a bedstead with a straw mattress—almost like home, if home was a notorious prison, where graft and corruption ran rampant.

Fortunately, she appeared to have landed on the right side of the graft and corruption—although the payout was as yet unclear. She was honest enough to admit she was mightily attracted to the necromancer, but had no desire to be the latest in a fleet of concubines, which was the way that powerful men displayed their power, in this uncivilized corner of the world.

One of the guards met her eyes for a significant moment, and Nonie was given to understand that he was her contact—either that, or he found her fetching, which seemed unlikely, given the current state of her poor hair. To test it out, she wandered over to look out the window, and stood close to him.

"*Les jeune filles,*" he murmured in an undertone.

It was French for "the little girls," and indeed identified him as her contact. "The necromancer has taken matters into his own hands," she murmured in response. "Stand down for now, and await instruction. I shouldn't be surprised if he knows who you serve, so behave accordingly."

There was a pause, and Nonie could sense the man's surprise at this turn of events. Inwardly, she sighed at the prospect of having to deal with a contact who was so inexperienced as to allow his startlement to show. No doubt good help was hard to find, here in Algiers, and so she should not complain, but instead try to make the best of it. Hopefully he wouldn't get one or more of them killed.

After the guards had departed, Nonie sent Fatima to fetch food, and then quickly crouched to run her fingers along the bottom edge of the bedstead. With a sound of satisfaction, she pried loose a thin knife, a small, round mirror, and a pillbox, its contents rattling when she tossed it in the air and caught it in her hand. With a deft, practiced movement, she flipped the knife in her palm and then tested its sharpness with a fingertip, before using it to slit the hem of her *kaftan* and slip it within, along with the pillbox. With the mirror in the palm of her hand, she then approached the window to experiment reflecting the sunlight off it, her elbows leaning on the plastered sill. Very good, she thought, as she watched the flash of light move along the building opposite hers. This should set the cat among the pigeons.

Fatima returned with a bowl of figs, and an air of suppressed excitement. "You are to be brought to see the Dey—I am to prepare you."

Nonie could muster little enthusiasm at the prospect, as she sank into the bench to finger through the figs. "It's humiliating, it is—to be paraded about like a prize pig; not to mention I've no idea of my lines."

"A pig?" asked Fatima, bewildered.

Her mouth full, Nonie winked at her. "Never you mind, Fatima—tell me what you'd like me to do."

The woman made a fluttering gesture. "We must cover your hair; and you must try to be—" here she paused, trying to decide what to say.

"—quiet," Nonie finished for her, laughing. "I can try, but I will make no promises."

"Sometimes—" Fatima continued delicately, "—you say things, because you are not afraid."

"I suppose not." Nonie entertained a sharp pang of sympathy for her companion, who had been forcibly wrested away from all she had known, presumably at a tender age. Fatima was right—Nonie should be a bit more wary and less unserious; things had gone altogether too easily, thus far, and there was nothing amusing about this place, particularly when it came to young women.

After her crowning glory had been carefully tucked away in the headdress, Nonie was escorted out the building, and through the central plaza of the government complex, the heat positively radiating from the whitewashed walls that surrounded her. She watched the people milling about her with interest; she'd never been to this part of the world before, but found that—aside from the clothes worn—the atmosphere was similar to any other government complex she'd experienced. Some men were grouped together in serious conversation, while others hurried to make appointments, or plead for favors. And who could say that the favors they sought were less civilized than those sought at Whitehall? Although the stiff-rumps at Whitehall would probably take great exception, if such a comparison were ever made.

Once they were within the confines of the Dey's palace, their party arrived at the same reception chamber where she'd been taken that first night—all onyx and ivory floors, with the great man himself seated in his peacock chair. The Dey was a thin, brooding man, wearing rich silks and with a ring on every finger, but no one would mistake him for a dandy; his face was framed in harsh lines, his eyes hard. One did not become the leader of modern-day Algiers without having successfully cracked a few heads together, and this man was no exception to the rule. At first blush, he was not one who would be suspected of having a deep affection for his late Mama, and it was certainly impressive that the necromancer had winkled out such a weakness. To what use that weakness was being put, however, remained unclear.

Several attendants flanked the Dey, amongst them the Agha and the necromancer, who smoked his pipe, and observed her approach impassively. As it was daytime, the fire trays were thankfully not lit, and Nonie let out a breath she'd not realized that she held. Not certain as to the proper protocol in this house of heathens, she bobbed a respectful curtsey, and then awaited events.

The Dey made a gesture, and one of the attendants stepped forward. "I am to help translate; your English is difficult to understand."

My English is perfectly comprehensible, thought Nonie a bit crossly, and perversely, she resolved to speak as distinctly as she could manage—which unfortunately meant she had to hold forth as though she held large marbles in her mouth.

"I am told you foresaw the sinking of the Dutch ship."

Doing a rapid assessment, Nonie decided she should appear cowed before the mighty Dey; if she continued defiant, it would not expedite matters.   She bent her head, as though reluctant to admit to such a calling. "Yes, it is true. I dreamt a dream, and attempted to warn the captain that the limmering moon would devour his fine ship. Being a reformist Dutchman, however, he paid me no mind."

She could sense a ripple of interest in the assembly, and the Dey leaned forward slightly, frowning in seriousness. "Oh? And you also foresee an attack, here?"

Here was a wrinkle, and she glanced at the necromancer for guidance, her confusion real and unfeigned.

"Speak," the necromancer commanded harshly, gesturing with his pipe. "Tell the Dey of the coming attack by the ships."

This seemed little enough to go on, but she was certainly game to give it a go—she could easily surmise what was referenced. Britain was at the forefront in pursuing the abolition of slavery worldwide, and even the late Admiral Nelson had brought his mighty navy to bombard Algiers, which served as a center of the slave trade. Tired of paying out huge ransoms, the Americans had also taken a turn at shelling the place; however, the British and the Americans were currently distracted from this noble pursuit by their war with each other. As a result of this unfortunate situation, the piracy—and the resultant slavery and extortion—was flourishing once again.

Nonie raised her face, and gazed solemnly into a distant corner of the room. "Yes—well, I foresaw an attack by warships; terrible explosions, that made the ground tremble, and the buildings crash to the ground—even this one." She paused, then lifted a hand, as though visualizing it. "There was a beautiful horse—white, with one blue eye, lying on the ground bleeding, whilst the birds pecked at its flesh."

There were audible gasps in the room, and the Dey recoiled in dismay. There you go, she thought with satisfaction; never doubt an Irishman's ability to tell a round tale. It was indeed fortunate that Lord Droughm had gone on and on about the Dey's favorite horse, whilst they'd been playing cards, and just as fortunate she'd paid any attention to what he'd said, horses being of lesser interest to her than the winning of stakes.

Unable to contain himself, the Agha sprang to his feet, and stalked over, subjecting her to an intense, hostile scrutiny. "Who brings this attack you speak of?"

She decided that a good prophetess wouldn't be well-informed as to the particulars. "I dinno' know, sir."

"She does not know," translated the translator.

The man needs to earn his bread, thought Nonie, and promptly broadened her accent. "Mi' be the gafty banshees, an' all."

While the translator struggled with this, the necromancer stepped in—apparently, she'd gone too far off script. "It seems likely she warns of a British attack."

But Nonie lifted her face, closed her eyes, and improvised, "Yes—there are enemies who beat their drums as they approach, but there is another enemy who is more deadly; one who lives in chains on an island, and who seeks to escape. This enemy should never be crossed." It is true, she thought fairly; say what you will about our friend the Dey, he certainly has some cheek, to be double-crossing Napoleon—he's a braver man than I am.

As could be expected, this news was most unwelcome, and the Dey sank back in his chair, covering his eyes with a hand, as the Agha turned upon the necromancer, his face mottled with fury. "This is your doing—do not think for an instant that I cannot see through it—"

"Silence," barked the Dey. With a brooding expression, he contemplated Nonie for a moment, then asked of her, "What of the pearls?"

"The pearls bind the hands of the doughty warriors," she replied in a solemn tone. "Woe unto them." Prophesizing was actually rather easy, once one got the hang of it; perhaps she could try her own hand at grifting, and learn at the feet of the necromancer—although if she were stationed at the necromancer's feet, she would probably be tempted to indulge in other impulses.

These pleasant thoughts were interrupted when the furious Agha put a rough hand beneath her chin, and forcibly drew her face close to his, hissing, "What nonsense is this? Where are the pearls?"

"She does not know," the necromancer interrupted in a terse tone. "I have already tried."

While Nonie appreciated the fact that he was trying to make the despicable Agha stand down, she had her own narrative to pursue, and so contrived to look frightened. "The captain did indeed have a casket of pearls. He was very proud of them."

She should know, of course. She'd helped the captain secure the casket of pearls with her own hands, before they'd gone up on deck to join Droughm, who was trying to man the helm in the stormy seas. She'd wound two strands of pearls around her neck, and with the wind whipping her hair, they'd toasted each other with a bottle of whisky. "*Proost*," said the Dutchmen; "*Sláinte*," replied Nonie, and then Droughm had helped her clamber up from the deck to stand on the ship's railing. The captain then fired two cannon balls straight down into the ship's hull, and Nonie had leapt out over the sea, clutching the pearls tightly in one hand.

Her thoughts were pulled back to the present by the Dey, who made an agitated gesture to the guard. "Take her away—I must think."

That's it? she thought in surprise. For heaven's sake, this was a dim-witted bunch of cutthroats; you'd think there'd be a bit more naked greed in evidence—she'd practically given them an engraved invitation to go find the sunken treasure.

She could feel the necromancer's thoughtful gaze resting on her, as she allowed the guard to lead her back to her quarters. A bit more prodding would be necessary, it seemed, but meanwhile, she needed to get to Jamie.

CHAPTER FOUR

"I hope it doesn't leave a permanent mark; I'll never catch a husband, else." Nonie was using her mirror to examine the bruise on her throat.

Poor Fatima was nonplussed, and repeated for the second time, "The Agha—the Agha tried to *choke* you?" She stood behind Nonie, who was seated in her quarters, and recovering from her harrowing ordeal by making short work of the remaining figs.

"He did indeed. He is not a kindly man."

"Oh no, Nonie—he is not." The distraught young woman couldn't conceal her extreme dismay and hovered, clasping and unclasping her hands.

Lowering her mirror, Nonie plucked another fig as she raised an inquiring brow at her companion. "For two pins, I think the wretched man would have choked your master, too. There is no love lost, there."

But Fatima was not going to indulge in any court gossip, and instead offered with all sincerity, "I am so sorry, Nonie." There was a slight pause, then she added in a gentle reprimand, "You were going to try to be quiet."

"I forgot," Nonie confessed, as she polished the mirror on the skirt of her *kaftan*. "Next time."

Suddenly aware of a presence behind her, she glanced up to see the necromancer, standing by the dressing screen, and silently observing them. Fatima did not seem overly surprised to see him, and steepled her hands before gliding out the door.

"I hope I do not alarm you." He tilted his head slightly. "I wished to give a briefing."

Unalarmed, Nonie lifted her brows. "There's a secret door, then? Lord, this place *is* like the Cat n' Fiddle."

"May I join you?" He indicated he would sit beside her on the bench, and she willingly moved so as to make room, thinking matters were suddenly looking up. It was a shame her bosom was covered like a nun's in winter, but there was no help for it—not to mention he seemed very self-contained, and not the type to be peeking down her bosom in the first place, more's the pity.

"There is a secret door," he confirmed as he settled next to her, drawing his long *djellaba* around him. "It leads to a series of tunnels that have existed for many years—tunnels that run between the buildings."

This was not a surprise; in her experience, nearly every center of government had secret tunnels—so much so that it wasn't much of a secret, truly.

He reached into his robes and produced a small orange, which he then proceeded to peel with the fig knife, balancing the fruit on his long fingers.

Leaning to breathe in the scent, she closed her eyes for a moment, and smiled. "I was in the north of Spain, once—I had to warn the 3rd Division of an ambush—and I'll never forget the way the orchards smelled; the orange trees were all abloom, as we rode through them in retreat. There is nothing like a scent, to bring back a memory." In a beguiling manner, she added, "Have you ever been to Spain?"

"I am not Spanish." He met her gaze with his own amused one.

"Process of elimination," she explained, settling back again. "Although I've a long way to go."

As he continued to separate the peel, the dark eyes flicked up to hers for a moment. "To whom did you signal, out your window?"

Easily, she shrugged her shoulders, noting that he had a better command of English than she did. "I'd rather not tell you—sorry." She certainly wouldn't be telling him she did it to throw him off, in the event he didn't already know that her contact was on site. Not that he would be fooled, now that she had his measure; she'd best step carefully. She was a good judge of such things, and she'd bet her teeth this particular necromancer didn't miss much.

He made the small movement with his head that she was coming to recognize as the equivalent of a shoulder shrug—he revealed very little of what he was thinking. From this proximity, she could study his high, flat cheekbones and his aquiline nose—North Italian, perhaps—and decided she was very much enjoying this unexpected tête-à-tête which didn't seem at all like a briefing. "Do you ever grow accustomed to the heat, here?"

"No."

With a gesture, he offered an orange piece, which she accepted from his palm with a small smile. "Ah—I have tricked you into admitting you are not from these parts."

But he was unperturbed, and popped an orange piece into his mouth—a lovely mouth, it was. "You already knew this."

"You won't tell me?"

"I'd rather not," he said, imitating her with gentle irony. "Sorry."

The orange was sweet and very much appreciated, as she took another piece from his hand. "Well, I wish you would have told me my lines, before I had to parry the

Agha's questions, sword and buckler. Why couldn't I've had my briefing beforehand?"

"I am afraid to tell you too much." He ate another orange piece, and met her eyes.

He is a libertine, she reminded herself as her breath caught a bit. Do not be misled by this polite flirtation, lass. "Is there indeed a British bombardment in the offing?"

"I should be the one asking you."

This was unexpected, but she answered anyway. "I honestly don't know—the war with America has been an unholy distraction. And anyways, the British navy is not going to be trusting the likes of me with their war plans."

With a nod, he handed her another piece. "I believe you made a reference to Napoleon."

"Did I?" She opened her eyes wide.

His lips curved into a small smile. "Yes; you implied that the deposed emperor is unhappy with the Dey, for some reason."

She sucked on a fingertip. "Got caught up in the moment, I did. It seemed to put the fear of God into him— did you notice?"

"I did notice."

They sat together in silence for a moment, and she knew they were each amused by the machinations of the other, as they continued to share the orange. It's like a friendly fencing match, she decided, and perhaps I am not so very jaded, after all—I am enjoying this far too much. "And where was my friend Saba today?"

"Saba has other tasks."

I'll bet she does, thought Nonie uncharitably, and was goaded to ask, "How do you decide who is the favored concubine, out of so many?"

He met her gaze with his own amused one. "Why would you wish to know?"

She hid her surprise that he would say such a thing, and was suddenly acutely aware of the bed, only a few paces away. With an effort, she pulled herself together and demurred, "Mere curiosity, I'm afraid, but I thank you for the kind thought."

He dropped his gaze, and she was aware he was pleased at provoking an unguarded reaction from her. Not one to shy away, she smiled in acknowledgment, and shook her head. "Now you've thrown me off—with such a remark."

"Forgive me; I could not resist. What is Mr. O'Hay to you?"

Immediately, she sobered. "He is the dearest thing in this world—we've only each other, you see. I travel quite a bit—" here, she glanced up in silent acknowledgement that he knew exactly why she traveled so much, and he nodded. "So, we see each other less than I'd like." She paused, and fingered the folds of her *kaftan*. "I can't help but think if I'd only been with him, he'd never have been captured."

"Please do not worry; we will extract him, with no harm done."

With a visible effort, Nonie threw off her sadness, and smiled up at him. "Don't give him the mist-in-the-cup treatment, though—he'd hate it worse than I did."

"You will not forgive me, it seems."

She dimpled. "On the contrary. If you can master-mind my escape with Jamie in tow, all will be forgiven, believe me."

Thoughtfully, he offered her the last orange piece. "How did you meet Mr. O'Hay?"

"He hails from my home town."

"Which is?"

"Dublin," she replied easily, as she popped the piece in her mouth.

"How did Mr. O'Hay from Dublin come to be in the Dey's *bagnio*?"

She sighed, hoping such an action would direct attention to her overly-clad bosom. "In the same way everyone does, unfortunately. He was seized by Barbary pirates, whilst traveling to India." Here, she paused, and gleamed up at him in amusement. "He is a missionary."

With a small smile, he shared in her amusement. "Ah."

"Yes; the two of us are like chalk and cheese. He's determined to convert as many Hindus as possible, to which I say good luck to him."

"You are Roman Catholic?"

This seemed an odd question, but she didn't want to put a halt to this thoroughly enjoyable conversation, and so she replied, "I was." Quirking her mouth, she confessed, "I'm not much of anything, anymore—the wages of sin, you see."

He made that sympathetic head movement again, and it occurred to her that he was probing for information, yet giving up very little about himself, which hardly seemed fair—it was past time to show some initiative. "I would like to see Jamie tomorrow, if that is possible— unless the Agha has a fancy to manhandle me yet again."

Her companion's mouth thinned. "His actions were inexcusable; it will not happen again."

With a sidelong glance at him, she observed, "He seemed to be aware that you were putting me up to it— and none too pleased, if I may say so."

He paused, and measured his words. "The Agha is unhappy with my influence."

With mock sympathy, she soothed, "Well, you mustn't dwell on it; I'd put my money on you, I would."

A gleam of humor returned to his eyes, as they met hers. "I thank you."

As much as she was enjoying this flirtation—Lord, the air was thick with mutual attraction—she needed to stay on task. "I believe we've wandered away from the topic of my visit to Jamie."

"Tomorrow, then. I will accompany you, if I may— we will go early, and we will dress as servants, so as to avoid discovery."

She made a wry face. "You'll come with me? It's a suspicious soul, you are."

But he met her gaze in all seriousness. "This is a place like no other, and you may not be prepared for its lawlessness. You will invite unwelcome notice, if you are a female traveling without a male escort."

Rather touched by this profession of chivalry, she nevertheless pointed out, "At the risk of sounding puffed-up, I've kept my own self safe for some years, now."

He made no response, his gaze was intent upon hers. With a surprised thrill of anticipation, she caught her breath and thought, he is going to kiss me, and I am going to enjoy it very, very much.

But the moment passed, and he leaned away slightly. "This is a place like no other," he repeated. "There is no other way, I'm afraid."

A bit surprised by the strength of her disappointment—she hadn't been kissed in a while, and she'd wager he was an expert—she mustered up a smile, and conceded, "All right; point taken. But I will give you fair warning; Jamie is not going to be happy that I am keeping company with a necromancer, and he may try to convince you of the error of your black-art ways."

But he shook his head slightly. "I would ask that you do not reveal my identity to any—even to Mr. O'Hay.

We do not wish to attract attention, or the Dey may take measures to curtail your freedom."

This was understandable, and she nodded. If the Dey guessed she was only here to rescue Jamie, he could lock them down, and then all bets would be off. Thinking along these lines, she cautioned, "Don't make me too valuable, my friend; I'd rather not live my days locked away as the Dey's private oracle—I must be in and out of this miserable place as quick as a cat."

"Where will you go next?"

His question was casual, his manner relaxed, but she thought she could discern a genuine interest, which was much appreciated. Perhaps the two of them could keep in contact, or even meet on occasion—with a mental shake, she remembered who he was and, more importantly, who she was. With a small shrug, she answered lightly, "I never know—I am bound by the whims of my superiors."

"As am I," he acknowledged with just a tinge of regret.

I believe he is teasing me—although it is difficult to tell, she thought, sliding him an amused glance. *It's as though behind this gravely courteous manner he is having a very fine joke*—rather like the Hospitaller's brooch that he wears on his turban. Reminded, she asked, "Are you indeed a Hospitaller, like Droom the cat?"

"I do not know of what you speak."

She wasn't sure if she believed him—but perhaps the brooch was stolen, after all; it was an expensive item, and didn't seem to fit his austere persona. "Such a shame—I was hoping to hear of secret initiation rites."

"I am sorry to disappoint."

Daringly, she teased, "I confess I have not been disappointed thus far." Except that he hadn't made the attempt to kiss her, which was more of a disappointment than she cared to admit.

But it appeared she'd been a bit too daring, and he gathered up his robes and stood. "I will not come openly tomorrow; Fatima will show you into the tunnel, and I will meet you there."

"I appreciate it," she said sincerely. "Truly, I do."

With his customary bow, he stepped behind the dressing screen with no further comment. I do like him, she thought, contemplating the screen with mixed emotions; it is a shame I am pulling the wool over his lovely eyes. But enough of all that—I've got to figure out how to secure this secret door, or I'll not catch any sleep, at night. Raising a practiced hand, she began to probe the wood paneling in the wall behind the dressing screen.

CHAPTER FIVE

E arly the next morning, Nonie found herself standing a few paces away from the necromancer, her gaze lowered and her face veiled, as he spoke briefly with one of the *bagnio* guards. The *bagnios* were communal buildings, which were used to house captured slaves whilst they awaited their fate—either to become galley slaves, or to be sold at the slave market in the large town square, depending on their potential usefulness.

As arranged, she'd descended the dark steps on the other side of the secret door to follow the necromancer— dressed in servant's clothes—through the narrow, musty tunnel, so low-ceilinged that her companion had to stoop to navigate it. After taking a final turn, they'd come upon a crude ladder that led up to a concealed hatch, in the floor of a small storeroom.

After his consultation with the necromancer, the guard gave her an indifferent glance, and allowed them entry, although she imagined the discreet pressing of a coin into his hand was the main incentive. It was an open secret that one's ability to bribe the guards was directly related to one's ability to survive here—although to be fair, it was much the same in the British prisons.

This place, however, didn't look like any prison she'd ever seen; there were all variety of men and women grouped about with little effort made to constrain them— apparently, there was no chance of escape, and so the prisoners were allowed to roam freely. Most of the inmates were European in appearance, because much of the slave trade was founded on extortion; indeed, sometimes entire villages would be seized and taken here to be held, pending a ransom payment by either the victims' government or their distraught relatives. In the course of her travels, Nonie had necessarily come across a great many people who were utterly heartless, but this—exploiting the bonds of family, and threatening a lifetime of slavery if a ransom didn't appear—seemed particularly cruel.

"This way, please." With a glance to ensure that she followed—a woman couldn't walk abreast with a man, here— the necromancer made his way along the perimeter wall, and Nonie followed him, noting the small rooms toward the back which seemed to be set apart as more private accommodations—even though they could not be described as comfortable, by any stretch. The place was noisy and the air was thick, as Nonie followed her silent escort until he finally paused before one of the private rooms. Drawing the cloth partition aside, he indicated she should enter, and Nonie stepped into the cramped, dim room. She made an involuntary sound, on sighting the figure who sat cross-legged on the pallet.

"Yes?" asked Jamie, as he warily rose. "Who is it?"

"Jamie." Nonie's voice was thick with emotion, as she dropped her veil. "It's me, Nonie."

Thunderstruck, he stepped to her and she glimpsed his incredulous smile for only a moment before he lifted her off her feet, and spun her around in a grip like a bear's—he was broad shouldered, with sandy hair and a handsome face that was currently the worse for sunburn. "Nonie—good Lord, Nonie; how on earth—?"

"Ye dinna think I'd liave ye here?" She brushed at tears with the back of her hand as he set her down. "Oh, Jamie—I am so glad you are in one piece."

Laughing, he clasped her hands in his. "Look at you—faith, you look like a Saracen in that get-up."

"Not with these freckles, surely."

He hugged her again, then set her at arm's distance, his hands on her upper arms. "How did you manage it? Are you here on business?"

Conscious of the necromancer, standing by the door, she lowered her voice and said, "You mustn't say, Jamie—I shouldn't have to keep reminding you."

"No—no, mum's the word, of course. Am I to be rescued, then?"

She placed a fond hand on his cheek. "You are, and as soon as I can manage it. First things first, though—I have some very fine digs near the Dey's palace; I'll see if I can have you moved over, and we'll work from there."

Subtly, his expression changed. "Oh—well, no need to move; I am quite comfortable here, actually."

With some surprise, she exclaimed, "Nonsense, Jamie; this place is probably teeming with typhoid or some such—"

"Nonie," he interrupted, and gently took her hands in his. "I've met someone." He could not suppress a broad smile. "Aditi—an Indian girl. You must meet her—she is an angel on earth."

"Oh." With a visible effort, Nonie pulled herself together. "Why—why that's lovely, Jamie."

"Who is this?" As if on cue, a young Indian girl stood in the doorway, taking in the tableau before her with a suspicious eye. "Why is she here?"

Jamie dropped Nonie's hands as though they were hot, and strode over to the newcomer's side, where he put a possessive arm around her shoulders. "This is Aditi, Nonie." Bending his head down to the Indian girl, he explained, "Nonie is a friend from home."

"Aditi; how do you do?" Hiding her dismay only with an effort, Nonie offered a friendly smile to the attractive young girl, who was dressed in gauzy trousers and a bare-midriff blouse that did little to disguise her form; it could not have been more evident that the girl was a concubine. Aditi offered no return greeting, but instead assessed Nonie with a mulish mouth, open hostility in her amber-colored eyes.

Into the awkward silence, Nonie ventured, "I cannot stay long, I'm afraid, but we should discuss your extraction, Jamie."

"I'll be going nowhere without Aditi," he pronounced firmly, and the girl wound her arm around his whilst giving Nonie an arch look of superiority.

"I'll do my best," Nonie replied, as evenly as she was able. "Is there any chance I could speak with you privately, Jamie?"

Aditi bristled, but Jamie drew her to him, and assured her it that was important to plan their escape. He then sent her away, as the girl threw a final, pouting glance at him over a pretty shoulder.

There was a profound silence in the tiny room for a few moments, and then Jamie ran his hands through his hair, and said with a touch of defiance, "I'm going to marry her, Nonie—of course. As soon as we can get to India, and find a priest."

"Jamie," Nonie said gently, struggling to sound reasonable. "She's using you as a mark—a dupe—for her own ends. Trust me, I know of what I speak."

With some heat, he defended, "I know what a 'mark' is, Nonie, and I assure you I am not a mark. She loves me, and I love her."

After pressing her lips together, she tried a different tack. "That is no missionary's wife, Jamie."

But clearly Jamie had already contemplated this angle, and was undaunted. "Nonsense; she serves as a redemption story, and I'll not hear another word."

Exasperated, Nonie tilted her head to look into his eyes—he was avoiding hers. "Jamie—perhaps you should think this through. I think perhaps you are enthralled, and for all the wrong reasons."

"Nonie," he chided, embarrassed, as he glanced over at the stone-faced necromancer, who gave no indication that he followed the conversation. "For heaven's sake; you mustn't speak of such things."

Struggling to regain her composure, Nonie managed to muster a thin smile. "All right—we won't pull caps; not now, leastways, when I am so happy you are safe and sound."

He lowered his voice and glanced at the partition. "Can you truly get the both of us out? You must have contacts here—"

With her smile now firmly in place, she assured him, "I will start working on it straightaway—and I'll let you know the plan, as soon as I have one. If this man comes to fetch you—" here she nodded toward the necromancer "—you can trust him."

After giving her escort a cursory glance, he lowered his head, and said diffidently, "About those pearls, the ones you told me about—I promised Aditi that I'd give her something special. I don't have much money, after all, and she loves jewelry—"

"Oh, Jamie—"

"Come now, Nonie; it's not as though there are not plenty—"

"Jamie," she said sharply. "You forget yourself."

He stared at her for a moment, startled by her vehemence. "I am sorry, Nonie." Contrite, he drew her into his arms, and rested his cheek against hers. "I know I've knocked you back, but you will see, once you get to know her."

She drew a deep breath, and tried to make light of this unmitigated disaster. "Yes, I've definitely been knocked back, but I'll recover, never you fear. We'll get it all sorted out."

"There's my girl." Drawing back, he ran his knuckles over the side of her face. "Lord, it is good to see you."

Her returning smile didn't quite reach her eyes, as she backed away from his caress. "I should go before they miss me, but I will be in touch."

After a final embrace, she followed the necromancer out the partition, and through the communal area until they descended once again into the cool darkness of the tunnel, much appreciated after the close, heated atmosphere of the *bagnio*. She followed him in silence for a time, and fancied that she could feel the sympathy emanating from him. "Well," she sighed. "That did not go well at all."

Apparently, he'd been waiting for an opportunity to offer advice, because he turned immediately to face her. "The sooner you can have them removed from here, the sooner she will leave him."

"Yes," she agreed. She lifted her face to his. "Is there any chance she does carry a true affection for him?"

"No."

They began to walk forward again, and she nodded thoughtfully. "No—I'm just wanting to make certain I am not prejudiced against her."

"Your friend is merely a stepping stone for her—a means to an end."

She made a wry mouth. "Poor Jamie."

He tilted his head slightly. "It is a common tale."

"I suppose." She walked a few paces in silence, and then remarked with some heat, "It is incomprehensible that men are so—so—" she caught herself, remembering to whom she spoke.

"Yes," he agreed. "I am sorry for your disappointment."

Taking a breath, she pulled herself together. "You are right, of course; she uses him as a passport out of here, so I suppose I should see to it she gets her wish. On the other hand, if he makes her pregnant, we are well and truly sunk."

"A girl like that will not allow herself to get pregnant."

Belatedly, she realized she probably shouldn't be discussing such a subject with him, although she'd never been missish before, and it didn't seem the time to start. "No—I suppose not. I am lucky you are well-versed in loose women."

"You were promised to him?"

Thrown off by the question, she felt her color rise. "No—no, nothing like that; he wouldn't do such a thing, if that were the case." She paused, and then added a bit bleakly, "At least, I would hope not."

They continued for a time in silence, the lantern making bobbing shadows in the darkness ahead, as they made a steady progress back to her quarters. "I will arrange to smuggle you out on a ship—the three of you—but it will take a few days to arrange."

She glanced up to him in appreciation, although all she could see was his shadowy outline. "I thank you—I confess I was a bit at a loss, as to how to proceed."

He nodded. "It is no easy thing for a slave to escape from here. I only ask that you draw no attention to yourself or Mr. O'Hay, in the meantime." He made a turn at an intersection, and within a few minutes, she recognized the narrow stairway that would lead up to her building.

After mounting the first step, she turned around so that she was on a level with him. "I thank you," she offered with quiet sincerity. "It's a miserable situation, and you have been very helpful."

He stood completely still, his face inches from hers. "It is my pleasure."

Lord, she thought in exasperation; it's giving him an engraved invitation, I am. Because she was an honest soul, she observed with some regret, "You aren't going to kiss me, are you?"

"No," he responded immediately.

She frowned, contemplating him, and genuinely curious. "And why is that, if I may be asking?"

There was a small pause while the shuttered dark eyes gazed into hers. "Because it is too tempting."

With a smile, she turned and began the climb up the stairs. "I suppose that is an acceptable answer, then." She decided she was rather enjoying this teasing game of civility between them, all in all. Unless she misjudged her man, he was battling his baser impulses, and if the history of civilization was any guide, it was a battle he would surely lose. Fortunately, she would be there to pick up the pieces.

CHAPTER SIX

S ilently, Nonie crept forward to join Jamie, as they peered over the rooftop's edge into the dark street below. The thoroughfare—expansive, by Algerian standards—was quiet, the inky darkness illuminated only by the occasional torch. Jamie whispered near her ear, "How did it all go? Do you think the mark took the bait?"

"I couldn't tell." Their faces darkened with walnut oil, they were dressed in nondescript black kaftans as they contemplated the French embassy, located across the street. Lying beside him on her stomach, Nonie rested her chin on her hands, and reluctantly revealed, "He knew who I was, which was a bit alarming."

Jamie stared at her in surprise. "The mark knew who you were? What do you mean—what did he say?"

She quirked her mouth. "He said, 'I know who you are'."

Incredulous, her companion continued to stare at her. "Lord, Nonie—was he bluffing?"

"No. He does indeed know who I am."

They considered this revelation in mutually dismayed silence; the only thing that kept Nonie alive was the fact that no one knew what lurked beneath her guileless, freckle-faced exterior. It was very unlikely that she'd long survive—that either of them would—once their identities became known, and they became recognizable.

Jamie was still trying to come to grips. "He knows, and he hasn't tried to kill you?"

"No—and he's had more than one opportunity, too."

Relieved, Jamie turned his face away, so as continue his watch over the quiet street below. "Then he may know who you are, but he must not know the assignment."

"No—I don't think he does. He thinks I'm here to rescue you, and he wants me gone, after that. Or at least I think that's all he knows—he's very hard to read, that one."

They watched the street in silence for a few minutes, until Nonie remarked, "I wonder if our information is wrong—it's very quiet. You do smell of fish, though; at least there's that."

He chuckled, softly. Their information-gatherers here in Algiers were posing as fishmongers, keeping an eye on the comings and goings in the harbor. The latest word relayed to Jamie was that a French merchant frigate was newly arrived on the evening tide, the ship not flying its insignia in the hopes of attracting as little attention as possible. "No, I think the information is accurate. The ship is here—I saw it myself. And it seems likely it's here to pick up another cargo of pearls—'*les jeune filles*'."

Nonie shifted, trying to find a more comfortable position on the patched-up rooftop. "Mayhap they're having second thoughts about the whole operation, what with Napoleon doing a bit of revenge-taking." During the recent war, the Dey had struck a bargain with Napoleon to supply his army with food and supplies—although both sides considered it a deal with the devil. Nevertheless, the allegiance had continued until Napoleon was defeated, and exiled to the Island of Elba. Unfortunately, the British had received intelligence that Napoleon's supporters were plotting his escape, and were gathering up riches and weapons from any source that presented itself. To this end, those supporters had struck another deal with the Dey, this time to smuggle in pearls shipped from the Orient, with the Dey keeping a respectable percentage of the profits for making the arrangements.

Napoleon's supporters soon learned that it was never a good idea to do business with the Dey, who then encouraged his fleet of Barbary pirates to simply seize the pearls *en route* from the Orient, and pretend they'd been stolen. However, in turn, the Dey soon learned that that one did not double-cross Napoleon's people with impunity; the brutal assassinations of several of the Dey's lesser officials had sent a very strong message that this sort of behavior was not going to be tolerated.

As a result, the Dey seemed to have mended his wicked ways, and was once again forwarding the pearls on to Napoleon's supporters. Therefore, it was a cause of grave concern that a priceless shipment of *jeune filles*—the code name for the pearls—had gone missing; the alliance between Napoleon and the Dey was precarious at best, and neither side trusted the other. On cue, Nonie had shown up with her tale of shipwreck and sunken treasure, but thus far, no one seemed motivated to act.

They waited, their eyes straining in the darkness, but there was still no movement below. Jamie ventured, "Do you think the mark is not coming? The place is quiet as a boneyard."

Nonie knit her brow, as she took another look up the street in the direction of the palace, high atop the hill. "I know the mark went out, and is not expected back until very late—or at least, that's what my contact told me. With the French ship newly arrived, I assumed he'd be over here, quick as a cat, to be meeting up with *Le Capitaine*—but perhaps I'm ahead of myself."

The notorious *Le Capitaine* was a former captain in Napoleon's now-defunct navy, a ruthless man who'd made himself useful by organizing various smuggling operations at the behest of the former emperor—ill-gotten goods, that would serve to finance Napoleon's next bid for world conquest. From what they'd been able to determine, the necromancer was in the very thick of the Algerian operation.

Jamie reluctantly voiced an unwelcome thought. "Do you think the mark's twigged us, and that's why there's no one stirring?"

Nonie had to smile. "I can't imagine, Jamie—you were so convincing, I was ready to slap your cheating face. No, I think he truly believes I'm here to rescue you, and nothing more."

Jamie chuckled in response. "Cheating with the likes of Aditi is my pleasure, I promise you. This is the best assignment I've had in a long time."

But Nonie warned, "Be careful, or she'll cling to you like grim death."

"No—as much as it pains me to admit it, she's not smitten. I think she's trying to make some pirate jealous. She's a first-rate schemer."

This was of interest, and Nonie glanced at him in amusement. "Well—then be careful the pirate doesn't rise up and slit your throat, for your sins."

"Believe me, that unhappy thought has crossed my mind." Carefully raising up on his elbows, he took another look around the shadowed area below. "Nothing. And here I thought we'd complete this assignment, and be back where they fight civilized wars in time for tea."

It was indeed disappointing, but Nonie had learned the importance of patience, in her line of work, and the importance of re-grouping. "I'll have to drop more hints, I suppose—Lord, they're a dense bunch."

"Or they're wise to you."

She drew her mouth down in acknowledgment of this alarming possibility. "Mayhap. I'd be surprised, but it's true that the mark plays his cards very close to his vest."

"That he does—we found little enough intelligence on him."

She thought once again about the man who had been the subject of her every waking thought for the past two days, well-aware that this was a foolish pastime, but unable, it seemed, to help herself. "I wonder where he hails from? He's very mysterious about it."

Jamie considered. "The Middle East, is my best guess. But he's mighty good at covering his tracks—it's as though he sprang from the bloody head of Zeus." Jamie shifted his position slightly, never taking his eyes off the quiet scene below. "He reminds me of the Flemish mark, a bit."

She quirked her mouth. "That does not bode well—we misjudged that one."

"Lucky no one knows how badly."

They both chuckled quietly at the memory, and Jamie added, "No harm done; the assignment was completed, with none to tell the tale."

"Not our finest hour," Nonie agreed. "Jamie—is there any chance that we've misjudged this one, too?"

Her companion glanced at her in surprise. "What do you mean?"

Frowning, she tried to put her uneasiness into words. "It's just—it's just he seems too *smart* to be involved in all this. And definitely too smart to be double-crossing Napoleon."

Jamie made a skeptical sound. "He's their point man, Nonie; the intelligence is irrefutable."

"I suppose so."

He squeezed her arm, briefly. "May as well pack it in—there's nothing going forward. A shame, it is; I thought I had good information that something was going forward tonight."

Carefully, they inched away from the edge. She contemplated their next move, and asked, "Shall I visit you in prison again? Or do you think we risk exposure?"

He shrugged. "Whatever you will; but I don't think I can mention the pearls again, it would be too obvious."

"He's offered to smuggle all of us out—including Aditi. I think I've no choice but to pretend to go along, else he may become suspicious of my motives."

But Jamie could not like this piece of information, and frowned. "And why would he go to the trouble?"

She glanced at him. "I honestly think he feels sorry for my jilted self. That, and he wants me well-away from his operations."

"All right, but let's not make the mistake of thinking any of them—*any* of them—has an ounce of human compassion. You'll be remembering what happened with the Saragossa mark."

"I won't be forgetting the Saragossa mark anytime soon. And it's true that this mark is as subtle as a serpent." Except he'd brought her an orange and teased her, in his grave way, and she couldn't seem to stop reliving every thrilling moment.

Lifting his arms, Jamie dropped through the trapdoor in the roof, and then stood to catch her when she followed him. "Do we have a timeline, or do we await events?"

She brushed her hands off. "As long as the assignment is not jeopardized, let's await events; surely someone's interested in the sunken pearls—I'll not believe otherwise." And not to mention she was bound and determined to convince a certain dark-eyed man that the world would not come to an end if he kissed her—for the love of Mike, it was not as though she was angling for the position of first concubine or something; he was making entirely too much of it.

"Off I go," said Jamie. "Don't forget that *Le Capitaine* is here, and perfectly willing to slit whatever throats he may. Have a care."

"I will, boyo—give my love to Aditi."

With a chuckle, he listened for a moment, then slipped through the access door that led out of the building. Nonie waited for a few minutes, then followed suit, making her silent way through the twisting, ancient streets back to her building. Because she suspected that her secret door was being watched from the tunnel side by the necromancer's people, she'd simply had her guard let her out by the door.

As Nonie slipped back into her rooms, she asked the guard, "Have you heard any rumors?" She'd learned long ago that it was never wise to have only one source; oftentimes it was a lower-echelon operative who came through with the best intelligence.

"The Dey is worried," the big man offered. "He has doubled his personal guard."

This was not a surprise; the poor man had heard tidings of bombardments and Napoleonic revenge, courtesy of her prophetic self. "Any Frenchmen skulking about?"

He thought about it carefully, and she could see he was pleased that she'd asked him. "There was a French sea captain over at the slave markets today."

This was of interest, as the infamous *Le Capitaine* had not arrived until evening. "What did he look like?"

The guard thought about it. "A good-looking man, brash, and with brown beard."

She nodded—not *Le Capitaine*, then.

"Should I try to discover more?"

The man was clearly eager to be given such a task, but she was equally eager to disabuse him, as he hadn't been trained for that kind of covert work—and oftentimes the training alone wasn't enough; the inclination had to be there, the ability to dissemble without a tremor. "I'm afraid you are to stay with me, so as to keep me in a whole skin. If you do well, then you'll be given more responsibility, next time."

Pleased, the man asked in a low voice, "Did you find the items under the bed?"

"You are never to speak of the items," she reminded him. "Good night, now."

CHAPTER SEVEN

Nonie watched, fascinated, as Fatima painted her toenails with a henna extract. They were resting in her chamber as the afternoon sun slanted through the window, Nonie chafing at the forced inactivity—apparently, no one was interested in prophecies or pearls today. As she observed Fatima's careful work, she asked with some amusement, "But how do I convince a gentleman to get past the hair and the freckles, so as to take a gander at my toes?"

Another brush stroke was applied with patient precision. "When everything else is covered, the men look at the feet."

"I suppose that can only work in my favor."

But Fatima would not hear it, and paused to lift her face. "You are so beautiful, Nonie—so fair. And I tried to curl my hair like yours, but it would not take."

Nonie lifted Fatima's thick, glossy braid from where it hung down her back. "I suppose we're always longing for what we don't have."

"Yes." With a smile, the woman placed a gentle hand on her own bosom. "I am envious of Saba."

"Yes, Saba has an impressive set." Nonie's tone was tart; she did not want to think of Saba and her impressive set, or who benefited from their undeniable impressiveness.

Tentatively, Nonie wriggled her toes, whilst Fatima began working on the other foot. "Saba comes to visit, soon. She will have messages for you."

"I'll try to possess my soul in patience, then. Are there any other visitors I'll be having?" In truth, she was hoping for one in particular; there'd been no word from the necromancer today, and she'd had no news as to his whereabouts.

Knowing exactly to whom she referred, Fatima glanced at her in apology, as she gathered up her utensils. "My lord is resting, today."

Suddenly alert, Nonie wondered if perhaps the activity she and Jamie had waited for in vain, last night, had taken place elsewhere—his intelligence may have been incomplete, or confused. With a casual air, Nonie propped her painted toes on the bedstead. "Was he up late then, last night?"

"Yes—he is very important." With some pride, Fatima leaned in to confide, "The Dey often sends for him, and heeds his advice."

Nonie decided she may as well see if any information could be harvested from Fatima, although it seemed clear that the woman was not one who would be trusted with any important information. "Do you know of any foreigners, visiting over at the Dey's court? I've heard there are some Frenchmen wandering about—have you heard the same?"

Fatima's smooth brow furrowed in confusion. "There are always Frenchmen at the embassy. I have friends, among the servants."

"Ah—I had forgotten you are French, Fatima, and I won't hold it against you; your wretched emperor has caused me no end of trouble."

"Oh, he was not my emperor, Nonie."

Intrigued, Nonie slanted her quick glance—it was the first time she'd heard an edge of sharpness in Fatima's tone. "Well then, I stand corrected. Do you know of anyone newly arrived at the embassy, then? I'm dying for a good gossip."

Fatima's soft eyes registered regret, as she shook her head. "I do not."

Nonie nodded, thinking it unlikely that anyone would entrust sweet Fatima with any state secrets, and in any event, the young woman was not in a position to observe events—not like her own contact, who seemed to be keeping track of the comings and goings even though it wasn't his job. In a way, the guard's earnestness reminded her of Fatima, and she wondered if the woman's status as a slave meant she could not pursue a relationship—perhaps even a marriage. With a gleam, she teased, "The guard who is posted at the door—he seems a fine fellow."

Ah—this evoked a definite reaction, and the other woman met Nonie's eyes almost eagerly. "Oh, yes—he is so strong."

Nonie leaned in, and suggested in a meaningful tone, "Perhaps you should send a smile his way."

The woman nodded, her eyes shining. "Would you like me to discover his name for you?"

Leaning back again, Nonie laughed aloud, and flexed her painted toes. "I'm afraid you misunderstand, Fatima; I was wondering if *you* might like him."

The other woman shook her head in abject surprise. "Oh, no, Nonie; I am married, and I cannot seek out another man—it is forbidden."

This was an unexpected disclosure, and Nonie stared at her in wonder. "Oh; I did not know you were married. I beg your pardon—" Something in the woman's eyes— a trace of bewilderment—sounded an alarm in Nonie's mind. "Who is your husband, Fatima?"

With a slight frown between her brows, Fatima offered with some confusion, "My lord. My lord is my husband."

With a supreme effort, Nonie managed not to fall out of her chair. "Oh; oh—I was not aware of this. How—how very interesting."

Touching Nonie's knee gently, Fatima leaned in, and said in her soft voice, "He said you have suffered a disappointment, and I should try to cheer you."

For a moment, Nonie thought she would surely strangle on the bitter knowledge that the necromancer was discussing her personal problems with Fatima, but almost immediately calmed herself; the woman could not be faulted—indeed, she had shown great patience in witnessing the closeted meetings between Nonie and the aforementioned husband. "Thank you," she managed, and wished she weren't so very disappointed—it was not as though there had been any possibility of anything more than a short-term flirtation. Perhaps she should indeed have another look at the guard outside the door.

"Saba, also."

Reining in her wandering thoughts, Nonie looked at her blankly. "Saba?"

"Saba is a wife."

"*Imigh leat*," breathed Nonie, finding this blow, hard on the last one, difficult to sustain.

"Pardon?"

"How many does the man have, then?"

"Three," Fatima answered, then added with quiet pride, "Only I can speak English."

Gazing out the window, Nonie firmly came to grips with her acute disappointment, which seemed all out of proportion to the situation, for heaven's sake. "What is your lord's name?" The words came out without conscious thought—although why it mattered was not clear.

"Tahriz," Fatima disclosed in a doubtful tone. "But you must not say; you are a woman, and cannot—"

"No—I won't. I was just curious, is all."

Aware that she had erred, in some unexplained way, Fatima hesitated for a moment, then offered, "May I brush your hair, Nonie?"

With a half-smile, Nonie teased, "Have at it, and good luck to you."

Taking up a brush, the woman stood behind her as Nonie sank into the chair, and let the rhythmic strokes pull her head back, as the brush worked its way through the resistance of her curls. It is lucky you found out, lass, she thought; before you became more invested—although you should never have been tempted in the first place. He is a mark, and you'd best remember your assignment, and that we're trying to stop a bloodthirsty tyrant, here, not dally about, entertaining romantic notions which may serve to interfere—ouch—with your work. You'd hate to be in a position where you might try to protect him at the risk of your assignment—unthinkable, and shame on you.

All tangles vanquished, the brush crackled through her hair, and she closed her eyes and enjoyed the sensation, trying to remember the last time anyone had been brave enough to brush it. Tanny, perhaps, back in New Ross, when she and Jamie and the others—don't be thinking about it, she warned herself abruptly. Not now—not on top of this other bout of bad news.

Opening her eyes, she observed Saba, watching from a small distance, her impressive breasts a bit more constrained, this time, in a very pretty silver tunic, tied at the sleeves and the neck. "Why, it's the missus," Nonie observed, sitting up. "Or at least a sampling."

Saba spoke to Fatima, who translated. "She has spoken to your friend in the *bagnio,* and you will be taken to visit with him, away from the girl."

"That is excellent, Saba, and I thank you."

Saba lifted her chin, eyes flashing, and said something in a sharp tone. Fatima translated, "She says the girl is a bad girl."

"You are exactly right," Nonie retorted in agreement, mollified that the beautiful Saba was apparently taking her side in this fictitious lover's tiff. "What is wrong with the man, that he would be so taken in, I ask you?"

With a turn of her head, Saba listened intently to Fatima, and then nodded vigorously. Her graceful hands gesturing, she added a few impassioned phrases whilst Fatima tried to keep up. "He is too naïve, and he cannot see past the bed."

Leaning toward Saba, Nonie punctuated her agreement with a finger. "Aye—that's it on the nail's head.

The foolish man cannot see past the bed." The two girls sat and fulminated together, and it occurred to Nonie that Saba seemed a little too interested in this faux contretemps. Leave it to Jamie, she thought, hiding a smile. Now I'll have to run interference, to save one of the necromancer's many marriages from an Irishman's wily charms.

Calming down only with an effort, Saba continued while Fatima translated. "My lord will come late tonight—he asks that you await him, and remain dressed, so that you may leave the building."

Nonie flexed her toes. "Lucky my toenails are painted—perhaps I can steal Jamie back."

Fatima said sincerely, "He sounds very foolish, this Jamie."

Foolish like a fox, thought Nonie, and did her best to appear thwarted in love.

CHAPTER EIGHT

It was past midnight, when Nonie heard a discreet tapping behind the screen—I should lie naked on the bed, and see if we can stir up a reaction, she thought uncharitably, but instead said softly, "Yes—come in; I am awake."

The necromancer entered, dressed as a guard again, and despite herself, she felt a pang of regret upon seeing him, as she stood to fasten on the hated headdress. You hardly know him, you nodcock, she scolded—take hold of yourself and recall, if you please, what is at stake.

When she stood ready to leave, however, her companion did not move toward the secret door, but instead stood still, regarding her with an air of concern. "What has happened?"

In the process of concocting a mild response, somehow other words came out. "I have discovered you have multiple wives." So much for discretion—it was hard to believe she was considered a decent spy, in some circles. "It is a grievous blow."

He looked into her eyes for a moment, his own holding a trace of some unidentified emotion. Why, I think I've finally thrown him, she thought; and I can't be happy about it, because I should never have said such a thing to begin with.

He tilted his head slightly, in his now-familiar manner. "It is the way of things."

"It is indeed—at least hereabouts, and I will say no more." She adopted a teasing tone, lest she give him the impression that she'd transferred her affections from Jamie—another reason she'd been a fool to make such a confession to him. Besides, there was no point in batting her eyes at him in the first place; she was not going to tie her star to a Muslim man with multiple wives who was willing to double-cross Napoleon—although this last was more an asset which could be toted up in his favor, despite its recklessness. It was strange enough that she felt they were so compatible; obviously, they inhabited different worlds, and if anyone thought for an instant that she would be willing to live in this miserable backwater, they were very much mistaken.

With her poise firmly restored, she asked, "Shall we go?"

She had the impression he was going to say something, but then thought the better of it. "Yes. Please follow me."

As they passed through the embedded door, she observed, "It that an orange, that I'm scenting?"

He dropped his chin in acknowledgement and silently drew an orange from within his robe—apparently, he would have shared it with her, but for her unruly tongue.

As she followed him down the crude steps, she found that her unruly tongue had no intention of behaving itself, any time soon. "I hope I haven't torn it. Do you think we can we be comfortable, again?"

There was a small pause, and then his voice floated back from the darkness before her. "I have not been comfortable since the moment I saw you."

His tone was not teasing or flirtatious, but instead was very grave. She made no response, because she was being foolish beyond measure, to goad him into a veiled declaration of affection that was doomed from the start—not to mention that he was also doomed; something she should try to remember, for the love of Mike.

When they came to the juncture with the cross-tunnel, he bent to light the lantern, but instead of going forward, he paused, and looked out into the dark passageway whilst she stood beside him, in the flickering shadows. After a moment, his quiet voice echoed off the walls, "What is it that you are trying to compel me to do?"

Acutely embarrassed, she stammered, "Nothing—pray do not think—"

He turned to her. "No—not that. I meant with regard to your work, here; what is it you try to accomplish, through me?"

She stared at him for a moment, a bit taken aback by the question, and bitterly regretting her comments, which had not only caused this confused awkwardness between them, but had jeopardized her assignment, to boot. "What do you mean? I don't understand."

Leaning in, so that he could watch her face in the lantern light he asked, "You speak Gaelic?"

"*Labhraím gaeilge*," she agreed, thinking this a bit off-topic.

"As does Mr. O'Hay?"

Ah—he didn't miss a trick, this man; he was wondering why they hadn't spoken to each other in their native language, when he'd been present. "Well, yes—but mostly we speak English to one another."

There was a long, silent pause while she knew he found her explanation lacking. "I am willing to help you, but you must not interfere with my work. Can you tell me what it is you seek to accomplish?"

Since she couldn't very well tell him they were intent on bringing all his well-ordered plans down in ruins, she struggled to choose the right words. "I'd rather not; it is possible that we are working at cross purposes, you and I." It was as close as she dared come to telling him his underhanded activities were known to her—perhaps she could scare him away from his wicked ways, and he needn't suffer for them.

He thought this over, his eyes upon hers. "I see."

She took a breath, and quelled any further conversation—she shouldn't have said what she already had, and—*truly*, this time—she would say no more. "I'm afraid I have my orders."

"I understand." He turned, and led her into the tunnel, and didn't raise the topic again. She followed in thoughtful silence, a bit taken aback by his willingness to confront her on these delicate matters. She was now aware that she should assume he knew some scheme was afoot—it was almost as though he had given her a warning to beware, much the same as she'd given him. What was truly alarming was the undeniable fact that she wasn't, in fact, alarmed by this realization—she would wager her life that he'd do her no harm, come what may.

After they emerged from the tunnel into the twisting alleyways of the Kasbah, he led her into a small, gated courtyard that smelled faintly of spices and burnt oil, as though it was a dining area, of some sort. After opening a battered wooden door, he stood back and indicated she should enter.

Once within the cramped kitchen area, the lantern light revealed a crude table, where Jamie was in the process of devouring a hearty bowl of some sort of stew. As she came in, he looked up with a grin. "Trust you to see to my stomach—many, many thanks."

Shamelessly taking the credit, she laughed, and noted that his eyes strayed behind the necromancer, to see if anyone else accompanied them.

"Is it the large-breasted messenger that you seek?" She spoke in Gaelic, just to serve the necromancer right.

He laughed, and answered easily in the same language, "She's a beauty—who is she?"

"I cannot say her name aloud, because she is married to the mark."

His eyes alight, as though they spoke of inconsequentials, he responded, "Is that so? Now there's a disappointment."

Preaching to the choir, she thought, but cautioned, "Best beware; the religious beliefs hereabouts do not take kindly to adultery."

But Jamie was Jamie, and was undaunted, as always. "It's not a real marriage; not according to our religious beliefs." With an air of self-satisfaction, he turned back to his meal.

Nonie placed a hand on his arm, and behaved as though she was concerned. "Turn your attention to more important matters, if you please. I think the mark is aware that he is a mark."

Pausing, he placed his hand upon hers, as though soothing her. "Well, there's a fine kettle of fish—now what?"

"We've little choice but to press on—perhaps we can outfox him; they still seek the pearls, after all."

Jamie's gaze held hers. "He can't know what your assignment is, surely?"

"I can't imagine he does, but be wary, and take nothing on faith."

He paused. "Do you think he's a danger to you?"

After a moment's hesitation, she thought she may as well confess, "No—in fact, I think he's rather fond of me."

"Is he?" Jamie lifted her hand from his arm, and kissed it tenderly. "Don't be stupid, Nonie—too much is at stake."

"No—I have no illusions, but it's a factor to consider."

"Then he's more like the Normandy mark, than the Flemish mark."

With a trace of brave sadness, she reflected, "The poor Normandy mark; no doubt he still stands at the roadside, and waits for me to return from Paris."

But Jamie had little sympathy and shoveled in another mouthful. "Man's an idiot—doubtful he's still alive." Without looking up, he added, "Any sign that this one has taken the bait?"

"No, he seems completely impervious to hints about sunken treasure." She gave Jamie a wan, brave smile. "And

I don't know whether it's worth it, to keep pretending that I'm only here to sway you from your foolish, besotted path."

He looked into her eyes with all appearance of sincerity. "Well, that was a faint hope to begin with. Aditi knows every bed-trick in the book."

As though dismayed, she shook her head. "And by the looks of her, it's a weighty book."

He bowed his head with a stubborn expression, sorry, but resolute. "Lord—it's exhausting, is what it is."

"Do spare me the details." She sighed and rubbed his arm with sad affection. "Then you'd best get back, before Aditi gets restless, and finds a worthy substitute."

"Tell me more about the other girl—the mark's wife."

"Sauce for the goose should be sauce for the gander," she reminded him with no sympathy. "Best to stand down; it would not end well, my friend."

In the midst of this touching scene, there was a coded tapping at the door, and with a long stride, the necromancer answered. Another man stood without, and the two had a murmured conversation.

"That's my fellow," Jamie informed her in an undertone, as he finished up the bowl of stew with two quick spoonfuls. "Works at the slave market; brought me here, but doesn't say much. I don't think he's a native, but I have no other impressions."

The necromancer shut the door and motioned for Jamie to rise. "We must leave quickly, and by the other way. We are being watched."

"By who?" asked Nonie and Jamie at the same time, turning to him like two hounds on point.

"Come," he said, and indicated they were to follow.

CHAPTER NINE

After exchanging a glance, Nonie and Jamie followed the necromancer through a narrow hallway toward the back of the building, and then onto a laundry deck, complete with linens laid out to dry, and a washtub that smelled strongly of lye. At the other end of the deck, Jamie's guard suddenly appeared, and motioned to him. "Go," said the necromancer. "We should leave separately."

Giving Nonie's arm a final squeeze of caution, Jamie followed the other man. Nonie then turned to watch the necromancer leap up to stand upon the deck's wash rail. Carefully balancing with a hand on the eave, he indicated he would help her onto the low, overhanging roof.

"Quickly," he whispered, and held out a hand to her.

Nonie didn't hesitate, as hasty and furtive escapes were her stock-in-trade. To this end, she clutched a fistful of his tunic to steady herself, and then stepped lightly onto the railing, peering upward onto the uneven roof with a practiced eye, so as to gauge the best handholds.

"Go." He bent a knee so that she could place her sandaled foot on it, and then launched her upward, his hand moving to brace her foot, as she was heaved over the roof's edge.

Carefully creeping away on her belly—the roof was patched, and creaky—she glanced behind to see that he followed, leaping up to catch the edge of the roof, and then swinging his torso so that the momentum brought him up and over in a smooth movement. He's done this before—and more than once, she thought, watching him. Why the necromancer was adept at eluding pursuit was an interesting question, but she didn't want to think about it just now, as she was still recovering from the feel of his warm hands on her bare legs—you'd think she could manage a modicum of composure instead of swooning like a Derry milkmaid.

"This way." He scrambled past her, and she followed close behind as they traversed the roof, crouching low so that they would not be silhouetted by the moon. Nonie was ready to cast off her constraining *kaftan* in frustration, but had to be content with ruching it up in front of her, as they leapt swiftly from one close-packed rooftop to another, the only sound being the occasional clatter of a dislodged tile, or the fluttering of birds who were forced to get out of the way.

Her companion halted upon coming to the edge of a roof that had a larger than usual gap between the buildings—she gauged it to be five feet across.

"I'll go first, and catch you." He leapt nimbly to the adjacent roof, and then turned with his hands outstretched. With a quick movement, she untied the strings of her *kaftan,* and pulled it over her head so that she stood in her shift; wadding up the garment to throw it to him. Then, taking a running start, she leapt across, catching his hands, and then standing quietly whilst he helped pull the *kaftan* back over her head. "We are almost to a tunnel entrance. Do you need to rest?"

"No; but I do need some answers." Carefully, she took a survey of the surrounding area for signs of pursuit. "How do you know it wasn't one of mine, watching us?"

"It wasn't. It was a French agent."

This was annoying, as she was intensely interested in catching the interest of any French agents who might be wandering about. She remarked a bit crossly, "You keep telling me not to interfere with whatever it is you do, but you are constantly interfering with me."

"That is unfair," he observed in a mild tone. "I was not aware that you wished to be captured by the French."

"For heaven's sake; of course, I don't wish to be captured by the French." She could be forgiven for being short with him, he was showing no signs of having been affected by his handling of her winsome, shift-clad self.

"Then why are you so interested in them, and what they do?"

So; he'd been asking Fatima about her, and she couldn't fault him—he was wary, and with good reason. After debating how much to reveal, she admitted, "The British are concerned about this whole region—about the alliances, and counter-alliances—and how they might end up causing a few more headaches, on top of the headaches they already have."

He gazed out over the rooftops for a moment. "Do you believe Napoleon's people are planning to take a vengeance against the Dey? Perhaps replace him with another?"

She glanced up at him, wondering how much he knew about who was watching whom. "Oh? Is that what you've heard? Or are you starting to believe my prophecies?"

He ducked his head for a moment. "The Dey is concerned, and with just cause. You are no doubt aware that others have been assassinated as a warning—lesser members of his court. He fears that Napoleon has lost patience."

Examining a blister that was forming on her palm, she noted in a practical tone, "I imagine that the threat of assassination is an everyday concern, for the likes of the Dey of Algiers." She paused, then added, "And it wasn't a very good idea to try and cheat the likes of Napoleon, in the first place. He's not one to forgive and forget."

"No," he agreed, and was quiet for a moment.

It was no surprise to Nonie that the necromancer was worried about this alarming possibility; if the Dey was thrown over, his own dubious role in the pearl-filching would no doubt be exposed, and the French were on a hair-trigger, nowadays. The long knives could then be drawn out against him, and even if he managed to escape, his easy days of grifting would be drawn to an abrupt close. She could offer him little comfort, and shame on him, for getting himself involved with this cast of villains—it was well-beneath him. "Well, they are definitely not getting along lately—Napoleon, and our friend the Dey. I don't think anyone would be shocked, if Napoleon came after him."

He brought his gaze back to her, the shadows playing off the planes in his face. "No. No one would be shocked."

She shrugged. "Exactly. It's the price you pay for consorting with tyrants and pirates; small wonder he feels a goose, stepping on his grave."

Considering this, he confessed, "I do not know what this means."

With a smile, she explained, "It's an old saying—to account for those sudden shivers one has, from time to time. It's akin to a premonition of death, and there you have it."

His eyes warm upon hers, he said unexpectedly, "I very much enjoy listening to you speak."

This was an unlooked-for compliment, and inordinately pleased by it, she couldn't contain a smile. "I do it a lot, I do. Although sometimes, I put my foot in it." She quirked her mouth at him in wry contrition, referring to her foolish outburst about his many marriages.

"You needn't guard what you say to me." He said it quietly, his sincerity unmistakable. "Please."

Oh, she thought, gazing into his eyes, as the silence of the warm night pressed in all around them; oh—I am in trouble, and if Jamie were here, he would take a switch to me.

"We should go." But the necromancer made no attempt to move, the attraction thick and palpable between them.

He is going to throw me down on this warm roof, and we are going to have at it, she thought, her heart thudding within her breast. And I will have no regrets—not a one.

But he stepped back, and broke his gaze away. "Follow me, if you please."

"By all means," she responded lightly, and tried to convince herself that it was just as well—the tiles had sharp edges, and didn't look at all comfortable. Besides, she was heartened to believe he would nevertheless have his way with her, sooner or later. She could be patient, certainly; it was second nature to her.

They descended from the rooftops near a market stall on the vendors' street, and entered into yet another hidden hatch, that led to the tunnel network, only this time they had no lantern, and so the journey home was pitch dark, and disconcerting. She held onto the back of his tunic as he made his way forward without hesitation, making turns at intersections before she was even aware there was one coming up. He knows these tunnels like the back of his hand, she noted; no doubt it came from his pearl-smuggling adventures, and trying to keep one step ahead of all the villains who were vying mightily to back-stab each other.

After a space of time, he finally spoke, his voice echoing in the darkness off the dirt-packed walls. "You will soon be called for an audience with the Dey—possibly tomorrow evening. I have advised him that you have been contacted from the afterworld by Nadia, who was his sister, and very dear to him. It will enhance your value."

"I am always one to enhance my value," she agreed readily. "Help me, then; whatever happened to our dear Nadia?"

He hesitated. "She was seized in the rebellion, and did not come to a good end."

Nonie winced. "Lord, it all seems a bit ruthless, this necromancing grift of yours."

They'd come to her stairway, and he paused with her at its base. "Yes, it is ruthless. But if you make the reference, it will help protect you, and in turn, you will have a greater ability to protect Mr. O'Hay."

Why, I believe I am being manipulated, she thought with a lively interest. I wish he'd make half as much an effort to manipulate me out of my *kaftan* again. "Mr. O'Hay is in my black books, if you will recall."

He tilted his head slightly. "He seemed fond, tonight."

"I spoke Gaelic for your benefit, did you notice?"

Turning to continue on up the stairs, he made no response, but she thought she heard him chuckle. "Lord—did I make you laugh? It is a miracle—I should build a shrine, to mark the spot."

"Nonie," he said. "Hush."

She obeyed, following him, and trying to contain her delight that he'd said her name.

CHAPTER TEN

With a sense of great satisfaction, Nonie observed the stir she'd created amongst the Dey and his entourage. She'd decided it was past time to put the fear of God into all these black-hearted villains, and so she'd thrown in a reference to the ghost of Admiral Nelson, who was on his way to the Barbary Coast, and none too pleased. The Hero of Trafalgar was dead, of course, but she could necromance with the best of them.

In response to this pronouncement, there was a sudden shuffle among the spectators in the Dey's receiving room—a worried murmuring. Superstition was frowned upon by the religious leaders here, but it was nonetheless embedded in the collective minds of these people;

she could relate, being the daughter of a superstitious people, herself. The threat of a ghostly and avenging Admiral Nelson could not be met with equanimity, despite the legions of Barbary pirates one might command.

As it was evening, the fire trays were lit, and Nonie averted her gaze from them, feeling the familiar knot of anxiety that always began to build, just below her breastbone. To ease herself, she focused on the upper corner of the room, as though preoccupied with the spiritual. I'm like a bloody Joan of Arc, she thought as she struck the pose; complete to the *bloody* fire.

The necromancer stood in his usual position behind the Dey, the smoke curling around his turbaned head, whilst the Agha paced in annoyance—he wasn't buying whatever Nonie was selling, and was doing his best to discredit the red-headed prophetess. As for the Dey— well, the Dey looked drawn, and uneasy. Haunted, she decided; that's the word. The man looks haunted, and small blame to him; I hear there are assassins, lurking about.

The Dey shifted in his chair, and commanded, "Describe what it was you saw."

Closing her eyes and lifting her face, Nonie intoned, "The great man comes to finish the task he started, lo, those many years ago. He approaches, holding lightning in each of his mighty hands—"

Cynically, the Agha interrupted, "You speak nonsense; Nelson had but one arm."

Nonie spread her hands, unfazed. "I can only tell you what I saw—he is made whole, and ten feet tall, with eyes aflame. He comes to retrieve the treasure of pearls from the bottom of the sea—he does not wish them in the hands of his sworn enemy."

Ah—this caught everyone's attention. Interesting that the necromancer had been impervious to similar hints—one would think he would be frantic to recover the missing pearls; he was going to drive her to distraction, that man. She resisted an urge to glance at him, as he would probably be unhappy with her for wandering off-script. If she was driving him to equal distraction, it was no less than what he deserved.

With a menacing air, the Agha approached to stand before her. "Speak, girl; can you tell us where the Dutch ship sank?"

Finally—*finally* they were getting somewhere. She knit her brow, thinking. "I don't know—it was very dark, and I nearly drowned." She paused. "But I believe Nadia will help me."

The Dey's gasp was audible.

"What do you mean? Who is Nadia?" barked the Agha, his uneasy gaze resting upon the Dey.

With a show of bewilderment, Nonie spread her hands once again. "A young lady—very beautiful—" From the corner of her eye, she could see the necromancer move his head slightly "—well, not so very beautiful, perhaps, but very kind. She greatly fears the jackals that are circling—"

"My lord," interrupted the necromancer with some urgency. "Perhaps we should continue this discussion in private."

But the Dey leaned forward, his hard, dark eyes fixed upon Nonie. "What does she say?" he asked in a hoarse voice.

"She fears the unseen enemy; the angry man, who watches from afar, and paces in his cage—he who seeks the treasure. She wants nothing more than to deliver it to him, so that her beloved will be safe from him." Take that, necromancer-whose-name-is-Tahriz; trying to curtail her prophesizing just when she was getting warmed up.

But the Dey leaned back in his throne-like chair with a perplexed brow, saying in bewilderment, "Nadia speaks of Napoleon—and the pearls?"

For once, Nonie could not readily find her tongue. Here was a wrinkle; apparently, she was mixing her themes, and should make a strategic retreat, until she could find her bearings. "No—not especially; mainly she is worried about whether her beloved can remain safe, from the many enemies who surround him."

This appeared to be the right tack, as the Dey nodded, less confused.

After cudgeling her brain for any tidbit of information Droughm had imparted when they'd sailed to Algiers, she added, "Nadia asks that you keep to mind your betrayal by the scrivener, and beware any others who may seek your ruin." That said scrivener had not so much betrayed the Dey as he'd been framed to take the fall for Droughm's misdeeds need not be mentioned—and good riddance to an enemy spy. Now, it only wanted for Nonie to put in place those who were slated to take the blame for the next round of mysterious deaths.

The reference to the disloyal scrivener seemed to have turned the trick, and the Dey nodded slowly, his expression intent.

But the Agha was more interested in laying hands on the sunken treasure than he was in the assorted dangers facing the Dey. "Tomorrow I will take this girl to the harbor, to show us where the ship went down. We will see if she speaks the truth."

"Take every precaution to do it in secret," warned the necromancer. "We do not wish to give hint of what is at stake—or of the girl's abilities."

The Dey's hooded gaze rested on Nonie. "Perhaps I should keep her in my quarters—I would listen to more of her words."

Oh, no, no, no; thought Nonie; I can't be anywhere near you, my friend. When you shuffle off this mortal coil, there can't be the smallest hint that I was in any way involved.

"Such a move would bring unwanted attention to her," the necromancer pointed out. "Better to behave as though she is of no importance, and send her back to her own chambers."

Pursing his lips, the Dey nodded at the wisdom of this, and then bestowed an angry glare on the assembled persons. "No one is to speak of what she has said. On pain of death."

I'm going to get an earful from the necromancer, Nonie thought, as the guards escorted her—more respectfully, this time—back to her chambers. But I can't be faulted—how was I to know he is advancing some storyline that is unrelated to my storyline, I ask you? And what is his Nadia storyline in the first place, if it doesn't involve the stupid pearls? You'd think the necromancer would be intensely interested in the missing casket— her people knew without a doubt that he was making all the arrangements for the smuggling operation with the French, so surely, he must be worried; his own neck was on the line, along with the Dey's.

Apparently, he had other fish to fry, and so she should step very carefully—it was possible he was pulling the wool over her eyes, in his own turn. I'd better not be the mark's mark, she thought with some amusement; although I suppose it wouldn't truly surprise me—nothing is unfolding as it is supposed to, in this wretched place, including the extraordinary fact that I'm behaving like a lovelorn lackwit who should certainly know better.

On the other hand, it did seem as though matters had finally fallen into train—why it had taken so long was a mystery, what with the hints that she had dropped—and she should send Jamie a message to let him know the pearls were soon to be retrieved from their watery resting place. Once they were, she'd complete her task and then—as Jamie had said—they'd be home where people fought civilized wars, instead of this barbaric place, where even those fighting on the same side were constantly plotting against each other.

Fatima was waiting in her chamber, and Nonie considered how to best speak with the guard outside the door, so as to send word to Jamie. "Fatima, do you think you could find me a bite of something? It's wearying work, having to make prophecies."

With a pleased smile, Fatima indicated a covered bowl next to the hearth. "I have prepared a bowl of *chorba* for you, Nonie. I thought you might be hungry."

"Ah, yes—well, that is excellent." Nonie had no choice but to take up the spoon with a show of gratitude, even though the miserable stuff tasted like the gruel Tanny used to make, when the pantry was bare. After a bite or two, she hit upon another plan, and said to Fatima with a show of maidenly modesty that was utterly foreign to her, "I think I'd like to speak to the handsome guard for a moment—perhaps he would like to share my soup."

Her eyes bright with approval, Fatima made a gesture indicting her whole-hearted encouragement of this plan, and then discreetly retreated to sit near the hearth, and out of earshot. Opening the door a crack, Nonie signaled to the man outside. "Hsst."

"*Na'am?*"

To her great surprise, the man who answered was not her contact, but was instead a stranger, who regarded her with an expressionless face that did not quite conceal the wariness in his eyes. *Danger*, she thought, and after rapidly assessing this disappointing turn of events, she offered, "I wanted to show you my beautiful toenails. Do you speak English?"

The guard frowned slightly, and shook his head, indicating he did not know what she'd said. With an inviting smile, she indicated her toes, and the man leaned forward, a crease between his brows, to observe her feet. With a swift jerk, she slammed the door on his head, and he slumped to the ground, unconscious.

Fatima leapt up from the hearth, gasping in dismay, but Nonie motioned her back. "I have to leave, I'm afraid. Stay there."

"Nonie—oh, Nonie, what have you done—"

"I can't explain just now, but you must be quiet, Fatima, and say nothing." Still clutching the bowl of soup, Nonie quickly exited out the door, stepping over the prone body of the unconscious guard.

"Nonie—"

"Say nothing, Fatima, and stay there."

Soft-footed, Nonie hurried toward the entrance to the building, listening intently for any sounds of alarm or pursuit. It couldn't be a coincidence, that her contact had been replaced the same night she'd spoken about the ship's location. Something was afoot, and anyone working in this business knew that a decent abduction plan never involved only one man, working alone.

Creeping to the entrance door, Nonie cracked it open, and then threw the bowl of soup, still hot, into the face of the man who waited outside. As he cried out and backed away, she kicked the inside of his knee as hard as she could, and had the pleasure of watching him collapse in a howl of pain. Swiftly, keeping herself within the deeper shadows that ran along the buildings, she raced down the hill, and toward the harbor.

CHAPTER ELEVEN

Nonie ran, twisting and turning through the narrow Kasbah alleys with the aim of confusing her pursuit and staying out-of-sight; a woman alone at night would invite the wrong kind of attention.

Her object was to continue downhill toward the harbor, and then enlist the aid of Jamie's contacts amongst the fishmongers to find out what had happened to her guard—he should not have been replaced without warning. Instead, there seemed little doubt that some sort of abduction plot had been put in motion, hard on the heels of her newly-revealed knowledge of the location of the sunken pearls, and her evasion of the French agent, the night before. Indeed, she'd not be surprised

if *Le Capitaine* himself was behind it, as the French undoubtedly had their own spies in the palace, and would
be motivated to seize control of any recovery operation.
After all, the pearls belonged to them.

It was still possible that this snake-bitten assignment
could be salvaged, but there was no mistaking that matters had suddenly taken an alarming turn—no honor
amongst thieves, it seemed, and these factions didn't
trust each other in the first place. Hopefully, she'd not
wind up being caught in the crossfire, instead of slink-
ing quietly out of town.

Running on her toes so that her sandals didn't slap
on the pavement, she was swiftly moving down the long
hill when she heard a shout behind her—she'd been
spotted. Blowing out a breath, she glanced around; there
were few options, unfortunately, as anyone pursuing her
would be faster, and have superior knowledge of the ter-
rain. Remembering their escape across the rooftops the
night before, Nonie glanced upward, and raced over to
a vegetable lattice, which she began climbing with grim
determination, aware it was unlikely she could scramble
upward fast enough, dressed as she was. For a moment,
she considered pulling the blade from her hem so as to
dispatch this fellow, but she'd rather no one knew she
had a knife, and was willing to use it—not to mention
she should try to avoid leaving a trail of corpses in her
wake. As a rough hand grasped one of her ankles, she

gauged her moment, then kicked out at her pursuer, hitting him squarely in the nose.

With a grunt of pain, he crashed down the flimsy structure and she released herself to land atop him, so that she knocked the breath from his body as he hit the packed dirt. For good measure, she took advantage of his momentary helplessness to crack his head against the hard surface, and knock him out.

Listening for other pursuit, she quickly untangled herself, and gathered up her *kaftan* to race toward the shadows. They would expect her to flee, so it would be best to go to ground for a while, and then circle back from whence she'd come. To this end, she needed a place to hide.

One presented itself in the form of a livestock pen, where several camels knelt in sleep, their bulky shapes illuminated by the faint moonlight. Ducking beneath the wooden railing, Nonie carefully crouched down and slid between two of the beasts—noting that they smelled to high heaven—and waited for any pursuit to pass by.

The camel she was pressed against made strange snoring noises as it breathed, and Nonie imagined, for a moment, what Tanny would say, had she been confronted with such a beast. "She'd say you were 'heathenish'," she whispered, and then smiled to herself.

Suddenly, men's voices could be heard approaching, and she released a frustrated breath, as this indicated she wasn't in luck; there was a perimeter being set up to contain her, and they must be aware that she was still in the immediate area. Hopefully, the searchers wouldn't think to look too carefully in the pen, and for a moment she toyed with the idea of leaping atop the camel if they saw her—surely, riding a camel was not so very different than riding a horse.

Carefully, she moved her head so that she could look toward the voices without disturbing her snoring beast of burden. She saw several men, holding torches and walking spread out along the alley, as they peered into nooks and crannies, coming ever closer. It was a bit surprising that the French would act so boldly, and it was a huge annoyance; the last needful thing was to be seized by the French, so that she no longer had access to the Dey.

As they came closer, she drew her head back again, and kept very still whilst the torchlight sent flickering shadows over the camels as the searchers passed by. Then someone spoke in Arabic from the opposite side of the alley, and with a sigh of relief, Nonie recognized the necromancer's voice—it was kind of him to mount a search and rescue effort; she liked to think she would do the same for him. Rising to her feet, she stepped away from the camel to reveal herself. "Here."

The nearest man made an exclamation, and then called out to the others, and she was soon surrounded by the search party as the necromancer strode forward, his gaze assessing her. "Are you injured?"

She was touched to see that he was worried, and hastened to reassure him. "No, although I do smell of camel."

He issued a short command to the others, who watchfully surrounded them, as they began their return up the long hill. "You should have called for assistance," he rebuked her gently. "There were others nearby who would have come to your aid. To flee into the streets—it is far too dangerous."

"Yes," she soothed, thinking his concern rather sweet. "I can see this, now."

She noted that he'd asked no questions about what had happened, and decided he'd probably come to the same conclusion she had. "The French grow bold, it seems. Mayhap I should be tucked safely away in the Dey's chambers, after all."

But this was not a teasing matter, apparently, and he shook his head a bit gravely. "The French have the whip hand in these matters, unfortunately. If they wished to seize you, there is little the Dey could do to prevent it. Therefore, we must remedy this problem, immediately."

She eyed him sidelong, as they strode up the hill. "Well, if you have a plan, my friend, I am all attention. But please don't ask me to truly conjure up the ghost of Lord Nelson, because that would be embarrassing, all around."

But he was not listening, instead issuing instructions to one of the men, who then ran ahead. In a short order,

Nonie was once again ushered into the Dey's presence, only this time, they were escorted into his private antechamber, and the only persons present were the Dey himself, and his guards.

The Dey was robed for bed, and it was clear he was already aware of Nonie's adventures this night, as his brows were drawn together in a fierce frown. "What has happened? Speak, girl."

Nonie had already decided she couldn't discuss the replacement of her guard, as to do so may put her contact—if he yet lived—in danger. "I was pursued," she recited vaguely, clasping her hands before her in dismay. "It was terrifying."

The Dey demanded, "The men who pursued you; what nationality were they?"

"I do not know," she answered truthfully. "I did not think to ask." Don't be flippant, she reminded herself— you've just had a traumatic experience. "They may have been French."

The Dey blew out his cheeks in chagrin, and the necromancer began a low-voiced conversation with him in Arabic. Nonie could only listen to its tone and watch the men pause, occasionally, to rest their gazes upon her. They don't dare pack me off somewhere, she assured herself—at least, not until I've told them where the ship sunk. And I honestly don't know what other options are available; it is true that the French hold the whip hand, and if they want to co-opt the prophetess-who-knows-where-the-missing-pearls-are, there's no good reason to resist. Hopefully, the necromancer can at least prevail upon everyone to leave me to my own devices after the pearls are recovered, which would be the best possible outcome.

Their conversation concluded, and the necromancer bowed to the Dey, then indicated Nonie should accompany him into the arched hallway, where he walked with her in silence for a few moments.

"Well?" Nonie couldn't like the feeling that some sort of decision had been made without consulting her—although in these parts, women were considered insignificant, which was one of the reasons she'd been given this assignment, in the first place. "What's the plan?" Whilst she awaited his reply, it occurred to her that— ironically—she fully expected him to tell her whatever it was, and that the necromancer, for all his faults, had never treated her as though she were insignificant.

Her companion met her wary gaze with his own level one. "The Dey is not as worried about the pearls as he is about the French seeking to gain control of your powers."

"Such as they are," she teased, inviting him to share the joke. It was his joke, after all.

"So, he believes he should take you to wife, so that you are protected."

All humor forgotten, she stared at him for a moment in blank astonishment. "What?"

He shrugged his shoulders slightly. "It would discourage any further attempts to seize you by force. The Dey would then assure the French that you will be made to cooperate."

Oh-oh, she thought; this particular plan would muck up my own plan no end—can't be penned in at the Dey's palace, with guards watching my every move. Affecting outrage, she retorted, "You are *raving* mad, if you think—"

Holding up a hand, he silenced her protestations. "I have advised him that his mother would be unhappy if he took a *kafir* to wife, and he has acknowledged the justice of this."

With a breath of relief, she thanked him. "Well, that was quick thinking, and well done. I cannot imagine—"

"So, he wishes that I take you to wife, instead."

CHAPTER TWELVE

In the ensuing silence, Nonie felt as though the air had been let out of the room. Pulling herself together, she quirked her mouth. "You are joking."

But the necromancer shook his head, his expression grave. "I am not joking, and it best be done quickly, as he may yet change his mind. The Dey is intrigued by the idea of—" here he paused delicately "—possessing a woman with such powers."

"Mother a' mercy," she exclaimed, much struck. "I hadn't thought of that—he's hoping that some magic will rub off, so to speak."

He gave her a glance that conveyed his disapproval of such indelicate imagery, and repeated, "I think you have little choice, if you'd like to avoid being seized by the French."

She had never been one to accept ultimatums, but managed to keep a light tone. "No, thank you kindly. Look about you, and find someone else willing to be wife number four—I'm sure some brave soul will step up."

He made a sound of impatience. "Come—it would protect you, and since such a marriage wouldn't be recognized by your own church, you would be free to disregard it, once you are rid of this place. You cannot tell me you would prefer the Dey?"

"I'm not one for marrying," she replied firmly. "Particularly when it comes to a man who collects women like handkerchiefs."

"It would not be like that." He spoke in a reasonable tone, his hands clasped behind him. "We both know that you will not be staying here long."

There was a small silence whilst she wondered, with a flare of alarm, if perhaps he knew of her assignment, and then decided that he couldn't—not possibly. On the other hand, she had already underestimated him, and more than once; it did seem that he was always five steps ahead of her. Perhaps it was past time to set him back on his heels, for a change. "Is this a scheme to wile me into bed, Tahriz?"

He showed no surprise that she knew his name, and offered up a genuine smile, his teeth flashing white. "In part."

Pleased by this rare dose of honesty from him—and basking in the smile—she teased, "Because you needn't, you know; I would think that another orange would do the trick."

"No."

The smile still lingered on his lips, and with an effort, she removed her gaze from his mouth and shook her poor head in confusion. "I wish I knew what you were about—aside from trying to vex me, that is. How can I go about my business—or see Jamie—if I am going to be guarded like St. Brigid's shoe, for heaven's sake? And what if Jamie won't have me, after I've made a mockery of the institution of marriage?"

"You will be free to travel about as before, only without the risk of being seized. You are not one for marrying, and Jamie has shown you little consideration on that subject."

"Touché." She bowed her head in mock-capitulation. "Aye then, I'll do it—but I refuse to marry anyone whilst I smell of camel." There was nothing for it; from the first moment he'd made the suggestion, she knew that she was doomed to agree—she was a reckless, reckless soul.

A flash of unguarded emotion flared in his eyes—a combination of heat and tenderness that made her feel a bit giddy. *I hope I don't regret this foolishness,* she thought, *and if this serves as a monumental mistake, it is nothing more than what I deserve for mooning after him—although it can't be helped, he is so—so solid; although why such an adjective comes to mind is unclear,* it seems evident he is my equal in underhanded shenanigans. Indeed, she'd not be surprised if it was all a set-up, and it was the necromancer who'd seized her contact in the first place. The fact that this didn't alarm her was in itself alarming.

After the momentary lapse, the necromancer was back to being his practical self. "You will be taken to my quarters, and bathe. I must make arrangements, and then I will join you." He added, very seriously, "It is very important you do not mention this to anyone."

She was in a flippant mood, and so made a flippant answer. "Who would I tell, between here and there, for the love of Mike? You give me far too much credit."

But he could not be easy, and searched her eyes with his own. "You will not attempt another escape? I have your promise?"

"That depends on events," she replied with perfect honesty. "You shouldn't be looking for promises from me."

He nodded, as though this was a reasonable answer from one's proposed wife, and then called for an escort. As the guard led her down the hallway, Nonie memorized the floor plan—the night's events had thrown her off-balance, and she should be far, far more wary with him. That she was being manipulated—and by a master manipulator—seemed apparent. On the other hand, there was no chance that she was going to pass up this opportunity to finally make her way into his bed, which seemed as good an excuse as any to throw caution to the winds. Up to now, she had avoided combining work with pleasure—it was never good for business, to indulge oneself with a mark—but in this case, she hadn't a prayer, and had known it from the first.

I'm not sure why I am so attracted to him, she thought; but I am, and that's that. And I'll have a fine tale to tell, next time anyone asks; why yes, I was married to a necromancer in Algiers once. A charming man—except for the preying on the bereaved, of course.

Once in the necromancer's quarters, Nonie was relieved to see Fatima waiting within, and gave the woman a warm and heartfelt embrace. "I'm so happy you are safe—I'm that sorry, for leaving you alone." Little doubt, of course, that Fatima had sped to report her successful escape to the necromancer, but Fatima was not one who could make decisions on her own, and so she couldn't be blamed for going along with the plan.

"Nonie—oh, Nonie, you are hurt." The woman's soft eyes were concerned as she focused on the red and raw scratches exposed on Nonie's forearm.

"I scraped it, shimmying up a lattice." Nonie bent her arm so as to examine the area—not so very bad; she would live to tell the tale.

"Lettuce?" Fatima repeated, her brow knit.

Laughing, Nonie added, "—and I made the acquaintance of a camel, although the camel didn't much care."

Fatima smiled as though she made perfect sense. "I guessed this; would you like a bath, Nonie?"

"More than anything, my friend."

While Fatima made the arrangements, Nonie quickly extricated the small knife, pillbox and mirror from her hem, since no doubt she'd be issued a new *kaftan*, after her bath. Looking about her, she decided to secret the objects in the hem of the silk curtain, and once this was accomplished, she investigated her new quarters—the necromancer's quarters. More spacious, certainly, and a nice window set off by intricately carved arches, but overall, not impressive. One would expect a candle guttering atop a skull at the very least, or a shrine littered with mysterious relics. Instead, the place had few appointments, other than a bed and an armoire—and provided no clue as to the antecedents of her mysterious bridegroom. Her gaze rested briefly on the bed, and she could literally feel her heart leap. Careful, lass, she warned herself; it is far too smitten, you are.

As the servants carried in the bath water, it suddenly occurred to Nonie that matters could become a bit awkward. "Where do you sleep, Fatima?" Hopefully she wouldn't be turning the other woman out of her bed—unless—certainly, Nonie wouldn't be expected to join the other two? She was aware that such behavior was not unusual in the *seraglio,* but Nonie would have to let them know she was just a country girl, and not at all cosmopolitan about such things.

The other woman looked up, as she laid out a brush and perfumed oil. "I sleep in the wives' quarters, Nonie."

Curious, Nonie asked, "Are the other wives kind to you? Do you quarrel?"

Fatima turned her tranquil gaze to her companion. "Yes, they are kind—there is no quarreling."

Now, isn't that interesting, thought Nonie with some surprise; I'd bet my teeth Fatima is hiding some secret—something big. It was a fleeting impression, but Nonie had learned to place great faith in her fleeting impressions—often, it was what kept her alive. As the woman continued her ministrations, Nonie idly fingered the brush and reassessed her initial impression; apparently, Fatima was indeed a keeper of secrets, and since she was French by birth, this did not necessarily bode well. Best to keep her wits about her—Nonie couldn't shake the feeling there was more here than she understood.

"Your bath," offered Fatima as the servant girls poured the jugs of hot water into the bath.

"And not a moment too soon," Nonie laughed in reply.

CHAPTER THIRTEEN

They assembled in the necromancer's antechamber for the wedding ceremony, Nonie feeling almost bride-like, after the scented-water bath, and the fussing by the servants. I imagine this is the closest I'll ever come, she thought with amusement. She meant it, when she'd told her purported bridegroom that she was not the marrying kind—there were far too many skeletons in her closet, and besides, she was a restless soul, and rarely in one place for any length of time.

Fatima had helped her dress in the green brocade *takchita*, the rich silk sliding coolly against Nonie's skin. Her hair—newly washed, and thus more unruly than ever—had been firmly tucked under a gossamer veil, although it was a faint hope, to think that it would stay thus constrained for very long.

"Tell me what I am supposed to do, Fatima, so that I don't shock the shaman."

"You must stand—" the woman hesitated, afraid to offer insult "—quietly."

Laughing, Nonie folded her hands before her, and adopted a demure posture. "I won't embarrass you, Fatima, I promise. Is there a ring involved? I notice you do not wear a ring."

The soft eyes met hers. "No—no rings," the woman replied, and again, Nonie had the uneasy feeling that information was being withheld. She couldn't dwell on it for long, however, because her purported bridegroom had appeared, looking very handsome in his own formal garment, the matching *taqiyah* atop his head only reminding her that she was doing something completely outlandish.

"Sir." Nonie curtseyed low, with a mock-solemn expression.

"Madam," he replied, and when his eyes met hers, she could feel a flood of warmth to the soles of her new silk slippers. He then turned to say a few words in Arabic to the servant who'd accompanied him.

Nonie—who was necessarily good at remembering faces—recognized the guard who'd brought Jamie to meet with her—the one Jamie said was posted at the slave market. As the man made a polite gesture, indicating that she was to come and stand beside the necromancer, she noted in a mild tone, "So; this slave-tender performs weddings, in his spare time?"

Unfazed, her bridegroom explained, "Under religious law, any man can officiate at a wedding—there is no requirement that a *qadi* preside." He nodded toward the other man. "Jamil is someone who can be trusted, and that is why he was summoned."

With a shrug of acknowledgment, Nonie moved to take her place beside the necromancer, and decided to say no more. She was no expert on Mughal weddings, but she had a vague understanding that the bride and groom were separated, whilst the ceremony was conducted. Therefore, it seemed likely that this ritual was nothing more than a hastily-put-together farce—although it didn't matter in the first place; it was only important that the French believe she was now the chattel property of the Dey's necromancer, and therefore protected, to some extent.

Jamil spoke the ritual, the Arabic words the only sound in the silent room. With a smile tugging at her mouth, Nonie glanced up at her bridegroom, but he did not return her glance, his own gaze intent upon the officiate. A bit chastened, she schooled her features to do the same, even though she couldn't follow the words. I should do him the courtesy of paying attention, she thought; after all, he is paying attention, even though this is completely routine for him. And he did act to save me from having to crawl into bed with the Dey—not that I would have stood for such a thing, of course.

She jumped slightly, when the necromancer made a response. He then turned to her and took her hand in his. "You must give your consent."

"I do," she replied, not certain if this was what one said. Apparently, it was, because the other man made a conclusory recitation, and then spread his hands.

"That's it?" asked Nonie in surprise. "Small wonder, that you do it at the drop of a hat."

The necromancer—now ostensibly her husband, by all amazing things—led her by the hand to a table. "You must sign a document, and then we are finished."

She signed her name in the perfect copperplate Tanny had taught them, in her determination to see them all educated. "What is my name, now; do I take yours?"

There was the barest hesitation. "*Fejn*—your name is *Fejn*, but it is not necessary to use it, if you would rather not."

Nodding, she was philosophical; it came as no surprise that he used a false name, which was yet another reason this ceremony would have no import. "Now will you tell me where you hail from?"

"No, I will not," he replied with a small smile, and met her eyes, the expression in his own unguarded, and warm. Why, he is very happy about this, she thought, and was rather touched. I suppose I am too—if I am not being led into a trap, that is; regrettably, it is hard to see past the bed in the corner, and my unbridled lust for this man.

She soon realized—with a twinge of disappointment—that he was not going to throw her down on that selfsame bed as soon as the others discreetly withdrew; instead, he invited her to sit with him on the thick carpet before the hearth.

She hesitated, then decided there was no time like the present to be honest with one's newly-acquired faux husband. "Could we sit by the window instead? I don't much care for looking into the fire."

"Of course," he said easily, and took her hand to help her settle on the cushioned window bench.

In response to his offer of wine, she raised a skeptical brow. "Are you allowed to drink wine?"

"No, but you may, if you'd like."

"You don't happen to have any whiskey?" she teased. "Irish whiskey?"

"Am I so frightening?"

There was that warmth in his eyes again; Lord, she was fast becoming addicted to it. "No—it's only that I should keep my wits about me. Although a dose of Dutch courage does come in handy, on occasion." Deciding she would offer him an equal measure of warmth, she replied honestly, "I'm not frightened of you at all—although perhaps I should be. I feel as though I've known you all my life. It is the strangest thing."

"Yes; I felt the same, when I first saw you."

She looked into his eyes, believed him, and felt a tightening sensation, within her breast. Fighting against it, she teased, "And then you coshed me out."

He tilted his head in acknowledgment, a small smile playing about his lips. "Regrettable, but necessary." With a gesture that seemed entirely natural, he took one of her hands in his, and with the other, stroked the top with his fingertips.

With some fascination, she watched his hand stroke hers, and struggled for something light to say. "I suppose it is a very effective technique for securing a wife."

"Nonie," he said softly, lifting his hand to trace her jaw line. "You needn't—" he paused, thinking about what it was he wanted to say. "You needn't entertain me; you may be yourself."

Tentatively, she lifted her own hand, and closed her fingers around his wrist, as he caressed her face. "It comes naturally, I'm afraid—it's the way I deal with the world." She closed her eyes, surrendering to the sensation of his touch on her skin.

His fingers traveled up the side of her face and gently, he pulled off her veil, loosing her hair. "You needn't." With light fingers, he stroked the hair away from her temple, raking through the thick curls, as though feeling the texture of it. "I want you to know that you can trust me—you can show what lies beneath."

She decided he was very astute, this Mughal husband of hers, and opened her eyes. "I think you'd be a bit shocked."

His hand followed her hair down to the side of her neck, and his thumb brushed her throat. "No; you are so alive; so vivid—like a flame."

With a mighty effort, she fought the inclination to melt into him and disappear completely—good God, what was she thinking? "That is a very fine compliment, and I am truly trying to refrain from making a smart remark about my freckles."

His lips softened into a smile. "If you would like to make a smart remark, you must do so. Please, do not be careful with me." To emphasize the point, he leaned forward and kissed her gently on the mouth, his hand cradling her face.

Oh, she thought as his mouth moved on hers. Oh—this is going to be *wonderful.* "I'm not very good at being honest," she whispered into his mouth. "It comes from having so little practice."

"You may practice with me, all you like." He tilted his head slightly and kissed the side of her face; the corner of her mouth.

"I am *dying* to get you into bed, Tahriz." There—now, there was a strong dose of honest honesty.

"Then let us do that." He took her hand, and as they rose, he pulled her into his arms and kissed her again—almost chastely—as she leaned in and tried to fight the urge to press herself against the length of him. He obviously wanted to take matters slowly, and she should allow him the lead on this—if she didn't explode from raw longing, first.

With an arm around her waist, he drew her over to the bed, and then began to undress her, pausing on occasion to kiss her mouth, her throat, her bare shoulder. "So beautiful," he whispered, and she sighed with delight, as she pulled at his own clothes.

And although he seemed inclined to linger in this upright position, there was only so much that a body could bear, and so she sank back onto the silken bed, pulling him atop her with gentle insistence.

Ah, that seemed to turn the trick, as the gentle and languorous kisses were now replaced by the more heated variety, which she met with an equal measure of heat.

"I don't want to hurt you," he breathed against her ear, in a ragged whisper, "You must stop me, if I do."

Not a chance, she thought in a haze, as she arched against him. "All right, Tahriz—but let's not be overcautious, here—"

He chuckled, and then she chuckled, as she clung to him, relishing the novel combination of lust and tenderness, and deciding right then and there that she was going to save him from himself, if it was the last thing she did.

CHAPTER FOURTEEN

"It is a fine thing, to be a wife." Nonie spoke sleepily from the bed, watching the necromancer as he stood by the window and gazed out, the lifted curtain allowing a narrow shaft of bright sunlight into the room.

"I am sorry—did I wake you?" He turned to faced her, a robe wrapped negligently around his lanky frame—Lord, he was a good-looking specimen, particularly now that she'd examined every inch of him.

"No. What is it you're thinking, over there?" She smiled, having a very good guess.

"I am thinking it is a fine thing to have a wife."

She laughed aloud. "Come here, then, and I will reward you for such a kind thought." Mainly, she wanted to test out her theory—although she was fairly certain of her theory. It would be fun to test it out again, though.

He left the curtain slightly open, and came to sit beside her on the bed, reaching to smooth down her untamed hair with a tender expression—she had come to the conclusion that he was very fond of her hair, which only demonstrated the depth of his foolish affection; not that she needed any more indicators, after last night. "I must leave; I have pressing matters, I'm afraid."

"They'd better not include pressing your other wives," she teased, grasping his hand and pulling it to her mouth, to kiss it. "It's a dangerous colleen, I am."

She could see that he was weakening, and lifted her face for his kiss. One thing led to another, and in a short space of time they were at it again, tangled in the silken bed sheets and ignoring the discreet knock at the door.

Afterward, he propped himself on an elbow, and examined the scratches on her forearm, his dark brows drawn together. "How did this happen?"

"I scraped my arm on a lattice, during my adventure in the Kasbah last night. It's a trifle, and nothing more than I deserve, for fleeing from you with all speed."

But he met her eyes very seriously. "This type of wound can be dangerous, Nonie— wood can cause a corruption of the flesh. I will prepare a salve for it." He bent and kissed her arm, for emphasis.

With a smile, she leaned back into the pillows. "I thank you—you are a very handy sort of husband;

and here I thought your only talent was grifting the bereaved."

His long fingers played with a curl that rested on her collarbone. "There will be a fruit tray outside the door—are you hungry?"

"I am." She watched as he fetched it, thinking again about her theory. Last night, they'd made love twice, and each time she was more certain of her rather surprising suspicion—that he was very inexperienced, for a man with multiple wives and concubines. Not that she was an expert, by any means—she was one who avoided entanglements—but she had indulged herself, on occasion, and it seemed clear he was not as aware of certain niceties as one would expect.

As she sat, cross-legged and nibbling on a date, she watched him dress, and considered this inexplicable phenomenon, and her tentative theory to explain it: the women were all for show, and in reality, he was some sort of ascetic. This rather made sense; his rooms were bereft of any ornamentation, and he wore no jewelry save the brooch on his turban, in direct contrast to the other men here—with their many rings, and earrings, and such.

She'd discarded her other theory—that he preferred another kind of sexual service to the old-fashioned one—because he gave no indication that he would welcome such attentions from her. And she'd also been a bit surprised—truth to tell—that he had not used a

French letter, or some other means to avoid pregnancy; it had not occurred to her that she might wind up with a token of his affection, at the conclusion of this little adventure.

"Do you have any children?" she asked casually, lifting another date from the bowl.

"I do not," he replied. "Do you?"

"No." She amended, "At least, not as of last night."

He met her eyes, and there was a long moment of—something; whatever it was, it made her feel as though part of her was standing and staring at the other part of her in stark disbelief. She shook it off, and briskly changed the subject. "What am I to do, now that I am a respectable junior wife, and not a crazed prophetess?"

He tilted his head slightly, and bent to pluck a fig from the tray. "You are free to continue on as a crazed prophetess; that was the entire point of becoming respectable."

"I may go about freely?" She tried to keep the edge of suspicion from her voice; she still felt that there was something here—something going on that she did not understand, and it made her uneasy.

"Yes—although the Agha will wish you to identify the ship's location as quickly as possible. I would like to suggest that you be brought to the harbor later today, so that everyone is assured that our marriage is not an attempt to undermine the operation. But it would be best if you stayed inside, until then."

She eyed him, thinking this over. "I was hoping to see Jamie, to explain what's happened, and why."

He nodded in understanding. "Very well; I will arrange for you to visit Jamie in the evening, after your return from the harbor. Jamil can escort you to him, although I'd like you to disguise yourself, again."

This seemed a reasonable plan, and—more to the point—indicated he would not seek to constrain her movements. "Thank you, I appreciate it." With a small smile, she confessed, "I was a bit worried there was an ulterior motive to this wedding business, and you meant to lock me down."

"No," he said immediately, his eyes meeting hers. "I seek only to protect you."

"Among other things," she teased.

"Among other things," he agreed with a smile. "I will mix a salve for your arm, but then I must go."

After she dressed, he returned with a small vial, and they stood next to the window whilst he folded back her sleeve to expose the red and angry scratches on her arm. With a slender application stick, he carefully smeared a small amount of the salve on them, and then wrapped a bandage around her arm. She was close enough to observe his long lashes and his mobile mouth, and found she didn't want him to leave—not just yet. "Tahriz," she whispered.

His dark eyes met hers. "I must go," he repeated, and put a palm up to her cheek. "I am sorry, Nonie."

"What is so important?" She knew she shouldn't make her longing for him so obvious—she was not one to wear her heart on her sleeve—but she couldn't seem to help herself.

"I must protect my interests," was the only answer he would give, and with a final caress, left her.

Although she was positively itching to follow him—no doubt he was arranging for the next shipment of pearls—she would have to possess her soul in patience; others would watch his movements, and Jamie would let her know if there was a need to expedite the assignment. She almost laughed aloud, thinking of Jamie's shock when he heard the latest news. He could not be blamed for thinking she'd taken an unnecessary risk, with this subterfuge marriage, but on the other hand, she was now in a better position to gather intelligence, and complete the assignment. That the mark seemed determined to give her as little intelligence as possible was a problem, but not an insurmountable one; he was smitten—she was certain of it—and it was very gratifying to know that she was the woman who had managed to infiltrate his self-imposed reserve.

I am going to save him from his fate, and convince him to mend his wicked ways, she thought with no small satisfaction. We would deal well together, and I'd love for nothing more than to have him close-to-hand, in my future travels. After all, I am the wife of his bosom, now, and it's only fitting.

How this was to be accomplished remained to be seen, but Nonie had full confidence in her own abilities, and in the strength of her faux-husband's attraction to her. With a contented sigh, she closed her eyes and settled back into the silken pillows, considering different schemes by which she could extract the necromancer from this nest of vipers.

CHAPTER FIFTEEN

"All right now, ladies—do you remember how to count them up? Fatima, you must try to do a better job of not showing me your cards."

Since the necromancer had left on whatever mysterious errand compelled him, Nonie was trying to pass the time until she would be escorted to the Bay of Algiers, so as to locate the sunken ship. She chafed a bit at the delay, because Jamie must be aware that there had been a disruption with her contact, and he would no doubt be concerned about the sudden failure of communication.

In the meantime, Fatima had offered to teach Nonie how to weave silks, but unfortunately this activity had not gone well at all, due to Nonie impatience with all things

domestic. Then, at midday, Saba had appeared and produced—stealthily, and with much self-consciousness—
a worn deck of cards. Nonie had no trouble guessing
its origin, and smiled at the girl in delight. "Jamie?"
Apparently, she needn't have worried about Jamie; he
had his own lines of communication, which were much
prettier than the fishmongers.

And so, Nonie was now trying to teach the two wom-
en how to play a simple card game, with mixed results.
Eying Fatima's discard, Nonie declared, "We won't count
this hand either—let me see your cards, and we'll have
another practice round." With more patience than she
had shown with the silks, Nonie explained, yet again, the
object of the game. Saba, on the other hand, seemed
to be catching on quickly, and Nonie soon learned why
this was, when the girl spoke to Fatima.

Her brow furrowed as she concentrated on her cards,
Fatima translated, "Saba wishes to know if Mr. O'Hay
knows how to play this game."

"He does indeed." Nonie demonstrated her discard
to the other two, and hid a smile at Saba's thinly-dis-
guised interest in all things Jamie. "He bilked me of a
quid, once."

Fatima met her eyes in puzzlement. "I do not know
what this means, Nonie."

"It means we played for money, and he beat me—but
not fairly, I suspect. Here, Fatima—do you see? Use this
one." Nonie then nodded, as Saba demonstrated the

correct choice with her own cards. "But since the two of you are not allowed to gamble, we will play for boasting rights only—or perhaps for pins, if that is allowed."

Fatima translated, and Saba made a quick response, which caused Fatima to look over at the other girl in mild alarm. Saba made another insistent remark, and after a moment's hesitation, Fatima said to Nonie, "Saba—Saba wishes you to know that she is not a Mughal."

Nonie suspected this information was not necessarily intended for her benefit, and gently probed, "I see—is she Christian, perhaps?"

There was a small silence, and glancing up, Nonie was surprised to see a silent battle of wills going on between the other two, with the gentle Fatima sending Saba what appeared to be a quelling message with her eyes. Lowering her gaze back to her cards, Nonie offered in a mild tone, "It is none of my business, and there is nothing more tedious than religious wars—believe me, I've been knee-deep in a few. Your discard, Fatima—let me see what you drew." With a hand, she lifted her thick braid off her neck. "Lord, it is hot in here."

They finished the hand, and as Nonie gathered up the cards, she asked in a casual tone, "How is Jamie, Saba? Does Aditi still cling like a barnacle?"

Saba's answer seemed a bit constrained, and Fatima translated. "Saba says that Aditi was not there, at the time."

"Ah. Do we have more water? Lord, I am parched." Nonie made to rise, but Fatima stayed her, and did the honors herself, re-filling Nonie's goblet, while Saba practiced shuffling the cards.

Because it seemed a bit odd that the subject of her wedding hadn't come up, Nonie teased, "Fatima—you shouldn't wait on me; I believe you outrank me, now."

Fatima smiled, but Nonie noted that she did not translate the comment for Saba. Never one to refrain from stirring the pot, she persisted, "Does Saba not yet know that I am a fellow wife?"

Fatima's clear gaze met hers, a trace of concern contained therein. "My lord said that you would not want this to be spoken of; he said it was not your choice."

But Nonie frowned slightly, and found this revelation a bit irritating. "On the contrary; no one forces me to do anything I don't wish to do."

Fatima stared at her in distress, and Nonie was instantly contrite, touching the woman's hand. "Forgive me, Fatima; I shouldn't be snapping at you—it is this wretched heat that has me out of sorts. Do tell Saba; I am certain she can keep a secret."

Fatima turned and made the explanation, and if Nonie hadn't been feeling so miserable, she would have laughed at the conflicting emotions which were revealed on the beautiful girl's face. She made an exclamation, and Fatima translated unnecessarily, "Saba is very surprised."

After a moment of recovery, Saba asked, and Fatima translated, "But what of Jamie?"

Nonie dealt another hand, a bit more slowly this time—Lord, her head hurt. "I wash my hands of that scoundrel—look at what he has chosen, for the love of Mike."

But Saba leaned in, and spoke in an earnest manner, so quickly that Fatima was having trouble keeping up. "She says you must not blame him; it is because the bad girl is his first woman and he is blinded—"

Afraid she would laugh aloud, Nonie interrupted to disagree with a shake of her head. "He's made his choice—let him suffer the consequences."

After a pause, Saba spoke again, and Fatima translated, "She says she will try to speak to him again tomorrow, to make him see."

"Good luck to her," Nonie replied gravely. "I fear he is a lost cause." The situation was fast becoming farcical, and it was a bitter shame that she could not appreciate it more fully, but her head was aching abominably, and she felt as though she was seated next to a roaring fire. Abandoning the card game, she dropped her hand and apologized to the others. "I must go lie down, I'm afraid—I'm feeling a bit peaky." On the way to the bed, she stumbled, and clutched at the bed stand, feeling lightheaded. Lord, she thought in alarm; here's a wrinkle.

Fatima and Saba expressed their dismay, and assisted her into the bed, Fatima manning a fan whilst Saba fetched more water. After conferring, the other women stripped her of her *kaftan,* and began sponging her with cool water, Nonie too miserable to do anything other than lie back and close her eyes as her hands restlessly clutched the silk coverlet. A short while later, she murmured in protest, as Fatima lifted her head and tried to convince her to drink from the goblet. "Please, Nonie," the woman soothed. "My lord said to give you this, if the fever came."

Too weak to argue, Nonie drank, and then sank back into oblivion.

It was some time later—and dark—when she managed to lift her eyelids again. The necromancer sat on the edge of her bed; his hand feeling her forehead, then her neck.

"I am unable to make a smart remark," she whispered, licking her dry lips. "Sorry."

"Drink this, *namrata.*" He held a cup to her lips, his voice rich with sympathy. She responded to his concern, and struggled to prop herself up and drink, as his hand cradled the back of her head. She lay back, and whispered fretfully, "Can you stay?"

"Try to close your eyes," he said, and, clinging to his hand, she drifted back into sleep.

CHAPTER SIXTEEN

"Nonie," Jamie whispered in Gaelic. "Nonie, it's me."

"I'm awake." She wasn't—not completely, and to obscure this fact, she struggled to remember where she was, and what was about to happen, so that Jamie would be waking her up. After a mighty effort, her memory came back—she'd spent a lethargic day sleeping in the necromancer's chambers, and now it was evening, once again. Only this evening, the visitor was not Tahriz, whom she hadn't seen all day, but was instead dear Jamie, and she shouldn't be so very disappointed to see him, for the love of Mike.

Propping herself up on an elbow, Nonie saw that Jamie crouched beside her bed, whilst Saba hovered by the antechamber, listening for anyone approaching, and looking very uneasy. "Jamie," Nonie scolded crossly, as she brushed the curls away from her face. "You mustn't cuckold my poor husband."

He stared at her in astonishment, having trouble finding his voice. "Then it's true? Saba told me you'd married the mark, and so naturally I assumed you were being held somewhere and tortured—"

Nonie decided the best defense was a counter-accusation. "And what is it you're doing, consorting with Saba, if I may ask?"

His eyes slid to his accomplice, and he lowered his voice. "There is no 'consorting', Nonie; I asked her to take me to you and she agreed, although I'm worried she'll change her mind and twig me out at any second."

Nonie made a wry mouth. "Unlikely—I think she's smitten."

Jamie's eyes gleamed blue in his oil-stained face. "Do you think so?"

But Nonie was having trouble sorting out this unlikely pairing. "How does Saba tell you anything, if she doesn't speak English?'

"We manage; she speaks some Italian—but don't change the subject, which is, *have* you run mad?"

With a toss of her curls—which only reminded her to keep her head still—Nonie retorted, "I have not, and you shouldn't be so provoking—not when my head aches like a jack-o'-the-clock's been at it. Think on it—what better way to establish myself behind enemy lines? To save me from the French, I was given a choice to marry the mark or the Dey, and how can I be faulted, for choosing younger and handsomer? You'd do the same, in my place."

"Don't give me your sauce," he warned. "You are in a hell of a fix."

With some spirit, she defended, "On the contrary, all is proceeding as planned. I've only been temporarily sidelined, because I scraped my arm on a lattice, and caught a fever—"

"He gave you the sickness, Nonie."

She stared at him in the sudden silence, having trouble assimilating what he'd said. "What?"

Jamie leaned in toward her, intent. "The mark gave you the sickness. He has some huge knowledge of potions and medicines—he knows how to do it."

Unbidden, Nonie had a sudden memory of the necromancer, applying the salve, and careful not to touch it himself. "That is utterly ridiculous—what on *earth* gave you this idea?"

Jamie's expression turned grim. "We have information that he was arranging for the transport of the *jeune filles* last night, and that he mentioned you were incapacitated—" here he paused, "—with smallpox."

Horrified, she stared at him for a blank moment, before righting herself. "But—this isn't smallpox, Jamie. Only look at me—I've no pox."

He frowned, but persisted, "I can only say what he said—perhaps you didn't get it as badly as he intended."

Nonie bowed her head so that her hair fell around her face, trying to fight the sick feeling that threatened to overwhelm her. Don't think about it, she urged herself; not now—and don't be defending him too much, or Jamie will think you've indeed run mad. "What's to be done, then? Do you think the assignment is jeopardized?"

Jamie glanced over to Saba, and lowered his voice, even though the girl certainly didn't understand Gaelic. "I haven't heard anything that would make me think so. Our reports say *Le Capitaine* is furious, because the French think they've been double-crossed."

As have I, she thought sadly, and firmly quelled the unwelcome thought.

Jamie bent his head, thinking. "But I can't like this— bloody hell; what do you suppose the mark is about?"

Annoyed by her own foolishness, Nonie replied, "Isn't it obvious? He is trying to thwart the assignment."

But Jamie could not accept this premise, and shook his head, slowly. "How can he know the assignment?

Nonie, you haven't told him?" He raised his gaze to hers, aghast at the thought.

With a careless blow, she cuffed the side of his head. "Of course not; good God, Jamie." She saw that Saba was regarding them with alarm, and lowered her voice. "He thinks I am here to rescue your sorry carcass—that we are old friends from home." She paused, and then added honestly, "Although I am certain he knows I am here for other reasons as well. He did tell me that he knew who I was, that first night; and things being as they are on the continent, he must know that I am up to my neck in plots and schemes."

Assimilating this with a frown, Jamie shook his head slowly. "Still—it makes no sense; if he wanted to thwart the assignment, he would just kill you. It is not as though he hasn't had plenty of opportunity, what with you following him about, all cow-eyed."

She cuffed him again, for good measure, and retorted with exquisite scorn, "Pot, meet kettle."

Jamie's blue eyes flashed with heat. "It's not like that, Nonie—and Saba could get in terrible trouble if anyone thought it, so I'll be thanking you to keep a civil tongue in your red head."

Oh-ho, Nonie thought; our Jamie is smitten, himself; it is a shame there is scant possibility this will end well for either one of us. "All right then; we are back to the nub of it—we know the mark purposefully made me ill, and in the meantime, he is making clandestine arrangements behind the scenes."

But again, Jamie shook his head. "No—the fishmongers tell me that no shipments were smuggled out last night—and *Le Capitaine* stayed at the embassy, drinking with the other Frenchmen."

This was unexpected, and Nonie thought about it for a moment. "So, what was the mark's aim in laying me out? Unless he *doesn't* want me to march down to the bay and raise the ghost ship—which is what I was slated to do yesterday, before he coshed me."

Jamie made a sound of frustration. "He's not a very good mark, I must say—he's gone back to reminding me of the Normandy mark."

Gingerly, she raised herself to a sitting position. "Not the same, I think; the Normandy mark was not cooperating out of sheer stupidity, and that is not the case here—quite the opposite, in fact. Perhaps he's trying to throw us off—I wouldn't put anything past him, he's a shrewd one. Where is he now?" She had no doubt that their spies on the ground were monitoring the necromancer's movements, and Lord, how she missed him.

"Yesterday, he was at the slave market, looking over the girls," Jamie informed her bluntly. "He's a rum 'un, Nonie."

Nonie hovered on the edge of voicing her own conclusions about the necromancer's collection of women, but drew back; Jamie would think her a besotted fool. "Ah. Charming fellow. So, where is he, now?"

Shaking his head in frustration, Jamie admitted, "We don't know—we lost him. Then I heard Saba's bizarre tale, and came to see if you were alive."

Nonie was touched, and with a fond gesture, laid a hand on his headscarf. "You're a good man, Jamie O'Hay—risking your health, to come look after me."

"No danger, actually—I already had the smallpox, when I was little." He pushed up a sleeve to show her a pock mark.

She examined his arm with interest. "Did you? Fancy that."

He lifted his gaze again, suddenly serious. "Do you have a weapon?"

"I do," she assured him. "And believe you me, I will put it to good use, if necessary." She hoped this was true; in her weaker moments, she admitted to herself that she would be very reluctant to take up arms against this particular mark. Reminded, she asked, "What does '*namrata*' mean? Do you know what language it is?"

"No, I don't—is it important?"

She sighed, and brushed her hair back again. "I've no idea. I'll need a new contact, if anyone's handy."

Jamie's brows drew together. "What happened to the old one—do you know?"

Pausing, she weighed how much to tell him, and once again felt that that strange sense of allegiance to her erstwhile husband, who had brought about her *many* problems and didn't deserve a shred of sympathy. "I think the fellow is being detained somewhere; I would be very surprised if he has been harmed."

"Nonie—" Jamie warned ominously.

Deftly changing the subject, she reported, "There is no love lost between the mark and the Agha; I have the impression there is a pitched battle going on behind the scenes, with the Dey in the middle."

The distraction did the trick, and Jamie cocked his head, thinking. "I'll see what I can discover."

Reminded, she added, "And my old contact mentioned a Frenchman hanging about; a laughing, handsome man."

Jamie gave her a look. "De Gilles."

Surprised, she stared at him. "De Gilles is *here*? After everything that went forward in Normandy?"

"Remember, there's a rumor that he's involved in slave trading."

She nodded, thoughtfully. "That would explain it, I suppose. This would not be the place to do any political scheming, after all—we're weeks away from the civilized world."

"So—he's just a coincidence?" His question held a hint of doubt; they'd been in their business far too long to believe in coincidences.

She nodded at the unspoken doubt. "Let's put a shadow on him, and see what he does."

Jamie glanced over at Saba, who met his gaze nervously. "I should go. For God's sake, Nonie; don't do anything foolish. Or, more foolish than you've already done."

She touched his arm. "I'll do my best. In the meantime, try not to give my husband reason to call you out."

With one last admonitory look, he rose, and followed Saba as she slipped through the door.

CHAPTER SEVENTEEN

As a result of her chosen line of work, Nonie was necessarily a light sleeper. Therefore, she opened her eyes in the faint light of dawn, staying very still, but aware that something—some slight movement—had awakened her. After a moment, she hid a smile and marveled that she was so far gone that she already knew his scent. "Tahriz?"

"Yes; I am sorry if I woke you."

Sleepily, she sat up on the bed, and saw that he sat on a stool beside her, watching her in the dim light. The quiet vigil didn't match with Jamie's theory that he had deliberately laid her low, but she knew better than to question Jamie's information.

"Are you still unwell? I have a draught, if it is needed."

Don't say anything, she warned her foolish, outspoken self—don't you dare. "I am much better, now that I've slept 'round the clock." With a lilt in her voice, she left an opening for him to explain where he'd been in that self-same space of time, but he didn't take it, instead leaning in to gently place his hand on her forehead, assessing. She examined the face so close to hers, and decided he looked tired. "And how are you?"

"I've been worried about you; have you managed to eat anything?"

Don't let him know you know, she warned herself frantically—if you let him know you know, you may put Jamie and the others in danger; you may jeopardize the assignment that they've been preparing for *months*. Please, please don't say anything, because you know how foolish you can be—

In a rush, she asked, "Did you give me smallpox, Tahriz?"

For a long moment, he stared at her with no expression, and she marveled at how well he could control his reactions—she should watch and learn, because she was just the opposite, as she had ably demonstrated once again. Slowly, he asked, "You will let me explain?"

"I suppose." She sighed, surprised that she wasn't more inclined to stab him through the heart, considering how miserable the fever had been—she was a lost cause, she was. "Although whenever I am with you, I believe all your dubious explanations, and then when you are away, I realize I am a complete nodcock for having done so."

He took her hands in his, and rubbed his thumbs on their backs. "Have you heard of the work of the English doctor—the work he has done with vaccinations?"

"Perhaps," she equivocated, having no idea what he was talking about.

He persisted, "He discovered that if a mild form of the disease is administered, the patient will never contract the more deadly version."

She thought this over. "You did this so that I would never catch smallpox?"

"Yes."

But her brows drew together in suspicion. "That won't wash, my friend; if that was your noble intent, why didn't you just tell me?"

He hesitated, then confessed, "Because it suited my purposes, if you were unable to leave the rooms for a day or two."

This made more sense, and had the ring of truth—although everything he said had the ring of truth, come to think of it. "And why is that, my friend?"

He met her eyes with a grave expression. "You said it yourself; we are working at cross purposes."

So—there it was, out in the open, and no refuting it—he was the villain of the piece, and all her wishful thinking would not change that hard, hard fact. If she was going to figure out a way to redeem him, she needed to do a better job than she'd done thus far; he had easily outfoxed her at every turn.

She squeezed the capable hands that held hers, and decided that perhaps it would be best to remind him of what he'd be missing, if he maintained his present course—anything to further the cause. "We've a problem, then. While we are deciding what's to be done, do you suppose you could join me, here?" Ah—there was an advantage to being so ridiculously outspoken, it was gratifying to see that he could not control the light that came up in his dark eyes.

"Are you well enough?" It was a perfunctory question; he was already shrugging off his *djellaba*.

"As long as I don't have to exert myself overmuch." She leaned back into the pillows, and caressed his bare chest, as he supported himself with a hand on either side of her, and lowered his head to kiss her. Willingly, she moved her hands to cradle his head, but she kept her kiss relatively chaste—he liked to take things slowly, and in truth, there was something almost unbearably sweet in the way he handled her; as though he could not be gentle enough.

Climbing onto the length of her body, he lowered his head to kiss her throat, and press his face into her neck as his arms came around her, and she could feel his chest expand as he breathed in—apparently, he liked the scent of her, too. Oh—this is heaven, she thought, feeling the rhythm of his chest rising and falling, warm against her breast. Despite his double-dealing ways, I have missed him miserably.

He didn't move for a few moments, and gradually she realized that his breathing had become deeper, his breath warm upon her neck—he had fallen asleep.

Carefully, she lay still, and smiled at the canopied ceiling. He was exhausted from whatever skullduggery he had been hatching this past day, and she could be patient, certainly. But she shouldn't get used to this—shouldn't get used to lying in his arms, and feeling protected and cherished—it would ruin her work ethic. Not to mention he was up to his neck in aiding and abetting Napoleon's latest attempt at world conquest—there was no mistaking that this constituted a serious hurdle in their relationship.

She shifted to the side ever so slightly—he was heavy—and tried for a moment to seriously consider the eventual outcome of this little interlude. Surely, she could protect him from ruin without jeopardizing the assignment. She knew on a fundamental level that he was not an evil man—she had known quite a few evil men, and flattered herself that she was a good judge of such things. It was the influence of this miserable place—where there was no honor or integrity, just greedy intrigues—that had led him astray; if he had seen the havoc and misery the last war had caused on the continent, perhaps he wouldn't be so eager to help Napoleon prepare for the next one.

And then—once she'd weaned him away from all this—perhaps he wouldn't mind living somewhere else, somewhere easier for her to visit, when she needed to feel the way she felt right now. She turned her head slightly, and felt his hair against her face. This is very unlike you, she admitted to herself—Jamie is right; you are cow-eyed, and the mark has been running circles around you. Don't let him see that you are weaving air-dreams about a mutual future, or he will sink you for certain. She closed her eyes and drifted back to sleep, the heat from his body seeping into her very bones.

She was awakened some time later because his mouth had rather roughly found hers, and he'd apparently decided to make up for lost time by dispensing with all preliminaries, as she gathered her wits and tried to catch up with him.

All too soon, their coupling was over, and he collapsed atop her, both of them panting and damp with perspiration. "Top o' the mornin'," she teased, once she'd caught her breath.

He chuckled—she *loved* it when he chuckled, and she could feel that he was trying to find the words to make an apology. "Don't you dare," she warned. "I'm that pleased to imagine I'm an irresistible temptress."

"You are an irresistible temptress." He shifted to lay on his back beside her, pulling her head against his shoulder, and sighing with deep contentment.

She lay with him, well-content, and her body still a-tingle. "So; am I to be plied with any other deadly diseases today?"

"Not today." He dropped a kiss on her forehead.

"Am I to hear where you are from? It seems only fair, after such a mauling."

"No."

The thread of humor remained in his voice, and so she pressed, "Why is it such a mystery?"

He thought about his answer for a moment. "Because you are far too shrewd."

This was of interest—where he was born shouldn't make a difference. Even if he were French, she wouldn't be surprised, and certainly many other nationalities had thrown in with Napoleon—that was the whole problem with the bloody tyrant; he inspired fanatical followers. "Well, then at least tell me that I am shrewder than all your other wives."

"You are." He kissed her head again, his hand moving along her arm. "It alarms me."

Then, because she was never one to let sleeping dogs lie, she ventured, "How attached are you to Saba?"

He clasped her hand in his. "How attached are you to Mr. O'Hay?"

She shook her head slightly in bemusement. "Is there anything you don't know?"

"I don't know enough about you," he answered immediately. "About who you are, and how you came to be who you are."

"I'm from Ireland, I am." She made the disclosure with the air of one revealing a deep secret.

She could feel another chuckle in his chest, and turned her head to kiss him on the shoulder, so as to reward this show of humor.

He persisted, "I would like to hear your story—I would like to hear—" he paused. "I would like to hear what happened to you."

She lifted her head slightly to look at him. "What do you mean? Lots of things have happened to me."

He met her eyes, the expression in his own tender and a bit grave, as he slowly raked his fingers through the curls on the crown of her head. "I think your—your manner, your lightness—I think it is a shield; that it protects you from feeling deeply about anything." He repeated, "I would like to know what happened to you."

She stared at him for a long moment, and then laid her head on his shoulder again, struggling to right herself. "Don't you dare try to redeem me," she warned lightly. "Better men have tried."

"As you wish." He propped himself up on an elbow and gently cupped her breast with a warm hand. "Would you mind—"

"Not at all," she assured him, and eagerly lifted her mouth to his.

CHAPTER EIGHTEEN

Without looking at Nonie, the young man said in a low voice, "I am to tell you that a ship did sail. It was spotted, along the north coast."

Nonie's gaze rested with interest on the slave who was pouring her bath, a wiry Moroccan man—in his early twenties, she gauged—who spoke polite English with a French accent. It was early evening, and the necromancer had left to conduct a séance with the Dey.

"Well; there's a wrinkle." The fishmongers must have gotten it wrong, then, and *Le Capitaine* must have known that he was being watched, which was why he'd spent the evening drinking at the embassy, so as to allay their suspicions.

As she watched the young man reach for another jug of hot water, she thought over this latest bit of bad news. The reason she and Jamie had landed in Algiers in the first place was because their people—those who watched the harbors of the world for signs of trouble—had discovered that French merchant ships were quietly taking cargo from Algiers to an unspecified location on the northern coast of France—ships sailing with no insignia, and not following the normal protocols. With that information, it had been relatively simple to piece together the pearl smuggling scheme—a scheme which was soon to come to an inglorious end, if Nonie and Jamie had anything to say about it.

She mused aloud, "It is so annoying, that the British and the Americans are busy warring with each other. If we could set up a blockade, and bombard a few people, here and there, we'd be done with this nonsense."

"Yes, ma'am," the young man agreed, glancing up to make sure that Fatima did not yet approach.

Shaking it off, she addressed him in a brisk manner. "Time to advance the assignment, then; please tell Jamie we'll be making a visit tonight." Assessing the fellow, she asked in French, "What is your name, and how are you in a knife fight?"

"I can fight," the slave assured her in that language. "I am called Ibram."

"Excellent. You may come along, too, Ibram; we'll have use for you. Tell Jamie." Usually she wouldn't recruit a contact she didn't know well, but he was custom-made for her purposes, and she was willing to take a chance—hopefully he wouldn't suffer the same fate as the last contact. Perhaps she'd say a word to Tahriz, now that she knew how to catch him at a weak moment.

Fatima stepped into the room, along with the slave girl who would assist with the bath, and with a bow, the young man left them.

"Who was that fellow?" Nonie asked Fatima, testing the water's temperature with her fingers.

Fatima lifted her gaze. "Ibram. He speaks English."

"Not as well as you, my friend."

Pleased, Fatima nonetheless demurred, "Sometimes I cannot understand you, Nonie, but I think I am getting better each day."

"You are indeed. Did you learn English from Tahriz?"

There was the barest hesitation. "No—I learned English before."

Stepped in that one, thought Nonie with regret; I shouldn't be bringing up her former life. Of course, since a captured female slave usually served as a concubine—or worse—Fatima had done well for herself, winding up as the necromancer's wife. Perhaps her tale wasn't too harrowing, and Nonie was frankly curious; while Saba was beautiful and intelligent, Fatima was not outstanding in either department. It would be interesting to discover why Tahriz had made this particular choice.

As the female slave helped Nonie bathe, she turned her thoughts to the dismaying revelation made by

Ibram—that the Dey had managed to slip another supply ship out to France, despite their watchfulness. It was no coincidence that she'd been laid out with a fever, and that the necromancer had been out all night—he was behind it, of course, not that any verification was needed. The only surprise was that the ship had sailed without the casket of *jeune filles*, which was currently sitting at the bottom of the harbor. They had miscalculated; the trap they were setting had not delayed this particular shipment, and therefore, they needed to step up the assignment. It was a bit embarrassing—that the pearls were getting through to Napoleon's people, despite their best efforts.

Hard on this thought, a commotion could be heard coming from the antechamber—men's voices. Fatima quickly snatched up Nonie's robe, and helped her out of the bath, as the Agha and another man in European dress strode into the room.

Speak of the devil, and up he pops, Nonie thought, hiding her satisfaction behind a flustered show of embarrassment. The others actors in this little drama must have also decided they'd like to expedite matters, and so they'll strike whilst the necromancer and the Dey are otherwise occupied—good on them.

Dripping water and wrapped in her robe, Nonie ventured, "Gentlemen—gentlemen, what is the meaning of this? If you seek my husband, he is from his quarters."

"It does not matter; it is you we wish to speak to." The Agha turned to the other man, and remarked in French, "This is the girl from the sunken ship."

Keeping her expression carefully neutral so that they were unaware she understood, Nonie covertly studied *Le Capitaine,* one of Napoleon's former naval captains, who was now overseeing the pearl-smuggling operation. It was he who had seen to it that those who'd double-crossed Napoleon were brutally punished, but in the Barbary pirates, the good captain may have met his match in brutality, and as a result the truce between the two sides was an uneasy one.

Nonie had met *Le Capitaine* once before, but he was not aware of this felicity, because she had been posing as a post boy, at the time. He was not a striking man; of only moderate height, and not one to stand out in a crowd—except, of course, for the unfortunate fact he'd lost an eye in an ambush on a dark road, and now wore a patch. It was a shame; he used to travel about unremarked, but now—now the poor man could not avoid recognition, and could not move about so freely. Such a terrible shame, it was.

The sharp gaze from his good eye traveled the length of her body with frank interest—never seen so many freckles in his life, Nonie concluded. She noted that Ibram had returned to post himself within the door—reinforcements were at hand, then—but it would not do at all to launch an attack on the Agha and *Le Capitaine* in the mark's chambers, not to mention her assignment would then lie in smoldering ruins.

With all appearance of bewilderment, she spread her hands. "How may I be of assistance?"

His mouth twisting cynically, the Agha eyed her. "I was informed that you were gravely ill. You do not appear so."

"Oh—I was ill, but I am much recovered, sir, and thank you for your kind concern."

The Agha turned to his companion to say in French, "The necromancer says the girl tells but a tale to preserve her own life. I disagree; I believe she knows of what she speaks."

"*Mademoiselle*," the Frenchman said in abrupt English. "Tell me what you know of the sunken pearls."

"I think I am more properly a '*Madame*'," Nonie ventured in a timid voice.

With a sound of impatience, the man circled around her, the expression in his one good eye cold. "You will answer me, before I lose my temper. Speak."

Her voice a bit tremulous, Nonie gathered her robe closer around her. "I would very much like to see the British Consul." She did not add that the British Consul's eyes would probably start out of his head, on seeing her—just before he swore he had never seen her before, of course.

The Frenchman ignored her request, and continued relentlessly, "You were wearing some fine pearls when you were rescued. Where did you acquire them?"

"From Captain Spoor," she whispered, glancing up at him, as he paused beside her in an intimidating manner. "He was very fond, you see."

"The Dutchman; yes. And where did he get them?" She hesitated, and watching her, he leaned in with an air of menace. "Speak."

With trembling lips, she confessed in a small voice, "He said—he said the Dey had given them to him—as his share."

"It is not true!" the Agha protested into the ominous silence. "He lied—or she lies!"

Clasping her hands, Nonie looked from one to the other. "He did tell me not to say—warned me that it was a secret."

Coldly, the other man addressed the Agha in French, "I will discover what is true and what is not, and those responsible will pay—and pay dearly, I assure you. In the meantime, let us attempt to recover the pearls." To Nonie, he said, "You will accompany us to the jetty, *Madame*—get dressed."

"Now? Oh—oh, but sir—what of my husband—"

He turned to Fatima. "See to it—quickly."

Gently pulling on her arm, Fatima led Nonie to the dressing area, and as she pulled the *kaftan* over Nonie's head, the other woman whispered, "I will send word to my lord. Do not fear."

"Tell him to be wary—'tis a dangerous pairing, we have here."

As they made to leave, Ibram opened the door for them, and Nonie met his eyes. "Thank you, Jamie." She then left with the Agha and *Le Capitaine* to—*finally*—seek out the treasure that lay on the bottom of the Bay of Algiers.

CHAPTER NINETEEN

"Come along," the Agha said with impatience. "There is little time."

I imagine he means there is little time before the Dey, or my husband—or both—makes an appearance to express their extreme displeasure at this high-handedness, thought Nonie. It is interesting that the Agha is willing to indulge the Frenchman in this—although it is possible he is willing to make any alliance, if he thinks it will bring discredit to the necromancer.

The party was making its way down one of the two jetties that had been built out into the Bay of Algiers, the large rocks piled high to create an artificial harbor between. As she trudged along—ruining her poor sandals on the rough surface—Nonie looked about her with interest, being as how she hadn't had a clear view on the night she'd arrived. Ships of various sizes were anchored in the harbor, and the jetty itself was illuminated with the occasional torch, the flames dancing madly in the persistent wind that blew off the water. Darkness was falling, and the ancient city of Algiers rose up from the shore, with newly-lit torches and lanterns illuminating the Kasbah against the coming night.

Ahead of her strode *Le Capitaine* and the Agha—both of their backs rigid with wariness—and a third man had fallen into step beside her, as they made their way along the narrow pathway atop the rocks. Like the Frenchman, he was dressed in European clothes, and she surmised he was on his staff, although she couldn't be certain of his nationality—a ship's officer of some sort, she guessed. Not a captain; a captain would not allow himself to be ignored by the other two.

She strained to listen to the conversation between the Agha and *Le Capitaine*—it was low-voiced, and intense—but gave up, as the wind carried away any tantalizing snatches of the French they spoke. Silently, she sized up the man walking beside her, and decided she needed to know more. To this end, she asked in a small voice, "Do you think they mean to do me harm?"

"Not if you cooperate."

English, she thought in surprise. Here's a wrinkle—nothing like a despicable turncoat, to add to the mix.

"Sir," she ventured. "You are British; please, I beg of you—"

"Quiet," he rebuked her in a sharp tone. "And do as you're told."

Stupid *sassanach*, she thought, subsiding into silence. It would be such a terrible shame, if you were to take a tumble into the choppy water; why, you might even drown.

The two men before them paused and turned to her, standing close so that she could hear over the wind that whipped around them. The Frenchman asked, "The night you were rescued—do you remember where the Dutch ship was, when it sank?"

Nonie gazed out uncertainly toward the darkening sea, clinging to the ends of her veil so that her head dress did not fly off. After hesitating, she raised an arm to indicate, "Off the far end, and over to the left a bit. I think that's the place; it was very dark, of course—and stormy." Truly, when she looked at it from this vantage point, she had turned quite the trick; despite the removal of her corset, it was no easy thing to swim in skirts, under such conditions. The Home Office didn't pay her anywhere near enough.

"How large a vessel?" The Englishman beside her asked. "How many masts?"

She pretended to consider this, even though she could have spared everyone the trouble and reported that it was a twenty-eight-gun frigate, that had been severely battered by action, and then had been stripped of its cannons with the exception of four portside nine-pounders, which had been left to sink it, so that it settled underwater on its side. "Three masts, I think; two large and one at the back, that was smaller." Her eyes wide with remembered distress, she added, "I hope none of the sailors drowned." Unlikely; unless she very much missed her guess, both Droughm and Captain Spoor had managed to find a tavern or a brothel—or both—in short order.

Viewing the area with narrowed eyes, the Englishman shook his head. "It makes no sense. Why was the vessel so close to the jetty that it ran aground? Were they landing?"

"There was a great deal of drinking," Nonie offered. Which was true, to an extent—it was a time-honored tradition to toast the launch of a new assignment.

"Perhaps the Dutch captain was making a delivery to the Dey, Mr. Peyton." The Frenchman allowed the sarcastic question to linger in the air, as he turned to face the Agha in an accusatory manner.

"*Monsieur le capitaine,* you are laboring under a misapprehension," the Agha insisted, his color rising. "I can promise you there was no such intent—"

"The Dey is double-dealing with the wrong people," the Frenchman interrupted in a voice that was all the more sinister for its softness. He turned, and addressed the Englishman. "Mr. Peyton, would it be possible to explore the cargo hold at this depth?"

Peyton took an assessing look at the area. "Yes—the depth along the shelf is perhaps thirty feet, only. So, either the masts are broken, or the ship lies on its side."

This was true, more or less, and Nonie was impressed, despite herself. Apparently, Mr. Peyton was an experienced seaman, and only served as a traitor in his spare time.

"We have divers here—very adept. They will recover the pearls," the Agha firmly pronounced, "—and this misunderstanding will be at an end."

"We shall see," said *Le Capitaine.* He then turned to Peyton. "Try to get an exact location from her; the Agha and I must have a private discussion." After holding Peyton's gaze for a significant moment, he then turned with the other man to retrace their steps down the pathway, the Agha wasting no time in launching into an impassioned defense in French.

Fancy that, thought Nonie, watching them walk away; apparently, I'm slated to be murdered by our friend Mr. Peyton. Comes from knowing too much about Napoleon's doings, it does—wouldn't they be surprised, if they found out I knew more about it than the three of them put together.

Dispassionately, she considered releasing her blade from its hiding place in her hem, but then discarded the thought; she needed to stay in the arena for the foreseeable future, and a stab wound could not be explained away, were it discovered—and she could not be certain it would not be discovered, as she was not familiar with the tides in the area.

"Come here to the edge," Peyton directed her with an impatient gesture. "Try to show me exactly where you think the ship is."

"Yes, sir," she responded nervously, and—carefully balancing on the rocks—followed him to the edge, losing her footing for a moment, so that she fell back on her hands, and managed to come back up clutching a good-sized rock. "Oh," she exclaimed in a startled tone. "Isn't that the mast, sticking up over there?"

Surprised, he followed her gesture, and as his head was turned, she clouted him on the temple where the skull was most vulnerable, and watched him slump down in a heap. Dispassionately, she kicked him with one foot, and then the other, so that he rolled off the rocks and into the water, the blood flowing freely, as it always did from a head wound. She then scrambled along the shoulder of the jetty back toward the shore, keeping low, and not certain how much time she had before someone would come looking for the despicable Mr. Peyton—hopefully he would drown, although she could not stay to be certain; she had some eavesdropping to do.

Keeping low, she held her *kaftan* bunched up in a hand, and swiftly leapt from rock to rock until she caught up to the place where the two men walked along, deep in conversation. Nonie decided she would very much like to hear what it was they said, and carefully scuttled along the rocks—she didn't dare lift her head—until she could hear snatches of their conversation.

". . . he is playing the both of us for fools—do not doubt that this is his doing. He has taken the girl to wife. . ."

But the Frenchman was not sympathetic. "How do I know this? You seek to have me take out your rival, but all I see is. . ."

The wind carried the words away, and Nonie crept as close as she dared.

". . . more problems, and you will reap . . ."

Suddenly, the Agha interrupted with a startled exclamation. "He approaches; be wary—he is not one to be trifled with."

"Come; I am not so credulous. . ."

Oh-oh, Nonie thought, her face pressed against the roughened rock. If I am not mistaken, my better half has arrived to raise a ruckus on my behalf, which is very sweet of him, although it would have been too little, too late.

On the horns of a dilemma, she considered how best to proceed—it might be best, all things considered, to maintain the fiction that she'd drowned. She'd succeeded in leading the enemy to the sunken treasure trove, and the other aspects of her assignment could be more easily completed if she were not constrained to the Dey's palace, but able to lurk about the city as a free agent. On the other hand, the mark would be very unhappy, poor man, and there'd be no more lovemaking sessions. After only a moment's debate, she decided she was a hopeless romantic, and began to crawl upward toward the pathway.

There was no mistaking that the necromancer was angry, and she had no problem hearing him in the wind, when he addressed the other two. "What is the meaning of this? I understand you seized my wife out of my chambers."

"Be easy," the Agha replied, a thread of scorn underlying his response. "She was not seized; *Le Capitaine* wished to learn what she knew of the sunken ship. . ." The man's voice trailed off, as he looked down the jetty, and suddenly realized that there was no one to be seen.

"Where is she?" The rough edge to the necromancer's voice overrode all other considerations, and with a sigh, Nonie gathered up her hem, and made ready to return to her gilded cage.

"Most unfortunate," said the Frenchman, in a tone that conveyed anything but sympathy. "I fear she has met with an accident."

Before her husband could react to this bit of bad news, Nonie clambered up the edge of the jetty, clumsy in her unwieldy garment. "Ho, there," she called out to the startled men. "I'll be needing some assistance."

The necromancer strode over to her, and helped her onto the pathway. "Are you injured?"

Standing upright, she brushed off her hands, which were a bit raw from the contact with the rocks. "No, sir; although Mr. Peyton fell, and hit his head—I was unable to pull him up by myself."

But the Frenchman did not go to his henchman's assistance; instead, he angrily moved forward with a hand out toward Nonie, as though seeking to wrest her away from the necromancer.

What happened next defied explanation; suddenly, there was a loud, crackling sound, and what could only be described as lightning seemed to emanate from the necromancer's outstretched hand. With a cry, the Frenchman fell to the ground, writhing, and the Agha stepped back, horrified.

"Mother a' mercy," breathed Nonie, staring in stark disbelief.

"You will not touch my wife," the necromancer said to the panting man on the ground. Then, he held out a hand to Nonie. "Come, we will go back."

CHAPTER TWENTY

A fter seeing to it that Nonie was seated beside him in the sedan chair, the necromancer signaled to the slaves to lift the poles, and they commenced the journey up the hill, back to the Dey's palace.

Aware that he was unhappy with her, she placed a hand on his arm. "Thank you."

He did not look at her, but she could see the contours of his profile in the flickering light—his jaw rigid, and his shoulders tense. "What were you about, Nonie?"

She couldn't very well explain to him that she needed the pearls—most of them fakes—to sail with *Le Capitaine*, so that Jamie could track where they went. Instead, she protested, "Pray don't blame me for this little dust-up; those two jackanapes brought me here without so much as a by-your-leave. Ask Fatima, she'll vouch for me."

"Do you know who the Frenchman is?"

"I do." She offered nothing further.

After a moment, he turned to her, and placed his own hand on hers. "Forgive me; I have no right to reprimand you."

Grateful that he was getting over his scare—which was what lay at the heart of his foul mood—she teased gently, "We'll have an agreement, instead; I'll allow you to reprimand me, if you'll allow me to reprimand you. Not in bed, though."

But he was not to be teased, and lifted his face to hers to say with quiet intensity, "You must be careful; these are dangerous people."

This, of course, was nothing she didn't know, and once again she wondered why he was not cooperating with the aforementioned dangerous people—it all made little sense. As she couldn't raise these matters with him, however, she replied in a light tone, "Ah—but I'm a dangerous colleen, Tahriz." For a moment, she dwelt fondly on the memory of the Frenchman's missing eye.

Thus prompted, he asked, "What happened to the other man?"

"I coshed him," she admitted readily. "But in my defense, he was winding up to drown me."

He bent his head forward, and brushed his thumb across the back of her hand in what was now becoming a familiar gesture. "You take such risks."

"As do you." She watched him, thinking about how they were both dancing around the truth, because neither one of them could be too forthright with the other without ruining their respective schemes. It is a shame we are on opposing sides, she thought; we would make a formidable pairing.

"Do you ever consider—do you ever consider not doing what it is you do, anymore?"

They were wandering into that-which-must-not-be-spoken-of, but she was loath to put a halt to this fine, semi-honest discussion. "Sometimes. But then Napoleon decides to march again, and all choices are taken away from me."

Choosing his words carefully, he persisted, "There are always choices; there are always opportunities to begin anew."

Surely, he couldn't be suggesting that she turn coat, and throw in her lot with Napoleon's forces? Almost immediately, she discarded the thought; he would know better, and besides, she couldn't shake the feeling that he hated this place; hated these people, and what they did—although it made little sense, as here he was, in the thick of it. Perhaps he was operating under some compulsion—he was being blackmailed, or threatened in some way. This actually made more sense than believing that he was willingly serving the forces of evil, and then grifting the Dey on the side, for good measure.

With an effort, she looked away, and took firm hold of herself; she needed to be clear-headed when it came to him, and to stop grasping at straws in the forlorn hope that it would all turn out well, somehow. To this end, she changed the subject. "What was that you brought down on him? It looked like lightning."

"Very similar," was his only response.

She smiled. "Remind me never to cross you, my friend."

But this only triggered another serious response from him, as he turned to say with all sincerity, "I would never harm you—never. You must believe me."

With a wry mouth, she was compelled to point out, "Yet you have coshed me out twice, thus far—and on very short acquaintance, I might add."

With quiet intensity, he insisted, "Believe me, I am only trying to protect you, Nonie."

For the second time, she pointed out, "I believe I am well-able to protect myself, Tahriz."

He held her eyes with his, and she thought, there is something here that I don't understand—some motivation other than greed, or ambition. But why wouldn't he confess it? He is a good man—it may sound foolish, after all that has happened, but he is a good man; I know it down to my bones.

She hovered on the edge of confronting him, but drew back; it was entirely possible he was exactly what he seemed, and she was going to destroy the assignment with her inability to control what she said around him. It was past time to remember why she was here, and how important it was.

Breaking off eye contact, she gazed out the window for a few moments, as the sedan chair lumbered its way up the hill. "And how was the Dey's mother, if I may be asking?"

In a grave voice that nevertheless held an underlying trace of humor, he replied, "She was in a mood to talk."

"That is excellent news; what sort of advice does she give him?" She had little doubt he was using his influence with the Dey against the Agha; in the same way that the Agha was trying to influence the Frenchman against him. It was always the way of it—in palaces, or other places where men vied for power; it was how these pesky wars kept breaking out.

He tilted his head, considering his response. "His mother wants only what is best for him."

"Then she was a—is a—a good mother." Despite herself, her voice faltered, and she ducked her chin to recover her poise.

He placed a hand gentle hand on her arm, and squeezed. "You have lost your own mother?"

The sympathy in his voice was nearly her undoing, but with her gaze focused on the floor, she managed to reply in a level tone, "I'd rather not speak of it, just now."

There was a pause. "Was it a fire?"

"Stop it," she snapped, and then was horrified by her loss of composure. "Oh—oh, I am sorry, Tahriz—"

"No matter," he responded lightly, his hand moving down to hold hers in a firm clasp. "I believe we have an agreement to reprimand, whenever it is necessary."

In the ensuing silence, she gazed out the window, and saw that they were nearing the palace. "Do you think you would ever want to live somewhere else?" So much for her resolve to mind what she said around him.

He chose his words carefully. "I think the future is very uncertain."

Which means no, she thought, and was embarrassed that she had asked him such a question—like a lovelorn lass, with more hair than wit, as Tanny used to say.

His hand tightened on hers. "You are very dear to me."

Quirking her mouth, she turned to him. "You needn't throw me a sop, my friend."

"It is not a sop—it is the truth."

But not dear enough, she admitted a bit sadly, and then chastised herself for putting on such a maudlin display. He was right; the future was very uncertain, and she shouldn't be looking for happily-ever-after. Meanwhile, she had an assignment to complete.

Upon arriving at their rooms, one of his guards—Jamil, the one who'd married them—moved his head slightly, and Tahriz stepped aside to confer with him in low tones. I hope there are no more crises tonight, thought Nonie, watching, and trying to gauge his reaction to the report. I am still a bit peaky from my brush with smallpox, not to mention my adventures on the jetty.

Upon returning to her side, Tahriz bent his head for a moment, considering, and then said, "I believe Mr. O'Hay hides within. Would you like to speak with him?"

Smiling in appreciation, she nodded. "If you don't mind." This was impressive; Jamie was usually very good at lurking about undetected. Poor Jamie—small wonder he was here; he must be wondering what had happened, after Ibram had given him the message that she was off to the harbor, with two villains in tow.

With a grave expression, her companion searched her face. "I would like to watch at a distance, if I may."

"There is no need for concern," she said gently. "He is like a brother to me—nothing more."

His expression softening, he admitted, "I'd rather you weren't out of my sight. Not after what has happened."

She nodded. "Right, then. Don't bring down the lightning on him, please."

"Don't give me reason." She had the distinct impression he was only half-joking.

They entered, and the necromancer shut the door, standing with his back to it. Nonie walked forward and said softly in Gaelic, "Are you here Jamie? Apparently, you've been twigged, but the mark doesn't mind if we speak."

With a twitch of a curtain, Jamie stepped forward, his wary glance noting the necromancer's position. "Hell, I knew it; I think he has some sort of tripping mechanism—threads, maybe."

"He's very crafty; we'd do well not to underestimate him."

Turning a shoulder to the silent figure at the door, Jamie drew her over toward the window, and assessed her with his brows drawn together. "What's happened—you look like something the cat dragged in."

"Then let me sit down—Lord, I've earned it. I showed those nodcocks where the ship went down. I practically had to take them by the hand and spoon-feed them, but in any event, it is done, so keep an eye out, and be ready to disembark from this miserable place."

His gaze flicked with irony to the watching necromancer. "You don't seem to be suffering, if I may say so."

She tossed her head, and said tartly, "None of your business, Jamie O'Hay."

He lowered his chin to look into her eyes. "You are telling him far too much, Nonie."

Stung, she defended, "I am telling him nothing—instead I am finding out, bit by bit, that he seems to know everything, all on his own."

"Obviously, he can't know everything," Jamie emphasized. "Think on it, Nonie."

But she had to disagree. "You mustn't make that assumption—I've been wrong at every turn, doing just that. I think instead there is something else at play, here; otherwise—you're right—he would be behaving in an altogether different way. We know that he's Napoleon's point man in the *jeune filles* operation, yet he's not even pretending to cooperate with *Le Capitaine,* who is Napoleon's agent, here. It makes no sense."

Jamie shrugged. "He's double-crossing Napoleon, then—like the Saragossa mark—and you'd best hope he doesn't meet the same nasty fate."

But once again, Nonie felt compelled to disagree. "I don't think so, Jamie—why would he be so openly hostile, then? He laid out *Le Capitaine* tonight, as a matter of fact—and a finer piece of weaponry I have never seen; it looked like controlled lightning, or something."

Jamie—who was always interested in the latest weaponry—allowed himself to be distracted. "Is that so? If that's the case, we'd best work on neutralizing him, Nonie; we don't know what he's about."

But Nonie warned, "You'll take no action without my say-so, Jamie O'Hay."

With a nod of his head, Jamie—bless him—did not argue, and she entertained a small qualm, hoping that her lovelorn foolishness would not end up endangering the both of them.

"We go forward, then? Even though the mark is not behaving like a proper mark?"

"We do," she agreed. "And despite everything, it is all working out perfectly—the Agha and *Le Capitaine* were observed openly quarreling this night, and the Dey will not be happy to hear that his red-headed prophetess was slated to be dumped into the drink."

Jamie raised his brows in amused surprise. "Someone tried to take you out? Who, and where is what's left of him?"

She smiled at the memory. "The good *Capitaine* tried to get his cohort to drown me, although it didn't work out very well for the poor man. He's since disappeared."

With another glance at the necromancer, Jamie hesitated, then asked, "Are you sure he's not the one who was behind it?"

"Completely. He lost his composure—which doesn't happen easily, I assure you—and brought down the lightning." She paused, then added, "The cohort was an Englishman named Peyton; you should alert the fishmongers, and see if anyone knows anything of him—see what his connections are."

Jamie nodded. "Any action needed? Ibram said we were to make a visit tonight, but I suppose now we'll need to reschedule."

"Yes—tomorrow, instead. Let's stir the pot to the boiling point, after the pearls are recovered. I'll meet you at the rooftop."

"Don't tell the mark," he teased.

"Not funny—but we would do well to assume he knows everything. He even knows of your meetings with—" she caught herself "—the female who must not be named."

Emotion flared in his eyes, and Jamie spoke in a low tone, his voice intent. "Nonie—look, Nonie, I've been talking it over with that female—"

Exasperated, she chided, "Lord, Jamie; who's being indiscreet now?"

"She thinks she may be able to convince him to set her aside."

Nonie stared at him in disbelief. "She can't leave with you, Jamie—are you *utterly* daft?"

"Of course, not," he agreed impatiently. "But I thought perhaps you could manage it, when it's your turn to leave. You could take her to London with you."

Her first reaction was to be outraged on her faux-husband's behalf. "I'll not do anything behind the mark's back."

"Come now, Nonie—the way this is unfolding, he probably won't survive anyway—"

Furious, she retorted, "Jamie O'Hay, I *swear* I will knock you down." From the corner of her eye, she could see the necromancer straighten up, alert, and so she endeavored to compose herself.

"I'm sorry," Jamie said immediately. "I shouldn't have said it."

Taking a breath to recover her equilibrium, Nonie admitted, "No—no; you are right, and I've thought the same thing myself, believe me. I've put out some feelers to him, but he does not seem inclined to turn from his chosen path, which is truly a shame, as I am very fond of him—but there is no room for fond attachments, in this business." She gave him a significant look.

"I'll make room for this one," Jamie disagreed in a stubborn tone. "One way or another."

"All right," she temporized, rather surprised he was so resolute, and firmly quashing a pang of envy. "I'll see what can be done, then."

CHAPTER TWENTY-ONE

With an ironic nod to the necromancer, Jamie turned and slipped back through the curtain, no doubt to descend out the window by way of rope—although he was very competent at scaling walls, and often didn't need a rope; it all depended on the composition of the wall.

Without comment, the necromancer moved over to the wardrobe, and began to remove his *djellaba* whilst Nonie watched with bemusement; it was as though they were an ordinary married couple—if you didn't count the necromancing, and the stealthy visitors—and it was a very strange feeling for her.

Nonie had already noted that he was very tidy in his habits, which did not match her own inclination, which was to leave things strewn about until they piled up so high that something finally had to be done. It is just as well—she told herself firmly—that they would not abide together for the long term; she would drive him mad.

"Thank you for letting me speak with Jamie, Tahriz; we were supposed to meet tonight, and when the Agha interrupted our plans, he was a bit worried."

But it seemed he was unwilling to discuss Jamie, instead saying only, "I will call a servant to bring hot water. I must visit my stillroom, but I will return within the hour."

There was a constraint in his voice—subtle, but she was alive to it. He didn't like the meeting with Jamie, and didn't like the life she led— he didn't like the fact he would have been too late to save her tonight, if she hadn't saved herself. In a strange way, she could sympathize with him, because she felt the same way; it was as though her carefully-ordered world had been turned upside down, and everything that used to be a priority suddenly was not. "And you'll be leaving me in my traumatized state? Is that very husbandly, I ask you?" She walked up behind him, and put her arms around his waist, leaning her cheek against his back.

He clasped her hands and she could feel his chest rise and fall, as he drew a breath. "Can I leave you to your bath? I have to think about what must be done."

Making a sound of disappointment, she moved her fingers gently on his chest, and noted that he didn't try to disengage from her embrace. "I will tell you what must be done, you should push me down into the bed, and work your magic; that's what must be done."

"Nonie—"

"You won't wear me out, you know—it's resilient, I am." There was a pause, and she could sense he was tempted. "*Namrata*," she added tentatively.

But this was a misstep, and she could feel the tension return to his body, as he turned to her in alarm. "You mustn't say," he warned. "Please; it is very important."

"Then pretend I didn't—I've no clue what it means, anyway, and you should be kinder to me, considering I almost drowned."

He ran his fingers through her thick curls, tugging gently so that her head tilted back, her face raised to his. "I would like to be kinder; I would like—I would like to see you away from all this, so that you could start anew."

His gaze held hers, and she could feel the honest emotion crackling between them like the lightning weapon—but her first instinct was to shy away from it. "You can't," she responded, trying not to sound defensive. "I have my orders, and I cannot walk away, even for you." She paused, trying to control the unfamiliar emotions that were roiling within her breast. "Don't make me choose."

He bent his head so that his forehead rested on hers. "No—forgive me. I don't know if I can endure many more evenings like this one; when I thought—"

In a panic, she only knew that she could not allow him to continue. "I can't be honest with you—I wouldn't know how." Irritated, she ducked her head into his chest. "So, what's it going to be? Are you staying or leaving?"

"Staying," he decided, and bent to lift her in his arms.

She kissed his neck, as he carried her to the bed, immeasurably relieved that he hadn't lost all patience with her. "I haven't washed." Aside from being tidy, he was also very cleanly, and there was no question that her hair smelled of sea salt.

"Not at all necessary; I am sorry I upset you." He lowered her onto the bed, and bent to kiss her, his fingers working on the strings of her *kaftan*.

She wound her arms around his neck, feeling a bit ashamed about her outburst. "No; I'm the one who's sorry, Tahriz—" she tried to think about how to explain everything to him, but apparently, he wasn't interested, and again, his lovemaking was a delicious combination of tenderness mixed with lust—they were becoming familiar with one another, and as result the touches were more certain, the surrendering more complete. *I trust him*, she realized in a haze; *at least in this, and this is wonderful.*

Afterward, she lay in his arms, drowsy and content—although she wouldn't have minded that bath, truth to tell—and they didn't speak, but gently stroked and caressed each other, the diffuse light from the curtained window the only illumination. She realized that he hadn't lit the candle beside the bed; in fact, he'd never lit another fire—not after she'd mentioned, that first night, that she didn't like looking into the fire.

There was an almost unbearable, tightening sensation beneath her breast, and turning so that her cheek rested on his bicep, she looked away from him, into the darkness. "I was born in New Ross—County Wexford. There was a big battle there—it was during the Irish Rebellion. I was seven, at the time."

She waited to see if he would make a response, or ask a question, but he didn't—instead he seemed to be intently listening, rather like a priest in a confessional.

"There was a big battle there—in New Ross." After a pause, she plunged on. "It was a terrible time, and the English—the English were brutal beasts. They wanted to send a harsh message to the rebels, and so many of the people from our town were herded into a barn in Scullabogue." She paused. "Have you heard this tale?"

"No," he said.

Of course, he hasn't, she thought; it was half a world away. She closed her eyes. "The English set the barn on fire, and massacred everyone."

He made a small sound of sympathy, and she added in a rush, "I was inside—inside the barn with my mother and my brothers and sisters—all of us so crowded, and so very afraid. My father—my father had already been killed at the battle, and it was so hard to believe that he was gone—he was gone forever. I was the youngest of seven—a skinny little thing—and my mother thought I could slip through a crack in the slats, if no one was looking—but I was so afraid; I could see that she was afraid, and that frightened me—I didn't want to go outside, alone. So, she told me to stop crying, and yanked hard on my hair, and—and pushed me, until I squeezed though." There was another pause. "Sometimes I wake up at night, and I fancy that I can still hear everyone screamin'."

His arm tightened around her, as she wiped tears away with the back of her hand. "You are not to tell anyone of this," she instructed.

"No," he agreed. There was a silence for a moment. "Who is Tanny?"

"Tanny?" It was not the question she was expecting, after such a revelation.

"Your voice changes, when you say her name."

Well then, she thought; we'll speak of Tanny, too. "Tanny was Miss Tannerby. She was the village school teacher—a very refined Englishwoman, who could spout out Shakespeare at the drop of a hat. She was a spinster, and took in the miscellaneous orphans who were left over after the massacre—a dozen of us—and managed it, somehow. There were times when she had to beg in the streets, but she would never allow us to."

"Mr. O'Hay was one."

"Yes, Jamie was another stray." The rough ground now behind her, Nonie continued with more confidence, "When Jamie and I were teenagers—angry teenagers, I suppose you could say—we started participating in the pockets of rebellion that still existed in the county. I think we were more bent on destruction than inspired by patriotism, if the truth be told. Anyway, our exploits were such that when I was arrested one fine day, a dour Englishman came to visit me in gaol, offering payment, if I would work for the Home Office." She paused. "I never caught his name, but I said some very rude things to him. With hindsight, I should have taken the money, but at the time I was filled with righteous principles."

"What changed?"

She sighed. "Tanny died. Well; she was killed— by two drunken Irish louts, who couldn't see past the fact she was English, and pushed her down for sport. Anyway, I decided there was no point to anything, and I may as well make some money, whilst the world burned. So, I grabbed Jamie, and we reported for duty." She twined her fingers in his, and warned, "There's a lot, in between then and now, but that's all I'm going to tell you, so don't be pestering me."

"All right."

He lifted his other hand, and began stroking her salty hair, whilst she let out a long breath she hadn't realized that she was holding. "Your turn," she prompted.

"I love you."

She blinked. "That's it?"

"That's it."

Unable to contain her smile at this confession, she teased, "You are trying to distract me from insisting on hearing your story—don't think I am not wise to you."

"Yes," he admitted. "But I do love you."

Again, she sighed. "Then you'll be tested, my friend."

CHAPTER TWENTY-TWO

There were no fire trays, and no peacock throne, this time; only the Dey, seated at his breakfast table on a shaded terrace, his thoughts unreadable as he gazed upon Nonie with his hard, opaque eyes. The necromancer had asked if she would give the Dey a debriefing about the events of the previous evening, and she was willing, because if the previous pattern held true, he would stay to conduct a séance afterward, which would free her up to meet with Jamie. It was time to stir up some trouble amongst the warring factions, and it was an unholy shame that she couldn't arrange matters so that they all killed each other outright—there was never a more deserving crew.

Thus far, the necromancer and the Dey had held a discussion in Arabic, whilst she waited patiently, and wondered what the governor's reaction would be if she helped herself to a sweetmeat, off the table. The tenor of the conversation was rather grave, but not heated, and she had no idea of what they spoke.

The Agha was absent, as he was overseeing the operation to recover the pearls from the bottom of the harbor. Yet again, it seemed apparent that the sunken pearls were of little interest to the necromancer, which was a puzzle, since he should be intensely interested in the pearls—it was the whole reason he was the mark, for the love of Mike. It was possible that he was somehow aware that the majority of the sunken pearls were fakes—in which case they had a serious breach of intelligence, as this was a very closely-guarded secret. But even in that case, why wouldn't he expose this fact to the others? There was something here she did not understand, and the mark did not want her to understand; she had the uneasy feeling that the current conversation was one she would very much like to interpret.

With an imperious gesture, the Dey beckoned her to approach, and Nonie dutifully stepped forward, her hands clasped nervously before her. "Last night—you showed where the ship rested in the harbor?"

"I did." She was tempted to give his deceased sister Nadia some credit, but then she remembered that

Nadia was apparently not interested in the pearls, in the same way that the necromancer was not interested in the pearls. It was all very strange.

"The Agha seized you out of chambers—and without your husband's permission?"

"He did." She wouldn't mention that she was perfectly happy to be seized, so as to finally get this bloody assignment on the bloody road. To be fair, she added, "Along with the one-eyed Frenchman."

The Dey leaned forward. "The two of them, they acted together?"

"Well, yes; although they were quarreling about the pearls, and very unhappy with each other."

At this, the Dey flicked the necromancer a knowing glance. I wonder what my pretend-husband is about, here, she thought. I wish I knew my lines.

"Speak, girl—what else was said by these men?"

Nonie considered. "They were unhappy with my husband."

The Dey nodded, narrowing his eyes. "Yes; I understand that violence was offered."

"That is true," she agreed in a solemn tone. "Violence was definitely offered."

The necromancer intervened to make a comment in Arabic, and the Dey shifted his brooding gaze to him. Her husband then said to her, "I explained to the Dey that—had I not appeared—you feared an attempt would be made on your life."

She kept her gaze on his for a long moment, and then agreed in a neutral tone, "Yes, this is true."

The other two then had a conversation that seemed to involve the necromancer offering advice, and the Dey gravely acquiescing, as he turned up his hands in capitulation. I believe—Nonie thought, watching them—I believe my erstwhile husband is manipulating the situation in some way, and doesn't want me to follow the conversation, which is not very sporting of him, I must say.

"Tell me," the Dey asked, leaning forward, and lowering his voice, "Have you had any other premonitions of my death?"

She blinked. "Which premonitions are those, sir?"

With a scowl, he made an impatient gesture. "Come now, you must recall what you have said. My horse, Admiral Nelson, the jackals who surround me—" he made another gesture toward the mark "—my necromancer tells me the import was clear, and that I must fear for my life."

"I—I suppose that is true," Nonie conceded. "Or—mayhap you are being warned not to do anything that would provoke the British."

But the Dey leaned back into his chair. "You would not understand what the messages mean," he informed her almost kindly. "Your husband—he understands."

"He's as gafty as the day is long," she agreed a bit grimly. "Gaftier, even."

With a frown of incomprehension, the other said in a brusque tone, "What is that? You must learn to speak more clearly."

"I should learn Arabic, I should. The three of us could hold long and enlightening conversations."

Oblivious to the irony in her tone, the governor nodded with dour approval. "Yes. My necromancer is fortunate that he has taken such a dutiful wife."

"From the moment I wake up," she agreed. It had come to her attention that her husband awoke with a burning desire for sex, first thing in the morning, to which she had no problem submitting, if not downright encouraging.

Swiftly, the necromancer intervened, and said in English, "If she comes to harm by the Frenchman, we will have no choice but to retaliate—indeed, we have already allowed him to levy insult without repercussion."

"Yes," agreed the Dey, steepling his hands, and staring at her with his brooding eyes. "I will see to it that he is warned—such behavior will not be tolerated. I am ruler, here."

Apparently satisfied, the necromancer bowed. "With your permission, I will see her out."

The Dey nodded, and made a negligent gesture with his fingers, whilst the necromancer turned to escort Nonie out from the terrace, and into the adjacent hallway.

As they exited past the guards, Nonie eyed her companion sidelong. "What are you about, my friend?"

But he was unperturbed, as he walked beside her. "Isn't it obvious? I cannot allow another situation like the one last night, where you were without protectors. It is best if the Dey takes a personal interest in your safety."

"And his own, apparently—what with my premonitions of death and destruction."

He tilted his head slightly. "It is important that he lives."

This seemed inarguable, at least from his point of view. "Of course, it is, otherwise your easy days of grifting will be behind you, and you'd be forced to find an honest way to earn your bread."

"Very true." He gave her a small smile, which warmed her heart, but did not dissuade her from her suspicions. "I have that feeling I have—the one where I'm wondering if you are trying to lock me down, again."

He thought about how to reply, as they approached the main entrance to the palace. "You must know I am concerned—especially after last night. Your safety is of paramount importance."

"I have to do my job, Tahriz—remember? You were not going to make me choose."

"No." He paused to face her, crossing his arms, and with his head bent. "Will you be careful? Will you take no chances?"

Touched, she laid a hand on his arm. "You needn't worry; I am very good at what I do."

But this did not seem to reassure him, and the expression in his eyes remained grave, as he signaled to the slaves to bring the sedan chair around. "I have no doubt of it."

CHAPTER TWENTY-THREE

"What's it to be—pistol, or rifle?" Jamie and Nonie were on the safe house rooftop across from the French embassy, and Jamie was looking over the various weapons that had been hidden in a canvas bundle under the catch-basin.

With a practiced eye, Nonie gauged the distance from the roof to the street below, and decided, "The rifle. It's a bit too far for a pistol—I learned my lesson with the Flemish mark." That was another target she was merely supposed to nick; instead the wretched man had dropped like a stone with a ball through his temple, and they'd been forced to improvise from then on out, with only mixed results. As Jamie had noted, the

Flanders assignment was not their finest hour, but despite that blot, their record was an impressive one.

During their wild and ragged years abetting the remnants of the Irish rebellion, they'd discovered that Nonie had remarkably good eyesight, and remarkably steady hands; the combination made her a lethal and respected sharpshooter—so much so, that a price was finally placed on her head by the frustrated British authorities. When she was inevitably captured, rather than a hangman, she became acquainted with a grey-eyed man who asked, very calmly, if she thought she could see her way fit to eliminating certain enemies of the crown who deserved such treatment. She would be well-compensated, on the understanding that she would never be officially recognized; assassins were not considered honorable players, in the arcane rules of warfare.

In the end, it had been a simple decision. Tanny had been ignominiously killed, and Nonie was tired of being poor and glad that she was good at something—even something that would have horrified Tanny, had she known. And indeed, she excelled at her craft; she and Jamie had an impressive tally of successful assignments that engendered not a drop of remorse—only a great deal of satisfaction that another evildoer had been vanquished, in what seemed like a never-ending list. The necromancer was right, when he made that wedding-night observation; she was good at what she did because she did not care deeply about anything. When he'd voiced the thought aloud, however, it resonated within her to such an extent that she began to think that perhaps she wasn't as far gone as she'd previously thought—irony of ironies, she definitely cared deeply about the Barbary mark.

With practiced movements, Jamie unsheathed the flintlock rifle from its oilcloth carrier, and inspected it. They'd visited America, on a brief assignment there, and had discovered that the Americans had created a rifled flintlock that was miles more accurate than the traditional British musket, due to the innovation of spiraling grooves within the weapon's barrel.

Satisfied, he handed it over to Nonie. "What did the Dey have to say this morning?"

Nonie quirked her mouth. "It was all very smoky. The mark is up to some scheme that involves setting the Dey against the Agha and the Frenchman—with me in the middle—but he avoided speaking English, so as to plague me to death."

"Sounds perfect," Jamie remarked, as he lifted his head slightly, to peer down the street.

"It couldn't be better—truly. The Dey was saying publicly that *Le Capitaine* must be warned to mind his manners." She practiced sighting the rifle, and smiled. "The mark has convinced the Dey that I'm having premonitions of his death."

Jamie met her eyes, and chuckled. "Has he? Lord, they all deserve one another."

"Villains, through and through." Carefully, she rested the flintlock's barrel on a tile near the roof's edge. "Speaking of villains, does *Le Capitaine* travel with a large contingent?"

"At least two guards, sometimes more. He's a cautious one, and small blame to him; a knife in the back is a commonplace, around these parts."

"Or a knife in the eye."

With a grin, Jamie's gaze met hers. "Little does he know—should we tell him where his eye rests, now?"

"We should not; let's not give him any reason to pay a visit to the Cat n' Fiddle."

Cautiously, he began to inch away from the roof's edge. "I've a rope coiled next to the balustrade, as a secondary escape route."

She nodded. "Many thanks; although I hope it doesn't come to that—hard to climb, whilst wearing a sack. Assignments are so much easier, when I can pose as a boy."

Pausing, he considered this. "Do you want to switch clothes?"

With a smile, she declined. "As much as I would pay money to see you in swathed in this potato sack, I think it best I stay within it—no one here would consider a mere female to be a suspect; easier to exit."

"Good point," he agreed, and tucked a pistol into his waistband.

"What is our timeline?"

"Ibram is at the bay, monitoring what's going forward. He will walk through below when the others are heading this way, so as to give us a preliminary signal. If his head is uncovered, they've brought up the pearls."

"How much does Ibram know?" She was inclined to be cautious; she would not be at all surprised if the necromancer had replaced her old contact with one more to his liking.

But it appeared that Jamie was of the same mind. "Not much; I don't like working with youngsters—they can't be trusted."

She smiled. "We were youngsters, not so very long ago."

"We were different; we knew we could trust each other."

This was inarguably true, to the extent that there was literally no one else they did trust. Although nowadays, this was not quite accurate; she trusted the necromancer enough to tell him about—about what had happened to her. I do trust him, she realized. I shouldn't, but I do, and if he winds up betraying me, it would be—it would be devastating.

Impatient with herself for making such a shocking admission, she quickly teased, "Best grab a fistful of pearls for Aditi, whilst you have the chance."

He shook his head. "There's no point; I wouldn't be able to tell which ones were real, and which were fake."

"Neither can Aditi," she pointed out fairly.

Jamie glanced at her in amusement. "She'd probably strangle Saba with them—she caught the two of us talking, and was not happy."

Nonie hid a smile at this revelation—that the steadfast Jamie, a veteran of many a false role, could not seem to hold his position, now that Saba had come onto the scene. "Where's Aditi's pirate? Let him take her off your hands, so that Saba has a clear field."

Jamie glanced up, casting an expert eye over the street below. "The pirate—whoever he is—is nowhere around, I'm afraid. I'll get Aditi back to India, and then call it even. She'll land on her feet—she's that type of girl."

"More properly she's the type of girl who lands on her back."

He glanced at her, as though weighing what he wanted to say. "Speaking of which; Saba is rather a puzzle."

"Is she? How so?"

Hesitating, Jamie confessed, "I told her that if she wanted the necromancer to set her aside, she'd best be certain she doesn't become pregnant, in the meantime."

Keeping her face carefully neutral, Nonie nodded. "That seems wise."

"I got the impression—well, she was flummoxed. Almost as though she doesn't—" His voice trailed off, and Nonie stepped in.

"No—I don't think she does. In fact—" frowning, she tried to put her vague suspicions into words. "I think there is something odd about the whole household. The wives and the concubines may serve an altogether different purpose—spies, perhaps." She added delicately, "Best be careful what you say to her."

He made a wry mouth. "Don't worry—I'm not that stupid. As far as she knows, she will be a missionary's wife."

With some surprise, she met his eyes. "You'll marry her? Truly?"

He looked a little embarrassed. "Would you mind?"

"Of course, I wouldn't mind—what a bloody nodcock you are, Jamie O'Hay. I was only thinking of the next war, and what it would mean."

"Oh, don't worry; I wouldn't leave you without support, Nonie."

"I'd hate to have to train another flanker," she teased. "I'd throw them off the roof, at the first mistake."

"I won't leave you in the lurch, I promise."

They watched the scene below for a moment. Now that the heat of the sun was dissipating, the foot traffic had picked up, which was going to make her job a bit more difficult. "I'll be needin' you to block out the bystanders, when the time comes."

"Done—and Tanny would be very unhappy, to hear you dropping your 'gs'." With a grin, he pulled out another object from his satchel—a small stone flask, with a cork stopper. "For luck."

Laughing, she took the flask from him. "Jamie, you are a saint—and I won't even ask how you managed it, here of all places. *Sláinte.*"

"*Sláinte.*" They took turns taking a pull of whisky, and as Jamie wiped his mouth on his sleeve, he asked, "Do you ever think about going back to Ireland?"

"No," she replied. "You?"

He looked into the distance for a moment. "I don't know—ever since I've met Saba, I've been thinking about how I'd like to show it to her."

"Then you should. I just don't know if I could bear it," she admitted.

His gaze returned to hers. "I'd be dead a hundred times over, if it weren't for you."

"Jamie," she said softly, placing her hand over his. "I could certainly say the same. I want nothing more than your happiness, so please don't be thinking that you are bound to me, in some way. Go, and take pretty Saba to Ireland with my blessing; only don't go until the crows are picking at Napoleon's carcass."

"Sorry I'm such a bleater." His grin was now firmly back in place.

With mock exasperation, she exclaimed, "Lord, man; next you'll be weeping at the stile. Take hold of your sorry self."

Suddenly, Jamie lowered his head, his hand shading his eyes. "There he is."

They watched silently as Ibram walked down the narrow street, his head uncovered.

"All right," she said. "Let's put the cat amongst the pigeons."

Gathering up the satchel, Jamie crept backward on his belly, as Nonie lay prone and carefully sighted down the rifle. They had a routine—although sometimes they altered it, it was never a good thing in this business to be too predictable—which meant Jamie would be on the ground to create a loud diversion from the other side of the street, so that it was unclear from whence the shot had come. He would then add to the general confusion, so that she could exit undetected. They were a good team; it was a shame he'd lost his bite for it. On the other hand, not a soul could complain; they had successfully completed many an assignment—none of which they could ever speak of again. It was a strange life, but it suited her; she would never be one to settle down in domestic tranquility with—with anyone in particular. Not that he was a likely candidate, what with his faux wives, and mysterious lightning-weapons. It was only—it was only that she hadn't met anyone she could even imagine settling with, and she could imagine it, with him. She could imagine it very easily.

There—the French contingent was approaching, and she needed to concentrate, as they began to unload at the embassy's entrance. *Le Capitaine* emerged from a sedan chair, easily distinguishable from the others. With a deliberate movement, Nonie rested her cheek on the warm wood of the rifle, and closed one eye. Think to murder me, do you; you have another think coming, my friend.

Carefully she sighted—she didn't want to wound him too severely. Any second, now.

There was a loud clatter across the way, as a bench stall collapsed, and an instant later she squeezed the trigger. Startled, her target had begun to turn toward the noise, and she winged his upper arm—let him think the last-moment movement saved his life.

Immediately, she scrambled backward on her knees and elbows, then slid the musket under the catch-basin and made for the trapdoor on the rooftop, crouching low.

As the commotion from the street could be heard rising up behind her, she lifted the hatch, and was confronted by the sight of a man, ascending the ladder. Almost immediately she recognized Jamil—the necromancer's guard—who froze, as he met her eyes.

There was no chance he didn't recognize her, and after a second's hesitation, she made a pretense of capitulating. "All right, step back; I'm coming down." She swung her legs around to sit on the edge of the opening, and as he turned his head aside to make his descent, she kicked him as hard as she could with both feet. As he fell backward, she slammed the hatch down, and secured the lock, listening as he tumbled down the ladder below.

Leaping to her feet, she fled to the balustrade, where the rope lay waiting, then tossed it over and shimmied down, hand over hand, with her feet braced against the wall, hoping no one would notice the unusual sight.

Fortunately, the noise and shouts from the street continued; bless Jamie, who would continue with his ruckus-raising until he was given an all-clear signal. After landing on the packed dirt, she turned to hurry away, putting her fingers to her mouth to blow two shrill whistles—hopefully, he could hear it. Keeping her head down and her veil up, she began to walk with a measured pace, but then she saw a man step out of the shadows to face her, a small distance ahead. Another one, sent by my wretched husband, she thought in annoyance, but then recognized him as one of the Agha's men—apparently, every man jack was keeping track of her whereabouts.

Thinking that she'd best find a place to make a stand, she ducked into a likely door, slamming it shut behind her. Unfortunately, the door didn't have a lock, and she looked around for a brace of some sort—it appeared she was in a storage room, with various misshapen items stacked up high in the dimness.

With a quick movement, she pushed a small wooden crate against the base of the door—knowing it wouldn't hold for long— and then lifted her *kaftan* and darted toward the back of the room, looking for another exit, as she heard her pursuer pounding and shoving on the door. Stumbling over a pallet, she barked her shin and stifled a curse, as she gave the walls an assessing glance—bad luck; no windows, and the back exit was blocked by bags of grain, stacked atop each other. She'd no choice but to prepare an ambush for her pursuer—an unwelcome complication; but no one could be allowed to connect her to the Frenchman's shooting.

Scrambling atop a packing crate, she leaned back against the wall in the darkness, carefully pulling up the fabric of her tunic to bring up her blade, hidden in the hem. With a final thrust, the door was forced open, and a shaft of light shot across the center of the room.

She was startled to hear a whispered voice, descending from the rafters above her. "Miss Rafferty."

With some surprise, she looked up to see Jamil, holding a hand down to her.

"Come along," he whispered in English. "I will see you back."

After deciding there was nothing for it, she put her hand in his, and allowed him to launch her upward.

CHAPTER TWENTY-FOUR

"You mustn't spy on me."

"You are always spying on me," the necromancer pointed out fairly.

"Don't be reasonable; I am out-of-reason cross." He was applying a salve to her sun- burnt face, and she was being short with him, partly because it was so very nice to have someone take such good care of her; it created mixed emotions within her breast.

He finished, and wiped his hands on a cloth. "Try to keep a thin layer over your face for a day or two, and stay out of the sun."

"This is not my first sun-burn, I assure you."

His gaze rested on her fair face, and his expression softened. "No—nor will it be your last, but you must be careful; with your skin, this climate can do a lot of damage."

"I don't intend to stay in this miserable climate a moment longer than necessary."

He made no reply, but stoppered the salve, and set it on the tray.

"I'm sorry," she offered quietly, her defiance at an end. "I keep looking for a way through this, and I can't find one."

"I understand," he replied, his tone a bit grave. "I feel the same way."

This wasn't exactly the response she looked for, and it prompted her to say, "It's not that I want to carry you away, to abide in a snug cottage—I don't. But I'd like to think I'll be seeing you again—and I don't mean visiting you when you're in prison, for war crimes."

He lifted his head, to gaze out the window. "I can make no promises."

This unpalatable response made her study him for a moment, perplexed. That he loved her she had no doubt—she could feel it in every touch, every glance. "Why do you do what you do? I've known more than my share of the most dedicated blackguards, and you are not cut from the same cloth—you'll never convince me of it. Do they have some hold over you? Is it your family?"

As was his wont, he ignored the question, and countered with his own. "What can I do to convince you to spare *Le Capitaine* from any further attacks?"

She blinked. "I'd no idea you were such fast friends. It certainly didn't seem so, when you struck him down."

He couldn't resist a small smile, and she couldn't resist smiling back—he had a lovely smile, he did—all the more so, because it was rarely bestowed. "No," he admitted with an ironic tilt of his head. "We are not friends. But you mustn't kill him, nonetheless."

"Tahriz," she said gently. "It is what I do." Almost immediately she wished she hadn't said it; but there was something about him that made her want to bare her soul, and she wasn't certain he knew.

He didn't seem shocked, so perhaps he was already aware. Instead, he suggested in a mild tone, "Perhaps you could do something else."

"I could run a flower cart," she mused, trying to tease her way out of this conversation that she should never be having with a mark, for the *love* of Mike. "Or sell pearls—I know where I can lay hands on a fine inventory."

"You are so clever, and so brave," he continued, as if she hadn't spoken. "You have so much more to offer."

Her brows knit, she stared at him for a moment, convinced that he was sincere. Of course, it shouldn't be a surprise that the mark—who was working hand-over-fist to help Napoleon—would try to convince her to find another line of work. It was a surprise, however, that someone as clever as he was would make such a ridiculous attempt.

"I promise I won't kill *you*," she compromised.

He turned aside with a smile. "I fear you will indeed be the death of me."

She watched him walk over to the carafe of water that sat on the table. "And where were you today, whilst I was misbehaving?"

"At the harbor." He made a gesture, offering her water, and she walked over to join him, as he poured them each a goblet.

He offered nothing more, and she prodded, "I hear they pulled up the pearls from their watery grave."

"I heard the same." Taking her elbow in his hand, he saw her seated on the window bench before he sat beside her—she noted he seemed weary; the fine lines around his dark eyes were more pronounced.

Unable to resist, she observed, "You don't seem very interested in the rescue operation."

His eyes rested on hers for a moment. "Should I be?"

"You could at least make a push to filch me a few strands of pearls—it hardly seems fair."

Lifting a hand, he ran a gentle finger along her jaw. "Next to your skin, even the finest pearls are dim imposters." The words were completely sincere.

For a moment, she couldn't find her voice. "Oh—oh, Tahriz; I am undone. That was a fine compliment—

perhaps you'd care to see a bit more of my skin? I can lie down, if that would help."

Smiling at the half-serious invitation, he demurred, "I expect to be summoned, I'm afraid." His gaze rested on hers thoughtfully. "The French are furious; they have demanded reassurances, and the alliance is very precarious."

Her clear eyes wide, she shrugged her shoulders. "There is no honor amongst thieves, I'm afraid—no matter what everyone says." If he thought she was moon-bit enough to confess her assignment to him, he was on a fool's errand; she may have opened her budget to him about her past, but business was business. Anyways, it was not as though he couldn't guess for himself that she was here to stir up trouble between these two reluctant allies; he was no fool.

Eyes gleaming, she glanced at him from over the rim of her glass. "I knocked your fellow down a ladder, did he say?"

Smiling, he shook his head. "No—Jamil is a gentle-man."

She made a wry mouth. "I owe him an apology; he whisked me from a tight corner."

With a fingertip, he gently traced her chapped lips. "Jamil was there to make certain that the Frenchman made no other attempt to harm you."

She couldn't help but laugh. "That *is* ironic. How was the poor man to know I would turn the tables, and then kick him down a ladder, for good measure?"

"Certainly, a surprising turnabout," he offered gravely, a light of humor lurking in his eyes. Delighted, she reflected that she had transformed this rather staid man into one with a finely-tuned sense of humor. Not to mention a finely-tuned desire for bed sport—she could see that he was regretting the lack of time, under the current circumstances. She'd also noted that he hadn't swallowed any water from his goblet—she may be love-lorn, but she was no fool.

A knock on the door interrupted the conversation, and he rose to answer. "Fatima?"

"Yes," the woman's voice could be heard.

As the necromancer opened the door to his more conformable wife, Nonie held the cup to her lips and watched them carefully—that something was afoot seemed clear. There was the discussion with the Dey that he didn't want her to understand, he had disappeared for the remainder of the day, and he was unhappy about her attack on the French mastermind of this little smuggling scheme. All in all, he was finally beginning to behave like a proper mark, which was a bit discouraging, considering she had been entertaining a vague theory that there had been a huge misunderstanding, and he was not a proper mark at all. Take hold of your foolish self, she chided, and be wary.

As she watched him lean in to speak in a low tone with the much shorter Fatima, she felt a twinge of jealousy that Fatima was a confidant, and she was not. Which was silly, of course—he had said himself that they were working at cross-purposes. Whilst the other two were conferring, she took the opportunity to splash the contents of her water goblet on the rug behind the bench. She may have a soft spot—a very soft spot—for this particular mark, but she'd also learned her lesson, when it came to taking drinks from his hand.

The necromancer approached with Fatima. "I must go, and I am not certain how long the Dey will require my services. Perhaps you should rest." From beneath lowered lids, he gave her a quick assessment.

Ah, she thought; I am supposed to be sleepy. Obligingly, she shut her eyes for a long moment, as though she found it hard to open them again. "I *am* tired." Tired of your shenanigans, that is—honestly, was it too much to ask for a husband who was not constantly dosing one?

"Fatima will stay with you—you may wish to re-apply the salve, in an hour." After exchanging a meaningful glance with Fatima, he was gone.

Nonie lay down on the bed, and Fatima pulled up the stool to sit beside her. "Do you wish to undress, Nonie?"

"I don't think so." With a knit brow, she studied the underside of the bed's canopy for a few minutes. "Where is Saba?"

Looking a bit self-conscious, Fatima answered evasively, "I will tell her that you were asking for her."

"We can't play our card game without a third," Nonie pointed out.

"Tomorrow," Fatima soothed. "Tomorrow, we will play cards."

Suddenly, Nonie propped herself up on an elbow and faced the other woman, as though much struck. "You know, Fatima; I think Saba is trying to steal my beau."

"Oh—oh, no, Nonie—" Poor Fatima looked horrified.

"Well, I am going to go find out." She swung her legs over the side of the bed.

Her eyes wide with dismay, Fatima's hands fluttered up in protest. "Nonie—you mustn't leave—my lord has said—"

"It's all right, Fatima; if you are worried, I will enlist Jamil to come along; I've a mind to give Jamie a proper dressing-down, I do." Fastening her head dress with an impatient movement, she threw a smile at the other woman, as she strode to the antechamber. "I'll be back in two shakes."

But her companion trailed behind her, protesting in her soft voice, "You cannot mean to go out now, Nonie— you mustn't."

"Don't worry, I'll stay out of sight." She opened the door, and Jamil, as expected, was posted outside. "Ho— Jamil, I've need of an escort. Come along."

In alarm, Jamil's gaze darted to Fatima and then back to Nonie. "I am sorry, Miss Rafferty, but you must not leave your chambers."

"Then you'll have to tie me down," she said cheerfully. "Good luck to you." With no further ado, she walked past him, and headed down the hallway.

CHAPTER TWENTY-FIVE

"We go to visit Jamie," Nonie explained over her shoulder to Jamil. "I'm going to scold him for leaving me in the lurch, today."

"Yes, miss." Apparently, Jamil had abandoned all hope of stopping her, which was just as well, since she needed him to act as a guide.

"It would be best to take the tunnels over to the slave market," she continued in a brisk tone. "That way, I can stay out of sight—I imagine there is an entrance here, somewhere?"

There was a silent pause, and she looked back at him with impatience. "Fine—if you won't show me where it is, I'll use the entrance by my old quarters—but I've an abysmal sense of direction, and if they find my skeletal remains months from now, it will be laid squarely at your door."

"This way," he capitulated, and led her through a door and down a set of servant's stairs, until they came to a narrow annex. After a quick glance around, he walked behind a set of shelves, and then lifted a hatch in the floor, exposing the entrance to a tunnel that looked very much like the one near the slave market. After pausing to light a lantern, he descended, then helped her down the ladder, and closed the hatch behind them.

Neither of them spoke for a few minutes, as she followed him in along the narrow confines of the tunnel. Nonie broke the silence, her voice echoing off the earthen walls. "I haven't thanked you for saving me at the warehouse, Jamil."

"It was my pleasure, miss."

Ruefully, she shook her head. "I don't know if I would have done the same, in your position—I hope there are no hard feelings, between us."

"Not at all, miss."

Not one to engage in idle conversation, was our Jamil. "Are you related to Fatima?"

There was a slight pause. "No, miss."

She eyed his back speculatively. There was definitely an affinity between the two, and it seemed unlikely that the naïve Fatima had taken a lover, amongst the guards. And then there was that unshakable feeling that

Fatima—for all her gentle naiveté—was the keeper of fearsome secrets. "I don't suppose you will tell me where the necromancer has disappeared to, this fine night."

"I'm afraid not, miss—here we are."

He turned at an intersection, and then led her to a ladder and another exit hatch, but it was not the one by the slave market; instead they emerged into a stable that smelled strongly of livestock and dust, and brought back an immediate memory of the camel pen.

She took a doubtful look around, as he doused the lantern. "Did we take a wrong turn?"

"It is a short walk from here," he explained, dropping the hatch closed behind them. "It is best to approach cautiously, to ensure that no one witnesses our entry."

She refrained from pointing out that the most cautious approach would, of course, be through the tunnels, where she wouldn't be exposed to above-ground eyes. But if Jamil wanted to avoid the tunnels, it seemed a likely indicator that the necromancer himself was somewhere in the tunnels, and wouldn't it be a lark, to run into him unexpectedly? But it probably would be best if she didn't—she was in an uncertain mood, just now, what with this latest attempt to cosh her out.

After a careful look around, Jamil led her down the street toward the towers of the government buildings. She could see the main square ahead, where the slave market was located—they were approaching the long way, from the opposite side, which only strengthened her belief that Jamil was avoiding the usual entrance tunnel into the *bagnios.* Never one to choose discretion when the other options were so much more interesting, she offered, "If we do run across your master, I will assure him that I forced you to accompany me, and that you'd little choice in the matter."

"Yes, miss."

Lord, the man was stoic—and I believe he is afraid to say too much to me, she thought. But little does he know that I'm a winkler of the first order, and will eventually unearth any and all secrets. "Aren't I more correctly a 'ma'am'? Being as how you did the honors, and all?"

Ah—this did seem to shake him a bit. He turned so that his eyes met hers for a moment. "I beg your pardon—ma'am."

With a warm smile that had softened many a stoic man's heart, she assured him, "I was only teasing—you may call me whatever you wish, Jamil." He'd seemed genuinely stricken there, for a moment, and she should control her impulse to tease; not everyone appreciated it. The necromancer did, though—he thought her amusing, and it pleased them both when she teased him, especially in bed. He would chuckle softly into her throat, so that it seemed to reverberate to the soles of her feet—

"Ma'am?" Jamil whispered, interrupted her thoughts. "We'll go across, now."

"Oh—sorry, I was woolgathering."

She ducked her head, and walked beside him as they crossed the square—there were only a few people scattered about, at this time of evening, but she could feel that her escort was wary, and alert.

"Are you expecting trouble?" she asked, matter-of-factly. "Have you an extra pistol?"

"No, ma'am." He slanted her an alarmed glance, and so she took pity on him, and followed the rest of the way in silence.

Once in the *bagnio*, they made their way through the throngs of slaves, and into the back area, where Jamie resided. It was not yet late, and so she was not wholly surprised to see that Jamie was nowhere in evidence. Her escort inquired of a guard, and then explained, "He is eating, and will be fetched back."

Nonie regarded him with a quirked mouth. "He dines out, again? Faith, he'll never want to escape."

Her escort bowed his head. "I believe that courtesies have been extended."

Thanks to the necromancer, no doubt, she thought. He probably facilitates Jamie's spying, so as to spy on Jamie, in turn—hopefully Jamie was better at that particular cat-and-mouse game than the mark—although she'd learned several times over that it never paid to underestimate her better half.

After deciding she may as well make herself comfortable, she settled in to sit cross-legged on the floor, her back to the wall, and a wary eye on the door—prisons always brought back bad memories. "Where do you hail from, Jamil?"

The casual question was met with a quiet disclaimer. "I would rather not say, ma'am."

So—apparently, the same mysterious place as the mark, which only made sense; the two were as thick as thieves. "You should make something up," she suggested. "Madagascar, perhaps—just to keep the conversation alive. Have you a cat?"

He shook his head, and there was the merest hint of a smile on his lips. "I do not."

With a sigh, she conceded, "Then I'm afraid we are fast running out of topics to discuss." Fortunately, in a few short moments, Jamie made his appearance, full of apologies as he walked past the curtained door, giving Jamil a cursory glance. "Sorry," he said in Gaelic. "I lost track of the time."

"All's well," she assured him easily. "Any debriefings to be had?"

"*Le Capitaine*'s arm is in a sling, and the embassy is armed to the teeth. The Dey has given assurances that his forces were not behind the attack, and has offered an escort of guards which the French—no surprise here—have declined. I am awaiting confirmation that *Le Capitaine* has decided to sail away when the shipment leaves—tomorrow, or the next day."

"Oh? Well, won't that be an interesting cruise." As Jamie was slated to board the ship and track where the pearls were going, it would make for some quality eaves-dropping. "Poor man; one can hardly blame him. He's probably rethinking this whole unholy alliance—there's nothing like a bit of bloodletting, to cause a change of attitude."

Jamie cocked his head with relish. "Not to mention he'll not be comfortable walking down a narrow street, any time soon."

"That he won't," she agreed. "But I am here to let you know that something is afoot; I think another phantom ship is being mustered out—tonight, perhaps. The mark tried to dose me again, and he's disappeared. There must be a reason he wants me to be fast asleep."

Jamie raised his sandy brows in surprise. "Tonight? Lord, does he never rest?"

"I think my arrival on the scene has caused him to step it up—I make him nervous, I do; he's worried that his days as an imperialist are drawing to a close."

Jamie smiled, as though they were engaged in casual conversation. "I'll warn the fishmongers, then, and make sure we don't miss this one, like the last one."

Fondly, Nonie reached for his hand. "Do you think the pearls pass through the slave market? My escort wanted to avoid the tunnels, coming in. And—come to think of it—the man is usually posted here at the *bagnios,* which seems a bit strange; if he's working with the mark, you'd think he'd be closer to the harbor, watching the pearls come in and out."

In a desultory fashion, Jamie played with her fingers. "I think it unlikely the pearls come through the slave markets, this is not a secure area." He thought about it for a moment. "Perhaps the mark keeps an ear to the ground—he wants to know who is brought in, by the pirates. The pirates earn their bread and butter by extorting ransoms, after all."

Nonie laughed, as though Jamie had said something amusing. "Hard to believe he's extorting his own ransoms, on the side. He'd be double-crossing the Dey."

As though teasing, Jamie tugged on a lock of her hair. "Make no assumptions."

She raised her gaze to his, and didn't have to feign her pensive reply. "No, I won't, but I think I know less than when I started. He's a walking bundle of contradictions, he is." She traced a finger on her bent knee, and confessed, "I'd like to extract him." There; she'd said the-thing-that-must-not-be-spoken-aloud.

Jamie, bless him, did not immediately question her sanity. "We're not exactly in the business of extracting people, Nonie; quite the opposite, in fact."

"You want me to extract—the female," she countered.

Jamie tilted his head. "That's not exactly the same thing—the female is willing. Whatever would you do with him? Put him in a cell somewhere, 'till the next war is over? He wouldn't thank you."

But she continued stubbornly, "I haven't thought it through, but I'd hate for him to stay here, once I've completed the assignment. There are some powerful people who would like to see him dead."

"That's exactly why he was chosen to be the mark," he reminded her. "Not to mention he's made his own bed."

Unable to argue with this blunt dose of reality, she decided to change the subject. "I was spotted by one of the Agha's men, coming down from the rooftop. Just so you know—hopefully, no one will be connecting the two incidents, but if they start thinking the shooter was female—"

"We'll have to accelerate. I understand."

Rising to her feet, she bade Jamie farewell with a fond embrace, and he whispered into her ear, "Take care, Nonie; don't get your head turned."

Too late, she thought, but Jamie is right; I'm having air dreams about happily-ever-after, and there is no such thing—at least not for me and the Dey's necromancer, who smuggles pearls for Napoleon, and indulges in some other skullduggery, on the side. And as I am spending most of my time trying to figure out how to save our mark from himself, Jamie is right to be worried. If I keep this up, I'll no longer be a legend, around Whitehall's hallowed halls.

Despite this stern attempt to draw her wayward impulses back in line, Nonie was preoccupied as she followed Jamil back across the square, and along the dark shadows toward the stable. Therefore, she was wholly unprepared when, as they slipped through the stable doors, an arm snaked around her neck, and the unmistakable tip of a blade pressed against her throat.

"Hold," said a heavily-accented voice beside her ear. "Or she dies."

CHAPTER TWENTY-SIX

Nonie immediately placed both hands on the man's arm, and made a small whimpering sound, thinking that it never rained unless it poured, but at least matters were starting to pick up—it would give her less time to lie around, mooning over the mark. From practiced experience, she'd already concluded that the man was French, and was working alone, since there was no flanker covering Jamil. It was always the way of it; the French were never very good at strategy—with the exception of their erstwhile emperor, of course.

Assessing the attacker, Jamil placed a hand on his sword hilt, but the Frenchman jerked Nonie slightly, to show he meant business. Meeting Jamil's eyes, she subtly raised her fingers, signaling to Jamil that he was to stay back. Fixing him with an imperative stare that was at odds with her voice, she whispered, "Oh—oh please, don't hurt me—"

"You will go tell your master that we will hold the girl at the French embassy," the man commanded Jamil with a jerk of his head. "Go."

Instead, Jamil took a small step forward, but Nonie frowned mightily at him, and lifted her fingers again, as she made a strangled sound of fear. Responding to the message in her eyes, Jamil stepped back again. "Let her go; I will come in her place."

"No—the girl will not be harmed, as long there are no further attempts on *Le Capitaine.* Now, go."

Lord—here's a wrinkle, thought Nonie. In light of the necromancer's reaction on the jetty, they must believe he'd not risk any harm to his red-headed wife, so they decided to hold her hostage, until *Le Capitaine* made his hasty departure. Truly, the irony of it all would be amusing, if she didn't have a blade to her throat.

She whispered in a tremulous voice, "Please; please don't hurt me." With a slight lift of her fingers she reminded Jamil that he was not to move, as she contemplated what was best to be done. The last needful thing was to be held captive at the French embassy, and the second-to-last needful thing was to allow this man to go back and tell the others that she was no ordinary Irish lass. Therefore, he had to be taken out, and in such a way that no one knew what had happened to him.

Nonie contemplated her options; she could twist the wrist beneath her hands, and thrust his own blade into the Frenchman's jugular, but the mess would be God-awful, and she never liked to leave a mess behind—messes were for amateurs. Best use a neater method. Faltering, she pleaded, "If—if I give you a pearl, will you let me go?"

There was a pause. "What pearls?"

"I have some pearls. I—I found them." She allowed the implication that she had stolen them from the palace to sink in. "I will give you one, if you let me go. Please, I beg of you."

Warily, the man released his grip on her—one should never underestimate the persuasive power of greed—although he kept the knife at the ready. "Show me."

With trembling hands, she bent to extract the pill box from her hem, at the same time sliding the handle of the small, slim knife into her palm. Nervously, she fumbled and dropped the pill box, which opened upon impact, sending several pearls the size of small pebbles skittering across the dirt floor. In the ensuing silence, the pearls glowed in the flickering lantern light; several were genuine, and could be used as bribes, or for emergency passage, if needed. The others only looked real.

"Stay back," the Frenchman warned Jamil, as he fixed his wary gaze on the other man. The Frenchman bent to collect the pearls, and with a quick thrust, Nonie plunged the blade of her knife into the base of his skull. With a guttering sound, the Frenchman collapsed forward; death was instantaneous, and had the advantage of producing very little blood.

With a gasp, Jamil knelt beside the fallen man, feeling for a pulse.

"He's dead," Nonie advised. "We'll need to dispose of his body." Normally, she would hold her mirror to his nose and mouth for a minute, just to be certain—sometimes a pulse was too faint to be felt—but in this case, there was no need.

For a moment, it seemed as though Jamil didn't hear her, as he cradled the man's head, and then gently closed the dead man's eyes with his fingers. Nonie watched in bemusement—not the behavior one would expect, from a slave master dealing with an unbeliever. "Quickly, Jamil. Shall I fetch Jamie, to help carry him?"

With a glance at the door, Jamil grasped the dead man's legs, and began to drag him toward the interior wall. "No—I will hide him in the straw, and return later. I must bring you back to the palace, and quickly."

After hesitating a moment, she agreed. "Aye then. But if you plan to toss him in the bay, he had to be weighted down, otherwise he'll wash up." She didn't want to hurt his feelings, but she didn't know how well-versed he was in the proper disposal of bodies.

When they emerged from the tunnel at the palace entrance, she could sense that Jamil was on the horns of a dilemma; he was probably entrusted with keeping watch over her—and had failed miserably, in his task—but there was a dead body to dispose of, in the meantime. "Go back and take care of it, if you wish. I'll stay in my room— my word of honor."

Her companion thought this over, and seemed to agree. "My lord must be told of this," he warned, as he opened the hatch for her.

"Definitely—he must be made aware that they are seeking leverage over him."

She arrived at the necromancer's chambers, and saw that Fatima had vacated the premises—probably to tattle to their mutual husband. The fact that—in hindsight—she should have stayed safely tucked away this evening did not improve Nonie's temper, as she settled in a chair in the dark room to await the return of her lord and master. Lucky for Fatima that she's not home, she thought; I'm in a mood, I am.

Upon reflection, it was actually good news that *Le Capitaine* wished to seize her—it showed he was indeed planning to decamp, as Jamie's spies had reported. Otherwise, there would be no point in holding the necromancer's wife as a hostage against his good behavior;

such a bold move could not be sustained in the long term.

Since one of the goals of their assignment was to turn the two factions against each other, this was a good sign, and she mustn't fret because the mark was now in the line of fire. As Jamie had correctly pointed out, he'd brought this on himself. Once Jamie sailed away with the pearls, she would complete her assignment, and then disappear from Algiers, never to be seen again.

This time, however, it would be different. Not only was she charged with extracting Saba, she very much doubted she'd be able to walk away from the Barbary mark, no matter the price she might have to pay.

It was in this uneven frame of mind that she eventually heard the necromancer's approach, and to send a strong message of disapproval, she threw her knife so that it landed with a thud in the wall beside the door, as he walked in.

Startled, his gaze flew to hers, and her heart seemed to twist within her breast, consumed with a yearning sensation that she'd not known for many, many years. Now look what you've done, she thought; Tanny would say that you've met your fate, and she'd have the right of it—how very unmanageable life is. I should be very unhappy with this wretched man, and instead, all I want to do is cast myself on his chest.

He stood still, assessing her. "Are you uninjured?"

To make up for her weakness, she replied in a steely voice, "You are going to swear by whatever you hold holy that you are not going to try to dose me again."

He approached to crouch down before her, taking her hands in his, and looking up into her face. "I do so swear. Forgive me, Nonie. I feared for your safety."

That his concern had been proved correct, only served to annoy her all the more, and she remarked with some irritation, "It's lucky, you are, that I love you." She'd been practicing, there in the dark, having not said the words since she was seven years old, but it still came out awkwardly, and she felt a bit foolish, and wished she hadn't said.

He lifted his hand and held it against her cheek in a gesture of silent reconciliation. "And I love you. You went to see Jamie?"

"Yes, I went to see Jamie—not that it did me much good; he's too busy dallying with your wife to do his job. I look about me, and I am mightily disheartened by the men folk, with the exception of Jamil, who can hold his position like the Rocks of Moher."

He closed his eyes, briefly. "You take such chances."

But in her need to reassure him, she disclaimed, "No—not truly. No one thinks me dangerous, and by the time they reassess, it is too late."

He bent his head, and traced a forefinger along her wrist. "If you had the chance, would you leave it?"

With a leap of her pulse, she wondered if he was going to suggest that they both strike out anew, together. "I suppose that depends," she offered carefully.

"Is it money? Because I can see to it—"

Biting back her annoyance, she interrupted, "You are a fool, if you think I would let another war erupt, without doin' my best to jibe the bit." In the ensuing silence, she took a calming breath, and confessed, "I didn't mean to snap; I thought for a hopeful moment that you were suggesting we run away together."

His gaze met hers in sympathy. "No. I am sorry to disappoint you."

"Why not?" she persisted, thinking that she may as well be hung for a sheep as a lamb—she had already made a fool of herself, when it came to him. "I won't believe you don't want to be with me—that this—this business of yours is more important to you."

"I love you," he said quietly, the expression in his eyes grave. "And so, I want you away from here with all speed."

"Away from you?"

His gaze held hers. "I'm afraid so."

Frowning, she considered this paradox. "I'll go—tomorrow, if you like—but you must come with me."

Ducking his head, he rubbed his thumbs across the backs of her hands. "I cannot."

They have some hold over him, she thought—they must. She had seen too many fanatical imperialists to confuse him with one; he was no ideologue, this man. And whatever it was, he could not disclose it, even to her—even to appeal for aid from the mighty British, who—and he must know this—were going to make their way to Algiers in the not-too-distant future, and bombard the daylights out of the knaves that held sway in this miserable place.

I won't tease him, she decided; I can see that it grieves him when I do. There's something here that I don't understand, and I've got to think about it, for a small space. Instead, she offered, "You mustn't be angry at Jamil; he did his best to dissuade me from my course, but I had the bit between my teeth, and I was annoyed with you."

He raised his face again, and said with a touch of humor, "No. I think that person does not exist, who can stop you, when you have the bit between your teeth."

"You could," she whispered softly, then wished she hadn't; she'd just decided she wasn't going to tease him, for heaven's sake.

"I am not so certain," he countered. "You are very good at what you do."

That it wasn't exactly a compliment was not lost on her, and she decided it was past time to change the conversation to more enjoyable channels. They were at a standstill, and the number of nights they would spend together were—sad to say—dwindling. "I know something that you are very good at—makes my toes curl, it does." She gave him a look from under her lashes.

Ah—that light in his eyes came up again—the one she lived for. "I'm afraid I cannot stay."

Teasing, she tilted her head. "You are wasting valuable time, then."

With no further demur, he stood, gathered her in his arms, and headed for the bed.

CHAPTER TWENTY-SEVEN

"My lord asks that you not leave your quarters," said Fatima apologetically. "He is concerned that the French captain will attempt to seize you again."

Nonie nodded, although she thought it more likely that Fatima's lord was worried Nonie would interfere with his misbegotten plans, now that she'd been proven uncontainable. They were seated at the window bench, Fatima sorting the inevitable embroidery silks, whilst Nonie watched, privately holding the opinion that she could hardly imagine a more tedious pastime.

With a teasing smile, Nonie suggested, "We could wear disguises, Fatima, and spend the day fishing off the jetty." She was actually rather fond of fishing, and while they were at it, she could see what the fishmongers had to report.

Her hands stilled for a moment, as Fatima wrinkled her serene brow in concern. "Oh no, Nonie; I have express orders that you must stay away from the harbor."

Perversely, this disclosure only fueled Nonie's desire to see what scheme was in play at the harbor, and unless she very much missed her guess, another phantom ship was in the process of being mustered out to Napoleon's supporters. With all appearance of docility, she reassured her companion, "Preaching to the choir, my friend; recall that I was fished out of the sea like a mackerel, once upon a time."

The other woman leaned forward and touched her hand in sympathy. "Were you very frightened, Nonie?"

"Terrified," Nonie pronounced, inspecting a fingernail. "I thought I was done for."

Fatima's soft heart was clearly wrung. "Is your family searching for you, do you think?"

With a shrug, Nonie confessed, "I have no family, truth to tell—or none who will admit to my acquaintance, leastways. Instead, I came here looking to rescue Jamie—not that he is in any hurry to be rescued."

With a stricken look, her companion quickly changed the subject. "If you'd rather not sew, perhaps we could play cards—oh; oh, perhaps not cards—"

Ruthlessly, Nonie did not allow the woman to side-step the subject. "Where is Saba? She's been playing least-in-sight, lately."

Dropping her hands in her lap, Fatima knit her brow, and gazed at the wall. "I do not know—it is strange that she is not here. Shall I call for her?"

"No matter—I've a good guess," offered Nonie darkly. "It's a sad day, when I can't trust my fellow wives."

Fatima's soft, expressionless gaze rested on her for a moment. "Would you be so very disappointed?"

A bit surprised by this dose of honesty, Nonie answered fairly, "No. Would Tahriz?"

The woman lowered her gaze, and fingered the threads with a small smile. "I think not; he is very pleased, that you are his wife."

As he'd demonstrated very thoroughly last night, thought Nonie with satisfaction, although he'd rolled out of the bed with real regret, and had not been seen nor heard from since—she'd a good mind to track the man down, and throw a spanner in his wheel, for God and country. The problem was, she had little doubt that her movements were being strictly monitored, after the set-to in the stable—although she noted that Jamil was not at his usual post in the antechamber. Thinking on this, she asked Fatima, "Tell me of Jamil—I wondered if the two of you were related, but he said you weren't kin."

"No," the woman replied, her eyes on the silks in her lap. "Jamil is not from France, Nonie."

"Do you know where he hails from, then?"

Her nimble fingers busy again, the woman asked in a mild tone, "Is he not from Algiers?"

"He wouldn't say—I've no idea why it is such a mystery."

Fatima paused for a moment. "Perhaps he would rather not speak of the things which are in his past."

Nonie shot her a swift glance, trying to decide if she heard a hint of innuendo in that last remark. In her own way, Fatima played everything just as close to the vest as did the wretched necromancer. "Well, Jamil is not on duty today, and small blame to him—I have shaken his faith in womankind."

Fatima's gaze lifted thoughtfully toward the antechamber. "I must call for Saba—I have not seen her today, and I hope she is not ill." She rose, and Nonie held her arms over her head to stretch, toying with the idea of an escapade to relieve the boredom—perhaps she'd nip down to the harbor, to see whatever it was that was going forward that she wasn't supposed to see. After all, another enemy combatant might present himself for her entertainment, and it would never do to fall out of practice.

Nonie quickly lowered her arms because she heard a soft signal whistle, and sure enough, Jamie slipped in through the window, which did not bode well—he must have a message he felt he couldn't entrust to Ibram.

"Mr. O'Hay," she exclaimed, pretending to be shocked, for Fatima's sake. "I don't believe the likes of you are allowed in here."

But Jamie was in no mood, and strode over to her, saying in Gaelic. "I'm worried, Nonie—I think that bloody French bastard has seized Saba."

She stared at him, then cursed herself for not thinking of this contingency—if *Le Capitaine* failed to secure the necromancer's red-head, the dusky Saba was the next best choice—not to mention the disappearance of the man sent to capture Nonie must have heightened his general sense of anxiety. "We'll soon find out; sit for a moment, and we'll decide what's best to do."

Fatima stood by the door, and Jamie belatedly turned to her, and bowed in a distracted fashion. "How do you do, ma'am."

"Please—what is it?" asked Fatima, looking from one to the other in concern. "Is it my lord?"

Nonie smiled to reassure her. "Have you sent for Saba? Jamie would like to speak with her, is all."

"Yes." Fatima turned to Jamie, and bowed her head. "She will be here shortly—may I offer tea?"

"She's been taken, Nonie, I am certain of it." Jamie's tone was grim, as he declined Fatima's offer with an abrupt gesture.

"Why you think they have her?"

Jamie could not be still, and so he paced back and forth. "We intercepted a communication from the embassy to the Dey, informing him of it, and seeking assurances that the mark is not going to rattle any more cages. Apparently, one of their men disappeared last night, and they suspect he was involved."

"That was actually me," Nonie confessed. "Sorry—they tried to take me, before they seized Saba."

He halted in surprise. "Did they? Well, that tears it, then." Frowning at the floor, he took a breath. "If they need her as a hostage, they won't hurt her—"

Nonie was quick to reassure him, moving to take hold of his arm with her hands. "Of course, not; they're spooked, is all. Once the pearls are delivered, and *Le Capitaine* is safely away, they'll all ungird their loins."

He nodded, and she gently squeezed his arm. It was a bit discomfiting, to see Jamie walking such a thin line—he was usually as steady as they came. On the other hand, if the French seized the necromancer, she'd no doubt be storming the embassy in short order, herself, so she couldn't lay blame.

A knock on the door revealed a servant, coming to relay a message to Fatima, and even though it was in Arabic, the tenor of the words made Jamie's head drop forward.

Her brow furrowed in distress, Fatima confessed, "He does not know where Saba is."

"I'm afraid she is probably at the French embassy," Nonie explained to the woman, thinking there was no point to sweetening the bad news. "They are holding her against Tahriz's good behavior."

Shocked, the woman looked from one to the other. "I cannot believe it—they would not dare."

"I'm going over there," said Jamie in Gaelic, his mouth pressed into a determined line.

Alarmed, Nonie grasped his shoulders. "Jamie, it's not thinking, you are. Let's plot this out, and decide what's to be done—come now, you know better."

Jamie stilled, and pressed his lips together. "Where's the mark?"

"He's gone—but he'll not be happy about this development, and he's powerful, Jamie—"

But Jamie was pent-up like a caged bear, and looked toward the door. "I'm going over there, to see what I can discover."

Nonie could not like the fact that this drama was being enacted before the others—even if they could not understand the language, they could easily perceive what was afoot, and that Jamie was a bit too interested in Saba's well-being. "Wait, Jamie; let's check with the fishmongers; someone may have seen something, and if we can discover what Saba's status is—that she's being treated well—then we can take a breath, and assess the best way forward. Some discretion is advised, my friend." This last said with a bit of emphasis.

At her implied rebuke, he made an effort to calm himself. "Aye, then." He glanced at the others, and ran his hands through his sandy hair. "Sorry."

"We'll get her back, Jamie, but we can't be jeopardizing the assignment."

"Would you like me to go over to the embassy?" Fatima interrupted in her soft voice. "I know many of the servants; they will tell me whether Saba is there. Perhaps I can speak with her."

But Nonie could not think this a good plan, and shook her head. "No, Fatima; they'll just seize another wife, for good measure."

But Fatima disagreed. "No—I will be careful, and wear a veil. The people I know there would not betray me."

While they thought this over, Jamie gave Nonie a look she recognized—he wanted to know if Fatima could be trusted. Nonie placed one hand on the opposite shoulder—their "safe" signal—and said to the woman, "I suppose so long as you're careful, such a visit would be helpful, Fatima. Mainly, we'd like to know if she's being held there, and if she is being treated well."

"We'll go too," Jamie said in English. "We'll watch over you from nearby, and you need only signal, if there is any problem."

Fatima agreed to this plan, but then added as an admonishment, "I must send word to my lord."

Nonie knew that if they cautioned for secrecy, Fatima would almost certainly back out, so she agreed in principle. "Of course—of course, Fatima; but Jamie is worried, and we'd rather not wait, if you don't mind—and we don't want to cause any more trouble between Tahriz and the French, so it may be best to scotch this attempt, before it goes any further."

Struck with the good sense of this, the small woman nodded, and then hurried to fetch her basket of embroidery silks, whilst Nonie donned her head dress, and took the opportunity to say to Jamie, "Try not to think the worst—they dare not mistreat her."

But Jamie had himself well in hand, and nodded his agreement. "No—you're right, of course; they'll treat her well, because if they didn't, it would set off the very firestorm they are hoping to avoid." He met her eyes, the expression in his own a bit rueful. "Sorry for the panic; I just hate to think she's frightened."

Feeling that it was now safe to tease him, she offered with mock reproach, "You wouldn't be half so worried, if it was me in their clutches."

"Of course, I'd be worried," he countered. "I'd be worried about the poor French."

CHAPTER TWENTY-EIGHT

"They don't dare cross the Dey—not here, surrounded by his forces," Nonie reassured Jamie in a low voice. "And the Dey relies heavily on the mark—I imagine as soon as he is aware of this little outrage, they will negotiate for her release, and she'll be home in time for tea."

They were once again lying prone on their rooftop station across from the embassy, watching for Fatima. The woman, the basket of embroidery silks on her arm, had slipped in the servant's entrance without notice—so at least she was within, and could report back. Nonie was not at all confident of Fatima's spying abilities, and so had impressed upon her the necessity of appearing disinterested, and of not raising the subject of Saba immediately. "Fatima's a little naïve, Jamie; I hope she doesn't tell her friends that we put her up to this, and that we're hiding outside, frantic with worry."

Jamie's gaze was fixed on the servant's door, and she could feel the tension radiating from him, despite his outward calm. "Yes—she'd not be my first choice, but it was kind of her to offer. I am a bit surprised he chose her for a wife, truth to tell."

"I'll not hear you criticize a fellow wife," Nonie chided, her chin resting on her hands. "It's a close-knit crew, we are."

"Perhaps she had a handsome dowry."

Nonie disabused him of this theory, which she didn't quite like, as it made the necromancer sound mercenary. "No—it's the opposite, in fact; she was captured by pirates. And recall that his wives aren't really wives in the first place; he uses them as spies, or something—she hides secrets, does our Fatima."

"I think your theory is right. I tried to ask Saba about—well, about how she doesn't sleep with him, and she closed up like an oyster. She won't say a word against him."

Nonie frowned behind her veil—she was keeping it carefully across her face, to guard against another dose of sun-burn on top of the last one, which would probably melt her poor face right off. "She's loyal to the bone—they all are. It's hard to explain; he should be knee-deep in evil doings, on account of who he serves, but instead he seems—I don't know—he seems very honorable and courteous, in an old-world sort of way."

"You're smitten," Jamie pronounced with a small smile. "Who would have imagined such a thing, I ask you?"

"Not me, that's for certain. But I'm going to cudgel my brain to come up with a way to extricate him, so that he's not hanged for his sins."

Shrugging a shoulder, Jamie cautioned, "Good luck to you—he doesn't seem in any hurry to be rescued."

There was a thread of warning in the words, which she took in good part—she and Jamie were nothing if not honest with each other. "No—but if anyone can do it, I can. The man has a soft spot for me, he does."

Their conversation was interrupted by movement at the servant's entryway, and they both lowered their heads and watched intently, as the handsome figure of Captain de Gilles emerged into the sunlight, deep in conversation with another man—a sailor, it appeared. The two paused in the street for a moment, de Gilles taking a quick, furtive glance around him, before leaning in to speak to the other. With a nod, the sailor turned to hurry down the hill, whilst de Gilles—with another quick survey of the area—strolled in the same direction.

"Bloody hell," swore Jamie in a soft tone. "What's he doing at the embassy?"

Nonie was equally surprised. "He wouldn't be transporting pearls for Napoleon, or we'd have heard about it. It must be something else, that brings him in."

"They may be seeking information—perhaps about the man who disappeared, last night."

She nodded, turning over possible explanations. "That. Or they may be trying to bribe him—neither side trusts the other in all this, thanks to us, mainly." She paused. "It's a wrinkle, though—I'd forgotten about de Gilles in all the excitement. Let's check with the fishmongers, to see what they know, and I'll mention him to the mark, to find out what he knows about him."

"Here's Fatima," Jamie said suddenly, all thoughts of de Gilles dismissed. The small woman headed across the street, and toward the rendezvous spot at the back of their building. "She doesn't look very happy," he observed with palpable disappointment. "All right, let's go."

"Hold," said Nonie, laying a hand on his arm. "That man there—isn't he the Agha's man?" She indicated a loiterer who was dressed in workman's garb, his sharp gaze at odds with his stance, as he scanned the passersby. "I think the same fellow was lounging about when I winged the Frenchman. Lord, it's like a gathering of vultures."

Jamie watched the man intently. "I imagine the Agha has his own spies, set at various locations. The French embassy must be high on the list."

"That's probably it," Nonie agreed. "*Le Capitaine* was ready to strangle the Agha on the jetty, and the both of them were ready to strangle the mark—it's a matter of mutual loathing, all around."

"We've got to get down to meet Fatima—let's go separately, since this fellow's keeping an eye out."

This was accomplished without mishap, and after carefully avoiding detection, Nonie caught up with a grim-faced Jamie, who was already speaking with Fatima in a shadowed alcove. Judging by Jamie's expression, Nonie knew what he was going to say before he said it.

"Saba's not in the embassy."

Fatima nodded, her expression stricken. "They have taken Saba away—and they have seized one of the Dey's wives also, although I don't know which one. They will hold them at a secret location as hostages, to prevent any more attacks."

"Fatima doesn't know where they're holding her." Jamie's voice was rough.

Nonie tried to soothe him. "It must be nearby, Jamie; and recall that they dare not harm her."

"No, they dare not," Fatima offered. "My friends overheard them joking that Saba would not wish to be rescued, from the man who holds her."

"Captain de Gilles," Jamie declared immediately. "That's why he was here—it all makes sense, now. Lord, Nonie; we have to follow him, and quickly—what if he's taking her somewhere on his ship? He was speaking with a sailor."

"Jamie." Nonie placed a staying hand on his arm. "We need to think about this in terms of the assignment."

But he turned to her, a fierce expression in his blue eyes. "She'll never find me again, Nonie—she thinks I'm a missionary in India."

"But we'll be able to track her, Jamie—my promise on it. Please be sensible; we can't storm de Gilles' ship, just the two of us."

"She's a beautiful girl," Jamie continued, his face a grim mask. "On a slaver's ship."

Nonie could think of no counter to this irrefutable fact, and so remained silent, thinking furiously.

"Should we enlist the fishmongers?"

Even as he said the words, Nonie could hear the doubt in his voice, and with good reason. "No—we can't start a pitched battle, Jamie; it would endanger Saba, and the assignment would be in ruins."

Looking into his face, Nonie realized he was going to go, one way or another. All right, she thought with resignation, if we're going to come to a bad end—me and Jamie—better it be for a noble cause, than for some petty foolishness. "Let's do a feint, then—I'll be another hostage, and you'll be a French sailor, delivering me."

"Perfect." Jamie nodded, his eyes brightening as they always did, when they were called upon to improvise.

After cautioning Fatima to stay close, they hurried down the streets of the Kasbah, carefully staying within the thick throngs of people, and moving as rapidly as they could toward the harbor.

"Where do we go?" Fatima finally asked, a bit breathlessly.

Briskly, Nonie instructed the other woman, "We'll board a ship to rescue Saba, and you must watch from the shore. If anything goes wrong, I will signal with a mirror, and if you see the signal, you are to go for help, as quickly as you can." This seemed the best use of her; she couldn't send Fatima back home, for fear she'd say the wrong thing to the wrong person.

Jamie must have had the same concerns, and asked in Gaelic, "Can she keep quiet?"

"I hope so, Jamie; but recall we wouldn't have known where Saba was without her, so you can't be resentin' her—she's doin' her best."

"Don't drop your 'g's'," he admonished. "You-know-who'd be unhappy with you."

She retorted with some heat, "I'll drop my 'g's' if I please, Jamie O'Hay; it's entitled I am, what with havin' to deal with the crossin's and double-crossin's in this bloody, *bloody* town—and a lovesick flanker, to boot."

"Lord," he exclaimed in disgust. "I'm a sorry excuse."

She smiled, and he smiled, and soon they were both chuckling, which is how it usually went, when they had to go in somewhere, and perform an impossible task. It broke the tension—usually with the aid of a bracing drop of whiskey, but as there was none to be had, they'd have to do without.

They carefully assessed the harbor from the shadows of a fish market stall—not the most comfortable viewpoint, because the fish under the awning were beginning to smell ripe, in the heat. It seemed to Nonie that none of the ships at anchor were in the process of mustering out, and so she waited to discover what their contact knew. Jamie had crouched to confer quietly with a man who was sitting beside the stall, mending his nets with a steady hand, and never looking up.

"Is he Irish, also?" Fatima whispered.

Nonie well knew that Fatima should be told as little as possible, and so she replied, "Not Irish—but he is a friend, who will take us out to the correct ship." She turned to the woman to emphasize, "You mustn't say anything of this, Fatima; if I signal with a flashing light, you are to go find Tahriz, and tell him we need help— but tell no one else. Do you promise?"

"I promise," the woman responded in a serious tone, her dark eyes opaque. She then gently took both Nonie's hands in her own. "You will be careful, Nonie?"

"I'm rarely careful," Nonie confessed with a smile. "And you mustn't worry—I'll be back before dinner. But remember, you are not to say anything to anyone; just wait here quietly."

"Yes," Fatima nodded.

Jamie came back to them. "He'll take us out—he knows which ship, but he says they haven't noticed anything unusual, going forward."

Nonie decided this didn't necessarily mean they were on the wrong track. "He's a wily one, is de Gilles. Let's keep on with the plan."

After reminding Fatima to wait and watch, they boarded the fishmonger's small dory, and sat without speaking whilst he rowed them out, and approached an unmarked vessel that did not appear to be manned.

"This doesn't look right," Jamie observed as they approached. "There's no crew on deck, and the sails are still furled." He spoke to the guide. "Are you certain this is it?"

"Yes," the man said, lifting his eyes for a moment. "This is de Gilles' ship—and he boarded within the hour."

"They'll want to keep it very quiet, if they're spiriting two high-value hostages away," Nonie pointed out reasonably. "Brandish your pistol; I'll be defiant—and don't forget you're French."

They sidled up beside the frigate, Jamie calling out a hail in French. After a few moments, one of the portholes opened, and a sailor leaned out, gesturing them away. "*Partez.*"

But Jamie insisted, "No—I've another hostage; *Le Capitaine* wants you to take this one, too."

The sailor eyed Nonie for a moment, then directed them to wait, as he closed the porthole. In a moment, the man appeared on deck, looking annoyed as he threw over a rope ladder. "Come aboard, then."

While their guide tied the boat to the ladder's end, Jamie prodded Nonie with his pistol. "Up the ladder."

"You'll not be looking up my *kaftan*," Nonie warned in a spirited voice. "Keep your eyes to yourself."

"*Tais toi*," snapped Jamie. "You will do as you are told."

"I demand to see the captain," Face aflame, Nonie appealed to the sailor. "This is an outrage—"

Jamie interrupted to ask, "Where is Captain de Gilles? I have instructions—"

"This way," called the sailor over his shoulder, as he descended the companionway stairs. "Quickly, we do not wish to draw attention."

With a flounce of defiance, Nonie followed the man down the stairway, and below the main deck, to where he lifted the trap door that led to the cargo hold. "The captain is counting inventory in the hold." With a careless gesture, the sailor indicated they were to descend the steps.

I don't have a good feeling about this, thought Nonie, as she followed Jamie down the rickety ladder into the darkness; it is altogether too quiet, for a ship that is supposedly guarding high-value hostages.

Once in the hold, the weak sunlight that streamed through the small porthole revealed a variety of young girls, huddled in the bow end of the cargo hold, and watching them with curious eyes. Blinking with surprise, Nonie heard Jamie call out in a soft voice, "Saba?"

With a bang, the hatch door slammed shut above their heads.

CHAPTER TWENTY-NINE

"Hey," called Jamie, pounding on the trap door with a fist. *"Qu'est que c'est?"*

"Mother a' mercy, Jamie—it's a trap." On high alert, Nonie whirled to face the occupants of the cargo hold, but she could discern no immediate threat; only several dozen young girls, crouched in a huddle at the far end, and watching them. "Saba?" she ventured, and Jamie paused in his endeavors to look down, but there was no response, only the creaking of the timbers, as the ship rocked slightly.

"They are slaves," said Jamie into the silence. "De Gilles must be transporting slaves."

"Where, though? *Away* from Algiers?" Frowning, Nonie tried to make sense of it, her gaze sweeping the silent girls. They certainly did not look frightened, the multiple pairs of dark eyes watching them with a lively interest, and a few beginning to whisper behind their hands.

"The left me my pistol; they're not very savvy for kidnappers, are they?" Jamie began to bang on the trap door again, but his heart wasn't in it; it seemed apparent that no mistake had been made. "All right, what's our strategy?"

But Nonie was fighting an idea that was—truly—too terrible to contemplate, and so she made no response, her gaze focused on the girls without truly seeing them.

After a pause, Jamie offered, "Not to worry, Nonie; if de Gilles is anything like the Normandy mark, he'll make some colossal mistake—like forget to take my pistol—and the assignment will soon be back on track." He glanced up at the trap door again. "We need to find Saba, though; we'll need to coordinate—"

"Jamie," Nonie whispered, having come to the reluctant conclusion that the terrible idea must be voiced, and bloody, *bloody* hell that she couldn't just ignore it. "I don't think Saba is on board."

"What?" Jamie's gaze flew to hers, but they both looked up, upon hearing activity above their heads, muffled voices and footsteps that shook the dust loose from the ceiling timbers. "Of course, Saba must be on board—Fatima knew it, and the sailor didn't argue—"

"I don't think its Saba they want. I think it's us."

"What are you talking about?" Jamie dropped down from the ladder, and approached her, a frown creasing his brow. "Do you think *Le Capitaine* has twigged us, and knows who we are? Then why aren't we dead?"

"Not *Le Capitaine,* Jamie—the mark. Let's say the mark wanted to remove us from the arena—"

Frozen for a moment, Jamie slowly ducked his head and swore, his hands resting on his hips. "You are never going to tell me that Fatima put us up to this? I'll not believe it—she's not capable."

Nonie pressed her fingers to her temples, trying to suppress the sick feeling of betrayal that threatened to overwhelm her. "She said something to me on the shore—she asked if I would be careful, and it seemed as though she was sad—as though we were parting. I thought it a bit odd, at the time." Pulling herself together, she lifted her face and scanned the girls again, some of whom were openly giggling at Jamie. "It makes sense, Jamie. The mark was unhappy about the abduction attempt on me—and he said nothing could stop me, once I'd the bit between my teeth. He was worried I'd be hurt."

Perversely, Jamie seemed impressed by this insight. "He said that? He has the right of it."

She was not amused, and pronounced in a grim tone, "Lord, Jamie, it's not funny. If he was here, I would strangle him with my bare hands."

The gleaming blue eyes met hers. "Of course, it's funny, Nonie. He's turned the tables, and now we're the marks."

"Yes—we're the marks," she agreed, much struck. "And we were as easily gulled as the Normandy mark." Despite everything, she responded to him, and made a wry mouth—she'd think about this little betrayal later; right now, she had work on turning the tables, herself.

Jamie's gaze traveled over the beams above their heads, listening to the movement above. "What of our information, though—about Saba and the Dey's wife being held hostage?"

"Planted," she declared. "I'll bet my teeth, Jamie."

"So—if the mark's behind this, then Saba is in no danger." It was evident this was the overriding concern for him.

"No—and neither are we, I daresay, which is why you still have your pistol. He just wants us out of commission, for the nonce."

He grinned at her. "I'll be sorry to disappoint him. Ready for a swim?"

"Not in this sack—I'll have to make do in my shift."

Jamie helped Nonie pull her *kaftan* over her head, and she carefully tied her pill box, knife, and mirror securely into a corner of her hem. "We'll do a double-back; make a fuss to distract them, and then when I'm in the clear, you can follow. Do you think you can get your shoulders through?"

Jamie gauged the size of the porthole. "I'll manage. If we're separated, we meet up at the fish market."

He reached to open the porthole, then placed his hands on her waist to hoist her up, as more giggling could be heard from behind them. Nonie wriggled her shoulders through the porthole, and Jamie retreated back to the trap door, to pound and shout for attention.

She took a quick glance above her, to note if there were any sentries posted along the deck, and then froze upon beholding the figure of a man, seating directly above her, his bare legs dangling over the side, as he whittled on a stick.

De Gilles flashed his charming smile. "*Madame. Bonjour.*"

"Captain de Gilles," she acknowledged politely, squinting up at him. "Well met."

"I have been given strict instructions not to trust you an inch," the Frenchman continued amiably, as he whittled. "And to keep you out of direct sunlight."

"Then I have every confidence you will not shoot me in the water," she replied, wriggling so that she was seated on the edge of the porthole. "Good luck, in all your future endeavors."

"*Arrêtez*; there is a young woman aboard." He sighed, and made a quick gesture, entirely French, which conveyed a sincere and masculine appreciation for large breasts. "I understand she is intended for the gentleman."

But Nonie was undeterred. "You must discuss it with him; I've a pressing engagement, I do."

He paused in his whittling, and his eyes met hers. "If you jump, I will jump also, and–make no mistake—I will catch you. Then, I will be forced to bind you, hand and foot, for the remainder of our journey." He went back to his whittling, and added, "You must lean back; I can see down the front of your shift."

"You may have the right of it," she conceded, squinting up at him as she thought this over. "Where is it that we go?"

He smiled, his teeth flashing white again. "We go to *la belle France, bien sûr.*"

"Wonderful," she said with great irony. "I have yet to make your emperor's acquaintance—perhaps we will arrive in France at the same time he does, after he slithers away from Elba."

The smile faltered for a moment, and he cocked his head in irritation. "He is not my emperor, *madame.*"

She eyed him, speculatively. "Then you and he must agree to disagree."

"You are too long in the sun," he chided. "I will have failed in my one task; please withdraw—you will hear from me, once we are underway."

Without comment, she squirmed her way back into the cargo hold, to be helped to the floor by a bemused Jamie, who'd been listening in wonder. "Well, at least we know that you were right, and that the mark is behind this. What now?"

She checked her palms for splinters. "We'll need to consult with Captain de Gilles, again, but we'll wait until we've sailed 'round the point. I imagine the mark has his people watching us like shrill kites, anyway, so after we've sailed out of sight, we'll pull a disease feint."

He nodded. "All right; who's diseased?"

"You are. Fortunately, you have the pock marks to prove it." She glanced up at him. "Saba is aboard—did you hear?"

"Yes. Thank God."

"So—apparently, the mark is going to hand her over to you, as a sop to make up for all the inconvenience."

There was a pause, as she watched him digest this much-welcomed news; there was no doubt he was battling conflicting emotions, and so she added in a sincere tone, "Jamie, if you want to continue on to France with her, I'll complete the assignment on my own. It's not as though I don't have supporters, here."

"No," he said immediately. No—I go back with you. I just need to see to it that she is kept safe." He glanced quickly over at the girls, who continued to watch them avidly.

Like little birds, thought Nonie a bit sadly; they seemed completely unaware of the fate in store for them—small wonder Jamie was worried about Saba. "Well, if it's any consolation, I don't believe the mark would be so petty as to refuse to set her aside out of spite, once he discovers that we didn't fall in with his little scheme."

But Jamie, bless him, was resolute. "It doesn't matter, Nonie—she's a Christian, and the Mughal marriage can be set aside on those grounds—it's not binding. We'll be married, one way or another, but I wish I felt better about leaving her aboard."

To reassure him, she pointed out, "I can't imagine the mark would place her here, if he wasn't certain that de Gilles could be trusted."

The deck beneath their feet tilted slightly, as the groaning of wood rubbing against wood could be heard, mixed with the excited murmurs of the girls. Standing next to Jamie, Nonie steadied herself with a hand on his shoulder, and stood on her toes to peer out the port-hole, as they watched the shoreline begin to recede. "We're underway—wait until we round the point, then let's put the feint into play."

With a calculating nod, Jamie looked for a good place to lie on the floor. "All right—I'm deathly sick. What are you going to say to de Gilles, to convince him to let us go?

With a grim little smile, she said only, "I'm going to appeal to his better nature."

Her companion grimaced in mock concern. "Katy, bar the door."

"Exactly," she agreed.

CHAPTER THIRTY

The ship had rounded the point, and was headed out to the Mediterranean Sea when Nonie hoisted herself out of the port hole, and shouted up toward the deck, "*Aide*; we have a sick man, below." She continued in this vein for a time, until a sailor leaned his head over the gunwale, above her. "The man is sick," she shouted in French. "I think it is the smallpox."

The sailor's eyes widened in horror, and then he withdrew. With a jerk, she clamped the porthole shut, and went over to sit beside the ailing Jamie to await events.

With impressive fervor, he sweated and tossed and murmured unintelligibly, his eyes rolling back in his head as she bent over him in mock concern. "Grifter," she murmured. "It would serve you right, if they tossed your sorry carcass to the sharks."

She looked up, as the cargo trap door opened slowly, the barrel of a pistol prominently displayed as two sailors warily crept down the ladder. "Please, *monsieurs*," she pleaded in a pitiful voice, weeping, as she clasped Jamie's hand. "He is so very sick." Lifting his arm, she slid his sleeve back, so as to expose the smallpox scars, and the sailors nearly tumbled over each other in their haste to ascend the ladder again.

As the girls murmured in distress, Nonie bent over Jamie, and hoped the captain's fear that smallpox would wipe out his human cargo overrode any warnings he'd received from the necromancer about her scheming ways.

After a short time, the trap door reopened, and two different men appeared—almost certainly two who had already survived smallpox. Once again, Nonie implored them for mercy, weeping over Jamie's hand in a distracted manner.

"Stand back," one instructed, and they bent to lift the writhing and incoherent Jamie by his legs and arms. As they shuffled from side to side, carrying the sick man over to the ladder, Nonie fussed over Jamie, stroking his head, and begging the men to be careful, with the result that the expressions on their faces were almost comical, when she suddenly held their own pistols on them, and instructed them to freeze in a cool voice. "I'd like to speak to Captain de Gilles, if I may."

In short order, Jamie and Nonie were assembled on the deck, their dispirited hostages shielding them, as they awaited the arrival of the captain.

"*Madame*," said de Gilles, as he approached with long strides. "I am not so very surprised, I must confess."

"Back," Nonie warned, cocking the pistol against her sailor's head. "I will have the truth from you, if you please. Where is it we go?"

Coming to a halt, he spread his hands in a gesture of surprise. "We go to France—fie; do you think I do not speak the truth? You sting me."

Having decided that it hardly mattered, she moved on to the nub of the matter. "I would like to speak with you privately, and make an offer. If you do not accept my offer, then we will escape nevertheless, and you will be the poorer."

They all stood for a moment in silence, as the French captain allowed a small smile to play around his lips. "By all means, then; let us go to my cabin, and I will hear what you have to say."

They followed him down the companionway to the captain's quarters, where they were offered wine, which Nonie politely refused for both of them. Nonie found him difficult to read, beneath his charming visage. They'd encountered de Gilles once before, in Normandy, but if he recognized them, he gave no indication. This was just as well; she would be hard-pressed to explain why two chateau servants were suddenly meddling around in volatile Barbary politics.

Without preamble, Nonie announced, "I will give you two very fine pearls for your troubles, if you look the other way whilst we escape."

At this, he cocked a brow, impressed. "Truly, you have stolen pearls from the Dey?"

Nonie was stung in her own turn. "Of course, I have; you can't think that I came upon them honestly?"

"*De vrai*," he conceded. "Although—they may have been a gift."

This said with a hint of innuendo, and Nonie was quick to disabuse him. "No—even I have standards. They were stolen, fair and square."

He bowed his head. "Then I commend you."

"So, if you will let us be on our way, we would be much obliged, and never mention that a deal was struck."

Thoughtfully, he considered her for a long moment, his expression unreadable. "I am given to understand, *madame*, that you must be saved from yourself, and to this end I must take you to France."

"Good luck to you," she said, almost kindly. "I've a score to settle with a certain necromancer, and I'll not be sailing to France with you, one way or another."

The captain shrugged a shoulder. "You are certain? I am to see to it that you are supplied with funds, and put on a ship to Ireland, if that is your desire."

"That's a very fine offer; but no thank you, just the same. I am going to return to Algiers, and take great pleasure in holding a blade to his throat."

He raised his brows in mock-censure. "Fie, you are bloodthirsty."

"I won't kill him," she promised. "But he won't know that."

Suddenly, de Gilles threw his head back, and laughed. "*Bien.* I think it would be prudent to take your pearls, and send you on your way."

"Thank you," she replied sincerely, and bent to untie the pill box from the hem of her shift. Plucking two large pearls, she handed them over to him.

"This one," he said mildly, "is not genuine." He handed it back to her, and waited expectantly.

Now it was Jamie's turn to laugh aloud, and Nonie couldn't help smiling, herself. "Isn't it? Well, here's another, then."

After tucking the pearls into his waistcoat pocket, he strode over to the cabin door. "This way; I will have a boat lowered for you. We are only a mile off shore, and it is a good place to land—there is a small town, at the point, and you will be able to hire camels."

"Saba comes too." Jamie spoke up, unexpectedly.

When Nonie glanced at him in surprise, he explained in Gaelic, "I'm not leaving her here with the likes of him—we've no idea what he's going to do with the girls, and I don't have a good feeling about it."

This seemed a valid point, and—although she probably shouldn't press her luck—Nonie turned to ask de Gilles, "What do you plan to do with the girls in the hold?"

"*Les jeune filles?* Since you have refused to accompany us, I do not believe I will tell you."

But Nonie was silent, because she had that feeling she sometimes had, when her instincts were telling her to pay closer attention. *Les jeune filles*—it meant "the little girls," and was the code name for the smuggled pearls. There was something here—something that nibbled at the corners of her mind—

"They will not be put to prostitution, if that is your concern."

She didn't care for his patronizing tone, but replied mildly, "It isn't my concern—my concerns are a bit wider-ranging. Nevertheless, we will take Saba with us, and relieve you of that particular burden."

De Gilles sent an amused, sidelong glance at Jamie which expressed his awareness that the man did not trust him. "Ah; I will be sorry to see her go." He then stepped out the door to issue instructions.

"I'd like to knock him down," Jamie commented into the silence.

Nonie's gaze was thoughtful, as she contemplated the door. "He's a puzzle, he is. I don't know what to think of him—which is very unlike me, you must admit."

But Jamie continued annoyed. "I've an impulse to free the girls, just to spite him, but I imagine they'd only be re-captured and taken back to the slave market, so I suppose it's not worth the effort."

"No," she agreed. "And pray let's remember our assignment, for more than a few minutes at a time. We can't be distracted by every tale of hard luck in this God-forsaken place—there's one behind every corner."

Any reply was forgotten as Saba entered, and in two strides, Jamie was over to her, clasping her in an embrace and murmuring in Italian, while she clung to him, her eyes tightly closed.

Fancy that, thought Nonie, observing the two; Jamie truly loves her. She felt a pang, as she considered her own lover, who'd lately tricked her into boarding a slaver's ship, and packed her off without a second thought. Perhaps she'd actually be angry with him, this time, instead of collapsing at his feet with a craven show of devotion—look where it had gotten her.

Shaking off this unhappy thought, she noted in Gaelic, "Between my red head and Saba's bosom, everyone will remember us, Jamie. Let's have Saba wear my *kaftan,* and I'll dress as a boy."

This was accomplished, and soon the three of them were boarding the tender to be rowed ashore. After

Jamie and Saba had descended the rope ladder, de Gilles bowed in an ironic gesture to Nonie. "*Adieu, madame.* It is my sincere hope that we never meet again."

There was something in his tone that told her that he had indeed recognized them, from their Normandy adventure. With a small smile of acknowledgement, she turned to descend. "Never is a long time, *monsieur.* I will say *au revoir,* instead."

"As you wish," he agreed politely, and watched her descend with an unreadable expression.

CHAPTER THIRTY-ONE

Nonie clasped the waist of her camel-driver, deep in thought, as the ungainly animal lumbered along the dusty road. They were traveling in the late afternoon to avoid the midday heat, having spent the earlier portion of the day at thievery, so as to amass some funds—she and Jamie were excellent pickpockets, particularly when they worked as a team.

Jamie and Saba rode the other camel, Saba sleepily resting her cheek against Jamie's back as they walked the long road back to Algiers. Nonie's hair was tucked into a boy's *taqiyah*, and they'd stained her face and hands with a batch of walnut dye, which had the added effect of protecting her from the brutal sun. That anyone who scrutinized her closely would conclude that she was not a boy couldn't be helped; she would try to avoid such scrutiny, and it was a mighty relief not to be constrained by the wretched *kaftan* anymore—Saba was welcome to it.

They were traveling back to Algiers along the coast road, the deep blue sea visible to their left as they passed vineyards, groves and the occasional village on their plodding, rocking journey.

Jamie shifted a hand to hold Saba's hands secure at his waist, as she seemed to be asleep, her head lolling against his back in rhythm with the camel's footsteps.

"I'm glad we have her," Nonie remarked softly, so as not to wake the other girl. "I have some questions."

Jamie turned to bestow a rueful smile. "I'm sorry to have pulled such a trick, Nonie, but there was no possible way I was going to leave her aboard."

Since this seemed the appropriate opening to give voice to some disturbing thoughts that she'd been entertaining, Nonie mentally girded her loins. "I don't know, Jamie; I think de Gilles isn't at all what he seems."

Jamie shrugged. "I suppose that's the rumor. Hard to believe it's true, though."

"No, that's not what I meant." She paused. "I meant that I don't think he's trading slaves."

With open skepticism, he glanced at her. "And he just happens to have a cargo-hold full of slave girls?"

Looking out over the serene blue sea, she persevered. "Hear me out, for a moment. What if—what if the mark is not supporting Napoleon?"

Raising a brow, Jamie replied diplomatically, "Then he is doing an excellent imitation of someone who is supporting Napoleon."

Alive to his tone, she made a wry mouth. "Don't think that I'm looking for an excuse to clear him; I've already leveled that charge at myself. But—if he *is* smuggling pearls for Napoleoon, then Fatima and Captain de Gilles are involved, up to their necks."

Jamie nodded in agreement. "What of it? He's a slaver, and she's the mark's wife—not a surprise, either way."

But Nonie persisted, "I made a comment to de Gilles about his beloved emperor, and he was quick to refute it; it was almost as if he couldn't contain his revulsion."

Jamie contemplated the back of his camel's head. "Go on."

"What struck me was that it was the same response I got from Fatima. She's French, and I teased her about her emperor." Frowning, she watched the road before them for a moment. "I had the same impression from each; it was as if the mask each of them wore suddenly slipped—just for a moment."

But Jamie remained unconvinced. "All right—let's assume, for the nonce, that they despise Napoleon, the both of them. But the mark is working hand-in-glove with the Dey to arrange for the shipments; our intelligence is irrefutable."

She turned to him, having decided there was nothing for it; she had to voice her suspicions aloud. "That's just it; the intelligence-gatherers thought he referred to the pearls—but what if the *jeune filles* were actually *jeune filles*?"

Jamie glanced over to her in surprise, his eyes flashing blue against his oil-stained face. "He's smuggling *girls*?"

"Think on it, Jamie. We saw a cargo-full of girls, and they didn't seem frightened or alarmed, did they? And de Gilles said they were sailing to France, where slavery is illegal."

"Prostitution," he said bluntly. "You are being naïve if you think anything else—no matter what he told us."

Nonie looked ahead again, and frowned. "It just doesn't fit, Jamie—the mark, Fatima, Jamil—even Saba; none of them are the type of people who would be involved in smuggling young girls for prostitution—I'd bet my teeth on it."

He contemplated this thought, as the camels plodded along, the placid beasts ignoring two dogs who ran alongside for a few minutes, barking. "You think he is freeing the slaves—like a bloody Moses? But that makes no sense, Nonie—why wouldn't he just tell you, if that was his game?"

Slowly, she replied, "Because we are working at cross-purposes—faith, he's said it to me, outright, and more than once. I assumed he meant Napoleon, but now—now I wonder if it has nothing to do with Napoleon. We want to put a stop to the supply ships, and he doesn't—because of the girls. He is using the supply ships to smuggle slaves to freedom—and he must be doing it without the Dey's knowledge."

But Jamie found this implausible, and fixed her with the same look that he usually gave her when he thought she was stretching their luck. "How is that possible? The place is infested with spies." That they were acquainted with many of them went without saying.

But Nonie was becoming more and more convinced of her theory, now that she was voicing it aloud. "The more I think on it, the more it makes sense—the mark has his own network, and his people are running their own, parallel operation, whoever they are."

Jamie contemplated the road ahead, thinking this over. "If this is true—and I'm not for a moment certain that it is—who, exactly, are they? French royalists?"

This was, of course, the thousand-pound question. "I don't know—perhaps, although I don't believe the mark is French. I don't know what he is, and he is very reluctant to let me know—as though it would give the game away."

Jamie met her eyes, and asked another thousand-pound question. "So how will this affect our assignment?"

She sighed. "I suppose it doesn't. But it would explain why some things never seemed to add up to me. Like how the mark seems so—I don't know, so honorable, I suppose, despite his dark doings. And how the wives and concubines are not truly wives and concubines. And how he is trying to influence the Dey, with his silly hocus-pocus—" She paused, suddenly struck, and asked, "Do you mind if we wake Saba? I'd like to ask her something."

"Of course, not; the assignment has every priority." This said in a firm tone, to make up for the fact that he had already demonstrated that this was not exactly true. Gently shaking the hands he held at his waist, he said, "Saba—*svegliati.*"

The girl raised her head, disoriented, and murmured a few words in a language unfamiliar to Nonie, which was a surprise; over the course of their work she and Jamie were able to speak at least a smattering of nearly every European language.

"What is that?" She asked Jamie in Gaelic. "Hebrew, perhaps?"

He seemed equally surprised. "I don't think so; she wanted me to know from the start that she was Christian." He rubbed the girl's arm gently and asked in Italian, "Are you awake? Nonie wishes to speak with you."

"*Si.*" The girl smiled a sleepy smile at Nonie. "*Bene.*"

Nonie's Italian was a bit sketchy, so she slowly translated out the question as best she could.   "The sister of the Dey—Nadia. Dead?"

The girl nodded, a faint wrinkle between her brows the only indication that the question was at all unusual. "*Sì.*"

"How?"

The girl struggled with the translation. "War—" She then made a clutching gesture with her hands.

"*Catturato?*" suggested Jamie. "Captured?"

The girl nodded. "*Sì, catturato.*"

With some excitement, Nonie turned to Jamie. "I stand corrected; the Dey knows about the *jeune filles*, Jamie. He is allowing the mark to smuggle them out, because of what happened to his sister. The reason the mark is posing as a necromancer is because the Dey believes that his dead sister wishes the girls to be set free. That's the whole point."

"Holy Mother," pronounced Jamie, shaking his head in admiration. "What a scheme—hard to believe he pulled it off."

But Nonie found that she was mightily heartened. "It all makes sense, now—the mark never seemed like a grifter who'd exploit the grieving, the way he did."

"I hope you are right," he replied in a tone that cautioned her. "Be wary, though; obviously, he wants us out of the arena."

But Nonie had the bit between her teeth, and smiled in a friendly fashion at Saba. "Tahriz—your brother?"

Startled, the girl disclaimed, but not before Nonie caught a glimpse of wariness in her dark eyes. "They are related," she pronounced to Jamie, still smiling at Saba. "Bet on it."

Jamie grinned, suddenly. "Then we'll be related by marriage—you and I; fancy that."

But Nonie firmly quashed a pang of regret. "Not really, Jamie—mine's a hoax, remember? Can you find out where she hails from, do you think?"'

"We'll see," he temporized. "I'll not be browbeating her."

Alive to his defensive tone, she changed the subject. "Lord, but these beasts are slow. Let's hope *le bon capitaine* hasn't already sailed with the pearls."

But Jamie was unconcerned. "If he has, he can't have gone far—I'll find a way to track him, never fear." He glanced at her. "You'll watch over this one, while I'm about it?"

She lifted her brows at him in mock reproof. "Like an angel at the cradle."

He looked ahead, hesitating, and then confessed, "It's only that I'm worried you'll do something foolish, Nonie. It's smitten, you are."

In a light tone, she replied, "Not so smitten as to insist we storm a ship single-handedly, and jeopardize the assignment in the process."

"Touché," he replied in a dry tone. "I'll say no more."

CHAPTER THIRTY-TWO

The fishmonger gathered up his ripe-smelling sacks, and prepared to depart. He'd brought them their supper, along with a briefing on the latest developments between the warring factions in the fair city of Algiers. They were staying in a small, nondescript residence which served as a safe house for any of their people who happened to be skulking in the area. The fishmonger had informed them that *Le Capitaine* was still in town, and that he and the Agha had publicly quarreled on the grounds of the embassy. Of the necromancer, there had been no sign.

"He's probably sleeping," Nonie remarked, as she picked the last bits of meat from the fish bones with her fingernails—Lord, she was hungry, after the day's adventures. "He's exhausted after staying up all night, to send off a batch of slaves. Leastways, he was the last time."

"What was the quarrel about?" Jamie asked, as he passed the jug of water to Saba.

"The pearls," answered the man. "There were accusations and counter-accusations about double-dealing."

This was not a surprise, as the Dey had a history of double-dealing; after all, it was the reason *Le Capitaine* felt compelled to make a visit, and bang some heads together.

Nonie observed in Gaelic, "A quarrelsome man, is the Agha; I believe he knows what the mark is about, and is trying to influence the Dey the other way."

Jamie nodded with satisfaction; a divided enemy was a weakened enemy. "That's an impressive tangle—the Frenchman against everyone, and the necromancer against the Agha. I imagine nerves are ragged at the palace."

But Nonie cautioned, "Not too ragged, I hope." She addressed the fishmonger in English. "Is *Le Capitaine* under guard? We don't want him to run into a blade in some dark corner, before he sails."

The fishmonger assured them, "He goes nowhere without a vanguard—four or five men around him."

"Do we have anyone close to him?"

"No—it was impossible to permeate. We have watchers at the embassy, though. The rumor is that he sails the day after next."

"Put me on the crew," Jamie directed him. "Even if I have to be a cook."

"You are not a very good cook," Nonie observed doubtfully. "You'll be found out, and you'll wind up in the drink."

"Hush, you—you're not exactly one to speak." He smiled at her and she smiled back; their spirits were always buoyed when an assignment looked to be heading for a successful close. This one, of course, had involved a few more twists and turns than some of the others, but nevertheless, it appeared that all loose ends would soon be tied up nicely. Except for her own loose end, of course.

They saw the contact out, then settled down to drink tea out of pottery cups. Jamie motioned for Saba to come sit with him, and with a happy sigh, the girl settled within his arms, the shadows only serving to accentuate the contours of her beautiful profile. Watching them melt into each other, Nonie felt a pang of yearning so strong she had to look away for a moment. "What of— the other girl?" she asked Jamie, not wanting to mention Aditi's name.

He pressed his cheek against Saba's head. "She's on a ship to India. I don't have high hopes."

"Ah, well; at least you managed to set her free. She can't ask for more."

But Jamie did not want to speak of Aditi. "It may be best that no one here knows that we have returned." The blue eyes slid over to her.

She didn't pretend to misunderstand. "I'm truly sorry, Jamie, but I could no more not see him again than you could allow this one to sail away with de Gilles."

He made no response, but absently stroked Saba's arms. He knows me all too well, she thought, making a wry mouth—dear Jamie. "And I'm so very tempted to confirm what I suspect—and confront him with his many, many sins."

Jamie nodded in resignation. "You do what you like— there's none to blame you."

She leaned to touch his arm, moved by his loyalty. "I'll not be foolish—I'll assess, and if I truly think he means to take me out of action again, I'll disengage."

He took another drink of tea from the chipped cup, and asked in a steady tone, "In the event you are seized, will you leave instructions for Saba?"

She had forgotten he had concerns other than her own foolishness, and loved him the more for his generosity. "Of course. If anything happens to me, she'll be packed off to St. Michael's as though she were a pearl of great price; my solemn promise on it."

After an assignment—if they were not immediately called to another assignment, elsewhere—they would meet up with the grey-eyed man in the basement of an obscure church in London, to hold a debriefing, and be handsomely paid. They never met directly with anyone from the Home Office—or even other agents—because officially, no one knew she and Jamie existed.

He nodded. "Thank you. I wouldn't be easy, else."

Watching him in the gathering dusk, with Saba resting within the circle of his arms, she suddenly felt compelled to say, "I told him, Jamie—I told the mark about Scullabogue barn."

There was a silence for a moment, and Jamie did not look at her. "I can't speak of it, Nonie."

Gently she continued, "I only said, because I thought you might want to tell Saba. It seemed—well, it seemed to help; to tell him of it. There was an easin'."

He did not respond, but lowered his cheek next to Saba's, and embraced her tenderly. That's my cue, thought Nonie, and with a brisk movement, she set down her cup and rose to her feet. "I'll sleep on the roof, then, and see you in the morning."

But Jamie rose also, disclaiming. "No—I'll sleep on the roof; you stay here with Saba."

Nonie stared at him in amused astonishment, as he explained self-consciously, "We are going to wait until we are married."

Smiling, she shook her head. "Lord; who are you, and what have you done with Jamie?"

But he stood his ground, embarrassed, but resolute. "It's important that I do this right, Nonie; she deserves no less. And she's so innocent—she'd be shocked, if I even made the attempt."

But Nonie was no longer listening, staring at him without seeing, as she felt the blood drain from her head. "Blessed saints and angels."

"What? What is it?" Jamie stepped forward to steady her, a hand under her arm as she sank back down to sit on the ground.

Pulling herself together, Nonie lifted her face, and said to Saba, who hovered over her in concern, "Jamil—" She struggled to make a translation, unable to put together a coherent sentence.

Slowly, Saba drew herself up, and took a step back, her expression shuttered.

"What?" Jamie looked from one to the other. "Nonie, tell me."

Her eyes on Saba's face, Nonie explained through stiff lips, "I think I've been tricked yet again, and this one's a corker." In exasperation, she bent her head, and pressed her fingertips to her temples. "Bloody hell, but I've never met someone who is so ahead of me at every turn; it shakes my faith, it does."

Raising her face to him, she explained, "Saba is related to the mark, and Saba wanted you to know she was Christian—even though Fatima didn't want her to say. And Jamil is—well, suffice it to say that Jamil is not what he seems, but is a holy man of some stripe. I—I think that it was not a Mughal wedding ceremony, but that instead I am well and truly married to the mark."

Astonished, Jamie stared at her. "But—why would he marry you? Did he hope to gain some sort of control over you?"

"He wanted to take me to bed in good conscience," she told him bluntly. "I am roundly an idiot."

Jamie turned to Saba and took her hand, speaking in Italian. "Saba—you must tell me." He made a gesture of reassurance that encompassed Nonie. "We will not tell anyone. But Nonie must know if she is married; it is not fair that she does not know—do you see? You must tell me, Is Jamil—"

"*Si*," the girl interrupted him with a stricken look. "Jamil *e prete*."

"Jamil's a priest," whispered Nonie, through dry lips. "Mother a' mercy."

CHAPTER THIRTY-THREE

"Let me see your hands," Nonie ordered Jamil, holding a pistol to the back of his head. "I've a bone to pick with you, my friend—not to mention I'm inclined to wring Fatima's sweet little neck."

She'd lain in wait near the slave market, and then followed him, dressed in her boy's clothes, until she could confront him where there were fewer people about—not that this was easy, considering this miserable town was positively teeming with miscreants and bad actors. Fortunately, he had diverted down a small alley, which had given her the opportunity. Despite everything, she felt a bit uneasy, holding a weapon to a priest—there must be a twinge of conscience left in me, somewhere, she decided, and drew back a bit.

His expression was a satisfactory mixture of chagrin and astonishment, as he slowly raised his hands. "Miss Rafferty."

"I think not; I'm a missus, thanks to you—Missus Something-or-other, I never learned my true name. Do you always dupe your brides?"

But Jamil was not one to be taunted into giving out state secrets, and stared straight ahead with a stoic expression. "What is it you wish from me?"

"I wish to have an audience with my erstwhile husband, but I am fearful that he will double-cross me yet again—the man can't be trusted to knot a string."

Jamil lowered his hands. "Where would you like to meet?"

She sheathed the pistol in her waistband. "Tell him I'll meet him at the storeroom where you rescued me— at nightfall. And you must swear to me on the soul of the Blessed Mother that there will be no tricks; my patience, such as it is, has worn thin."

"My promise on it," he said immediately. "He will be anxious to speak with you. The ship—did it founder?"

"De Gilles' ship is en route to wherever it was headed; I had other plans."

She saw that he hovered on the edge of asking how on earth she'd managed it, but thought the better of the question. It was just as well, she'd learned that half of one's reputation in this business was built on mystique; to this end, she rarely made explanations.

"Off you go." She watched as he walked away, then she quickly disappeared into the busy street, doubling back several times in the crowds until she arrived at the safe house, followed closely by Jamie, who had tailed her the entire way.

Jamie's eyes were sparkling, as they greeted Saba. "What did he say? He looked as if he'd seen a ghost."

"I imagine a ghost would have been more welcome." There was nothing like turning the tables to give one an acute sense of satisfaction, especially after one had been made to look foolish. Nonie took off her *taqiyah*, and shook her curls out. "And anyway, he's a priest, so he doesn't believe in ghosts."

"The Holy Ghost," Jamie teased.

"I'll Holy Ghost him one, the feckless mackerel-snapper."

"All is well?" asked Saba in her halting Italian, as she looked from one to the other.

"*Si.*" Jamie took her hand and smiled reassuringly. "All is well."

But this reminded Nonie that they had a problem. "Lord, Jamie—what should I say to the mark about Saba? He'll be that worried—"

"Nonie," said Jamie with deceptive calm. "He doesn't deserve an instant's concern, after the trick he's pulled."

But Nonie found she was unwilling to abandon the necromancer to Jamie's scorn. "He was trying to protect his own assignment, Jamie; surely you can give him credit for that. And he was willing to give up Saba to you—and even though she's not his wife, she's a relative of some sort, I think."

"Then we'll leave matters as they are; I'm not willing to give her back, only to have her used as a bargaining chip against my good behavior."

This did make sense, and Nonie had to reluctantly concede. "All right, then—but you must lay low until you sail; he seems to have a very efficient spy system of his own."

"You needn't warn me; until I have to leave I'll spend every moment I can sequestered with Saba." Upon hearing her name, the girl looked up, and he smiled into her eyes.

"You probably shouldn't tell her you're about to depart for parts unknown," Nonie warned. "I know it's wrenching, but we don't want anyone catching wind of the assignment, or putting two and two together."

Jamie nodded in agreement—even the fishmongers didn't know the particulars of the assignment; the residents of Algiers were infamous for their shifting loyalties.

They sat in silence for a moment, and as Saba had the good sense to have tea brewing on the brazier, she rose with a graceful gesture to pour them out a cup. As they smiled their thanks, Nonie asked, "Are you ever going to tell her what you truly do for a living?"

Jamie took a sip of tea. "I think she already knows."

Startled, her gaze flew to his. "Surely, you haven't said?"

"No, nodcock. But haven't you noticed that she asks no questions?"

This was true; despite abandoning ship, returning to Algiers by stealth, then being left alone with strangers without explanation, the girl had shown neither dismay nor curiosity.

"She's a brick," Nonie pronounced with a small smile. "It hardly seems fair—I wish mine were a brick."

But perversely, it was Jamie who was now willing to defend her husband. "He was a brick to explain it to Saba before she made her choice—not many men would have, I think. Or would have allowed her to marry the likes of me, in the first place."

Nonie could not agree with such a viewpoint, and was moved to protest hotly, "She's carried off the palm, Jamie O'Hay. She'll never find a better man, and I'll not hear another word."

He chuckled, and she chuckled, and Saba smiled over her teacup to see them laugh. Nonie rose to her feet, and stretched her arms over her head. "Talk to her as long as you like; I'll retreat outside to sit with the fish, whilst I rehearse how to play my rendezvous with my better half."

He watched her walk to the door, his gaze sympathetic. "Will you be needing reinforcements? Do you want anyone on site?"

She considered logistics, while running her fingers over her scalp—the woolen boy's hat made her head itch. "No—the mark and I may come to blows, and the fewer to witness it, the better for my dignity. And I truly don't believe he'd try anything again, so I think we'll need just a man on the perimeter." She glanced down at him. "If it goes wrong, you're to sail with the pearls, regardless, and never mention to a soul that it was my own foolishness that did me in."

"Understood," he said easily, then couldn't suppress a smile. "Lord, Nonie; what will you say to him?"

She put a hand on his shoulder to steady herself, and removed a sandal to as to rub between her toes—the dust got into *everything*, and she would be certifiably insane to consider staying here for any reason, particularly for a man who'd duped her every bloody chance he got, and she had to stop—*stop* allowing such a ridiculous notion to keep creeping into her brain. "I will try to have him confirm my theory. And I will explain to him that he is interfering with the king's business—although he probably doesn't much care. But mainly, I'm going to comb his hair with a joint stool about duping me into marriage."

"Good on you," he grinned. "I wish I could be there to see it."

CHAPTER THIRTY-FOUR

B ut when Nonie pushed open the door to the store-room, matters did not go quite as planned. She saw Tahriz immediately, seated on a crate, and waiting for her; a lantern on the floor beside him, to illuminate the dim room. He was dressed in servant's clothes, and stood when he saw her. She had the swift impression that he was weary, and tried to remember that she'd promised herself to be ruthless with him—the worthless, miserable—

"I am so sorry, Nonie."

Although she'd carefully rehearsed what she would say, for some reason, different words entirely tumbled out of her mouth. "You—you sent me away—" *I am going to cry.*

she realized in amazement, and began to weep, her mouth working so that she could no longer speak. Wholly embarrassed, she ducked her head, and covered her eyes with her hands, as her shoulders shook, and she struggled for breath between sobs.

Swiftly, he strode over to take her in his arms. "Nonie," he whispered, holding her close. "Ah, Nonie— *nomrata; nomrata.*"

Sobbing into his shoulder, she managed to gasp, "Ye shouldna' ha' sent me away." Even to her own ears, she sounded like a broken child, but could not seem to help it—seeing him again had made all her resolutions fly out the window.

"I wanted to keep you safe," he said, near her ear. "Forgive me, my love."

This, for some reason, started a fresh onslaught of tears. "I don't want a husband—I don't want a home—I don't want anyone who can twist my heart—"

"I know," he murmured. "I know."

Clinging to his tunic, she wept unabated for a space of time, whilst he murmured in his strange language, and stroked the small of her back. When the storm had passed, she managed a shuddering breath in an effort to calm herself, and then said into his chest, "You mustn't send me away again; it was horrid."

"Yes," he agreed in a somber tone. "I watched the ship sail from my window—it was nearly unbearable."

Glancing up at him, she sniffled, and rubbed at her eyes with the heel of her hand. "Why then, did you do it?"

"I cannot allow you to assassinate the Dey."

For a brief instant, she stared at him, then decided it was no surprise he knew—or had guessed—the assignment. For a moment, the conversation they'd held on the rooftops flashed into her memory—the one where he had probed about her knowledge of any plans—supposedly French plans—to assassinate the Dey; he must have known, even then. "I don't know what you're talking about," she disclaimed, her clear eyes wide.

He did not respond, but drew her to him again, and she rested her cheek against his shoulder, wishing the world and all its wretched warmongers would just go away. "I know about the *jeune filles.*"

"I don't know what you are talking about," he replied with gentle humor, in imitation of her.

She ducked her head, resting her forehead against his chest. "Do you remember that first night, when you said you knew who I was?"

"I do." His voice rumbled in his chest, his strong hands stoking her arms, her back.

"Well, I knew who you were, too—you were the mark. We thought you were the point man, smuggling pearls to Napoleon." She raised her face. "It was a mis-translation, a mistake in intelligence-gathering."

But he wasn't interested in this irony, and instead stated bluntly, "I need the Dey to survive, and I need the supply ships to keep sailing."

She lowered her head again, and rubbed her face against his tunic, breathing in the scent of him. "I'm afraid it's all doomed to come to a crashing halt, *fear ceile.*"

His hands moved gently on her back. "What does that mean?"

"Husband. And what was the point of that, if I may ask? Or did you just want to have me to bed, in good conscience?"

He bent his head to kiss the area where her neck was exposed, near her shoulder. "I cannot deny it. But also—" he paused, thinking over what it was he wanted to say. "I wanted you to have something—something of your own. I have land, and wealth. You would have a home, and a reason not to do what you do." He lifted his head to look into her eyes, the expression in his own very serious. "I wanted to give you the freedom to walk away from it."

This made perfect sense to her; he was chivalrous to a fault. "And where is this happy slice of heaven, if I may ask?"

He hesitated for only a moment. "Malta."

"Malta?" This was an island mid-way between the coast of Algiers and the European continent; it seemed suitably obscure—small wonder she hadn't recognized the language. Maltese, he was—fancy that. What she knew about Malta couldn't fill a thimble, except, of course—

Her gaze flew to his in astonishment. "Why, you *are* a Hospitaller." She'd teased him about the brooch on this turban, that first night; it was the Maltese cross, which was the symbol for the Knights of Malta, the Order of Saint John. An order that was famous for its efforts in fighting slavery—

"God in heaven," she exclaimed, closing her eyes, briefly. "I'm roundly an idiot, but so are you, for wearing it for all to see."

He smiled slightly without responding, and she could easily conclude that the brooch was his small defiance—his way to fly his true colors, amidst all the treachery and evil. Everyone would assume it was stolen; there was not the smallest chance that the Dey's necromancer was a Knight, operating right under everyone's nose.

She took a long breath, then chided, "Little good it would do me—to have this option of a home, and a hearth—if I didn't even know of it."

"You would have been informed. The moment I am exposed, I will be killed."

The words were said almost matter-of-factly; but she had already come to this conclusion when she had figured out his role—he was already at daggers-drawn with the Agha. It was a wonder he hadn't already been dispatched by a swift knife in the night; presumably, the only thing that stayed his enemy's hand was the Dey's anticipated reaction to such a development. If the Dey himself was dispatched, then all bets were off.

She leaned her head back, and met his eyes, her own twinkling. "That doesn't impress me, my friend; it is the same story for me. The instant I am exposed, I can expect a knife in the back, or worse."

A smile played around his mouth. "What will I inherit from you?"

She laughed, amazed that she could. "Nothing. The Home Office will disavow any knowledge of the likes of me—you've made a bad bargain, and let this be a lesson."

"No." He kissed her temple, leaving his mouth to rest against her head.

She lifted a hand, and fiddled with the clasp on his shirtfront. "Perhaps we should try to avoid the certain death and destruction that awaits us—lately there seems to be so much more to live for."

His chest rose and fell beneath her hand. "I cannot stop my work."

But she persisted in a practical tone, "It's going to be stopping, one way or another. Admiral Decatur is itching for the war with England to be over, so's he can come here and bombard the pirates, yet again."

"Yes," he agreed—no doubt he had better information on the subject than she did. "And those that meet in Vienna are working to stop the slave trade, altogether."

"Good luck to them, they'll have bigger worries, soon." The Congress of Vienna was an on-going meeting of all the allies who had defeated Napoleon, getting together to discuss how to restructure Europe so that such a thing could not happen again. Ironic, it was, since Napoleon was soon to be raising another ruckus, whilst the Congress meandered along, politely ignoring this possibility.

He tilted his head in acknowledgment. "Nevertheless; I believe the slave trade will not survive for long—the British are very determined."

"Come away with me," she said, suddenly tired of speaking of the inexplicable politics of war. "When I leave here—"

"I cannot," he said softly. "I am sorry, Nonie."

But she persisted, her eyes intent upon his dark ones. "You can't risk your life for this—you've so much to offer; you know so much. The medicines—you know about the vax—the vaxy—oh, whatever it was—the smallpox cure. You can help so many—"

He interrupted, lifting a hand to caress her cheek. "Do you know what happens to these girls, if we do not intervene?"

She made a quick, impatient gesture with her head. "Tahriz—there's human misery and wretchedness all over; we can only do what we can."

"Every ship that sails is a victory."

"You are so *bloody* noble," she declared. in exasperated wonder. "To risk everything for this—what if you are ignominiously slaughtered, and nothing comes of it?"

The timbre of his voice was completely sincere. "What happens in this life is not important."

Now thoroughly irritated, she tugged at the clasp between her fingers. "Then we are not slated to coexist in the next one; I have absolutely no hope of heaven."

"Of course, you do. Everyone does."

He said it with such conviction that she was tempted to cuff him, for such a foolish thought. "I'd be in the confessional for a week, my friend; they'd have to allow the priests to take shifts, in order to hear it all."

"I have every confidence in you." He embraced her again, and she sighed into his neck. In a strange way, she respected him—even understood him, as much as he frustrated her. Speaking of frustration, she had noted that he couldn't seem to stop caressing her—and she was mighty tired of discussing the perilous state of her soul. There was no point in being married, unless you put it to good use.

"Do you have anyone on site?" she whispered, her hands trailing in a suggestive motion down the front of his tunic.

She heard a sharp intake of breath in reaction to her touch, and then he smiled into her neck. "No—do you?"

"No."

He lifted his head to glance around them. "Nothing looks very comfortable."

"Not important, just now, Tahriz," she breathed, and pulled his mouth to hers.

CHAPTER THIRTY-FIVE

It was almost comical, if it hadn't been for the unadulterated lust. He began to kiss her in earnest, his hands pulling up her boy's tunic, and his mouth urgent upon hers as he pushed her down on the crate, but she caught her foot on a rope, and stumbled, so that they went down to the dirt floor in a heap, neither of them willing to relinquish their hold on the other to right themselves.

"Let me douse the lantern," he murmured into her mouth, getting his legs beneath him, so as to lift her again. "Ah, Nonie; hold—just a moment."

"Mmm," she replied, paying no attention to him.

"Hold, Nonie—Nonie; let me put the light out—if anyone comes—you are dressed as a boy—"

She giggled, and he chuckled in response, while he righted them, holding her with one arm and lowering her onto the crate, as he stretched to douse the lantern.

"Ouch—there's a nail, or something," she whispered, shifting away from it, as he wedged his hands between their bodies so as to slide her trousers off her hips.

"Should we move to the floor?"

"No—I'm all right. Hurry, please, I am *dyin'*—"

But his own need was urgent, and he required no encouragement. After a few frantic, heated moments, the coupling was complete, and they lay entwined on the rough wood, recovering; his breath ragged in her ear. She shifted subtly, and he propped himself up on his elbows. "Sorry—I'm crushing you."

"No, you are not." She pulled his head to hers, and kissed him. "But you'll be needed to pluck splinters."

She couldn't see his face in the darkness, but she could sense his playful mood—there was nothing like a raging round of lovemaking, to cheer a man. "You shouldn't encourage me; I am unable to resist you, *mara*."

"So I've noticed, believe me. What does '*mara*' mean?"

"Wife."

She spread her hand on his cheek and rested a thumb against his mouth. "Should I be trying to learn

Maltese, or is there no point, because this will all end in disaster, anyway?"

He sighed, his breath warm against her hand. "I would like to avoid a disaster, if it is at all possible."

"Not this side of that heaven you speak of, I'm thinking." She then paused, afraid to go on. Coward, she chastised herself; get a hold of your craven self, and trust the man.

As he lowered his head to nuzzle the side of her face, she ventured, "Saba says she is not your sister, but I am not so certain."

If she surprised him, he hid it well. "No; she speaks the truth."

So—he was not going to tell her what the relationship was, which was annoying but very much in keeping with his manner—as close as a clam, he was. She tried again, "D'you mind very much, about Jamie and Saba?"

His fingertips moved gently on her face. "She knows her heart."

"As I know mine." She raised her head to gently kiss his chin, his mouth. "I knew it straight from the first."

He cradled her head in his hands and admitted, "I must confess that I tried to resist—my plans had no room for someone like you."

With a light laugh, she grasped one of his hands and turned her head to kiss the palm. "Now, there's an understatement—I landed in a bedraggled heap on the jetty for the express purpose of upsetting your plans; that is, until I found out we had it all wrong."

She gathered her courage, and lifted her head to kiss his mouth again—it was now or never, now that she'd softened him up. "I wonder, my husband, if we could do a bit of compromising, you and I—if we could rethink our strategy so that we could—we could survive this, and stay together." Listen to yourself, she thought in bemusement; it's hopeless, you are—no one who knows you would recognize this soft, silly creature you've become. Except perhaps Tanny.

He took her hand, and squeezed it, his voice soft and exultant. "Yes; you could stay here, with me. You could start a new life—"

"We could stage a feint," she interrupted, as though he hadn't spoken. "I must see to it that Napoleon and the government of Algiers break it off—never to trust each other again."

"You were going to frame *Le Capitaine* for the Dey's murder," he agreed, as though they were discussing the weather. "But you mustn't, Nonie."

Without admitting this was the assignment, she said carefully. "There are other ways to skin that cat. For example, if *Le Capitaine* seized the Dey's necromancer—that would turn the trick." She paused for a moment. "And no one need die, except the necromancer."

He lifted himself on his elbows, and she could feel his scrutiny, even in the dark. To his credit, he didn' immediately suggest that she was insane. "I'm afraid I don't understand."

Focusing on his shadowed face, she urged, "You are doomed anyway, you said so yourself—the Agha wants you dead, and soon; perhaps you should grant him his wish."

He lowered his chin, thinking, and then said slowly, "We stage my abduction by the French—"

"And there is a terrible mishap—"

"I am killed. The ship sinks—"

She corrected, "No—the ship can't sink, because my people need to track the pearls to whoever's on the other end."

He tilted his head. "If the ship doesn't sink, then what happens to my corpse?"

"Your poor corpse is swept out on the tide, and the French are run out of town, dodging cannon fire from the jetty, never to return."

There was a pause while he thought this over. "And what of my work?"

"I'll go tattle to the Dey that Nadia has informed me 'twas the Agha who plotted your downfall with the French, and she is rightly furious. The Agha gets expelled from the palace, and your work continues, only you are now working behind the scenes—since everyone thinks you are dead—and the Agha is powerless to put a stop to it. Hopefully, it all works out so that I won't soon be a wealthy widow."

He kissed her, but he was distracted, as he considered this plan. "You have a gift for this."

"You may be better," she admitted with some modesty.

With gentle fingers, he pushed a wayward tendril behind her ear—her cap was all askew, due to being repeatedly bumped against the wall. "And what of you, then?"

She took a breath. "I've decided to retire from the ranks. Instead, I've a fancy to help you save people, in an ironic twist that should not go unappreciated." In the comfort of his arms, she spoke aloud a thought that had occurred to her more than once, lately. "My usefulness is coming to an end because too many have heard of me; without the element of surprise, I'd soon be a gone goose."

He rested his forehead against hers. "So, you will instead stay with me, and be a happy goose."

She frowned against his head. "Fah—I *hate* this place. I hate everything about it."

"So do I."

They both chuckled for a moment, and she then confessed, "They'll be no more French ships, coming through, though; that's the flaw in my plan."

"No matter; there is an alternate route we've used—overland, to the port of Azir."

"I was in Azir," she interrupted, very pleased to tell him this. "It's where I landed, when I plagued de Gilles into letting me go."

Reminded, he lifted his head. "How did you manage it?"

"Can't say. Professional secret."

He contemplated her for a moment in silence. "I am sorry I hurt you," he said softly, "but I didn't know what else to do."

"No more of it," she begged, completely serious for once. "Please. I will be a good helpmeet, I promise. But I would like to believe that we will begone from here, some day. I would like to see Malta."

"Soon," he soothed, his long fingers playing with the errant tendril. "Soon, the tide will turn."

After a poignant pause, she said slowly, "I will tell you a secret, my friend. You can wait for it all you want, but the tide never seems to turn." She had seen the world from a different perspective than his, and wasn't at all certain it was salvageable. With a mental shake, she chided herself for being so melancholy—he was going to regret his whole plan to snatch a bride by trickery, and that wouldn't do at all.

With some reluctance, he raised himself off her, and helped her to sit up, so that they could re-adjust their clothing. "I would like to speak with Mr. O'Hay, if I may."

Guilelessly, she explained, "Jamie is on de Gilles' ship."

There was a pause, whilst he turned his head to her.

"You are so annoying," she retorted crossly. "Don't you dare let him know he's been twigged."

"It is not his fault." He rose to take her hand, as she stood also. "He cannot blend in easily, here."

"What are you going to say to him?"

"I wish to speak to him of Saba."

"Oh." This did seem to be a legitimate request, particularly if he was her closest male relative, and the girl was soon to leave for parts unknown, to join up with an Irish assassin's flanker. "All right, then—don't mention the new plan, if you please; allow me to break it to the poor man."

After determining that the coast was clear, they stepped outside, and began to walk up the alley, Nonie resting her right hand on her left shoulder in the signal to Jamie that it was safe to approach. There was no immediate response, and so she said to Tahriz, "Step apart from me, if you please; it's worried, he is, that it's a trick."

Taking a look around, the necromancer strode over to lean against a shadowed wall, whilst Nonie wandered down the alley.

In a few moments, Jamie materialized by her side, wary. "What's happened?"

"He would like to discuss Saba with you." She braced herself, prepared for a serious dose of swearing, but Jamie instead paused thoughtfully, and looked over toward the mark. "Yes—I should speak with him, I suppose. Wait here."

This seemed unfair, after all she had been through to help bring this about. "Can't I listen in?"

"No," he said bluntly. "Stay within sight, and try not to cause a ruckus."

"Aye, sir," she teased, but he wasn't listening, and walked over to join the other man in the shadows.

To pass the time, she imagined the conversation between the two men, with Jamie saying, I have a tidy sum set aside, being as how I am an accomplished pickpocket, and raider of treasures. I am owed favors from various heads of state, but none will ever acknowledge me. There've been a few women—well, more than a few—but there is no better man in a tight corner; no better supporter and friend—

Lord, she thought, feeling the prickle of tears yet again; I am going to miss Jamie, when all is said and done. Everything is changing, everything except for Napoleon, who fancies he can make history bloody repeat itself. Letting out a long breath, she waited for the men to finish their discussion.

CHAPTER THIRTY-SIX

"They are cousins," Jamie told Nonie, as they returned to the safe house by a circuitous route. "And she has a fine dowry, which I explained was not necessary, but which he insisted I secure."

"Lord," laughed Nonie, shaking her head. "Leave it to you to land on your feet—Tanny always said you'd charm some poor girl out of her senses, and best of luck to her."

"He wanted to know if I would allow Jamil to marry us in the morning, so that he could attend. Apparently, he's aware that I'm leaving on the tide." He glanced at her sidelong.

She tried not to look self-conscious. "Yes; well— here's the thing, Jamie. I've agreed not to kill the Dey, and in return he's agreed to stage his own abduction and death at the hands of *Le Capitaine*."

There was a pause, whilst he digested this startling pronouncement. "I thought we didn't collaborate—don't you remember the riot at the clothworker's guildhall?"

"I do indeed—and how the Flemish mark nearly did us in." She sighed. "I know we don't collaborate. But the mark is set on a course that would result in his death— sooner rather than later—so I compromised with him. I can be honest with him, Jamie; he packed us off with de Gilles because he'd already guessed our assignment, and the Dey is too important for his own project, being as how His Excellency the Dey of Algiers is tied to his dead mother's apron strings."

Jamie cast a practiced eye along the rooftops around them, as they turned a corner, and she trudged along beside him in her boy's trousers. Cautiously heartened by his silence, she continued, "I'd like to accommodate him if I can, since I can't like the idea of young girls being sold, and I can't like the idea of my poor husband's murder at the hands of the Agha, or any other blackguard. Since the whole point of the assignment is to stir up so much trouble between Napoleon and the Dey that they no longer do business, I decided there were other ways to pluck that bird."

Jamie nodded as though this made perfect sense, even though she had never countermanded an assignment before. "So; the mark will go back to London with you, then?"

She glanced up at him, and decided that there was nothing for it; he needed to know that nothing would ever be the same. "No. I'll frame *Le Capitaine* and the Agha for his death, and then we'll both continue his work here, behind the scenes—smuggling the girls overland, by a different route."

Jamie thought it over for a moment as they walked along. "All right."

Enormously relieved, she teased, "Confess—you think me mad as a hatter."

He smiled. "No. I think you are smitten, but since I'm also smitten, I can't cast a stone—not to mention I don't want him to rethink that fine dowry."

She laughed aloud, relieved that she'd cleared this particular hurdle—if Jamie had been unhappy about her plan, she would do anything in her power to ease him, perhaps even change her mind. "Will you look at us, Jamie—what has happened, I ask you? This is exactly what I deserve, for finding myself married to a bloody saint."

He smiled, but his mood turned pensive, and his pace slowed, as they approached the safe house. "It's true, though; everything is different, now—the way I look at our work is different. I used to heap scorn on the paltry diplomats, and their attempts to head off the next disaster because I welcomed the war—I needed it to keep me busy; to keep from thinking about—about everything." He paused outside the door, and she stood silently beside him as he continued. "It was almost a relief to hear that Napoleon would make another attempt—d'you know?"

She nodded, understanding completely, as no one else in the world could. Out of habit, he glanced into the shadows, and continued, "But now I'm hoping it stops before it starts, because suddenly I'm seeing a future that's worth surviving for."

She stood, silent and uncomfortable, because he had touched on the one subject they couldn't discuss—the one, terrible memory that overshadowed everything that had happened ever since. And he was right; suddenly there was a tantalizing glimpse of happiness, and they were terrified by it—almost too terrified to hope. "You've lost your bite, if you're hoping for help from the diplomats," she accused in mock outrage, trying mightily to steer the conversation back toward a lighter tone. "Take hold of yourself, man."

With a small smile, he shook off his pensive mood. "No—you're right; the moment we lose our bite, we've signed our death warrants. Not to worry, I'll not go wobbly." He did not turn to enter the building yet, but bent his head toward her. "Since you won't be bringing Saba to London yourself, would you make sure whoever does is aware that she's my wife? And perhaps they can find someone to translate for her, so it's all not so strange."

"I can't imagine Maltese-speakers are thick on the ground, but I will do my best," Nonie promised.

Jamie looked up in surprise. "Maltese? She is Maltese?"

Surprised in turn that he did not know this, Nonie nodded. "Yes. The mark is a Hospitaller."

With dawning comprehension, Jamie said slowly, "Of course. It makes perfect sense, that he'd be a Knight."

Nonie nodded. "I never knew anyone who was—or who admitted to it. I know that the Knights Templar—the ones who survived—were folded into the Knights of Malta. It does make sense; they're rather secretive, and abide by their own code."

Jamie raised his head. "Raike's man—the one he picked up in Spain—he's a Knight, I think."

"I never met the man, I'm afraid. Well then—mystery solved." But she was eyeing Jamie, who had suddenly looked away, as though he found the buildings across the way to be of extreme interest.

The subject shifted, as he asked, "How many men will we need tomorrow, and stationed where? I'll head over to the fish market, later tonight."

"What is it?" she asked, not distracted by his question.

He turned back to meet her eyes, his own guileless. "Nothing—I'm thinking about tomorrow, is all."

"James Michael O'Hay," she pronounced in an ominous tone. "Tell me."

Hesitating, he lowered his voice. "It's just that Raike's man—well, he's a priest."

Nonie fixed him with a hard stare. "The mark—the mark is not a *priest*, Jamie."

"Of course, not," he assured her hurriedly.

"Oh, my God," she returned.

But he took her by her upper arms and was quick to point out, "No—no, Nonie; you said so yourself, he's too honorable. He wouldn't marry you, if he were a priest."

"No," she agreed, righting herself with an effort. "Although Jamil is a priest, and he's one of them too—"

He ran his hands up and down her arms. "I shouldn't have said it—I'm roundly an idiot."

But she was still trying to reassure herself. "He likes sex too much to be a priest."

"Nonie," Jamie chastised, laughing. "I'd rather not hear it, if you please."

She laughed in return, and the door opened to reveal Saba, who smiled to see them so merry. Jamie gently kissed Saba's cheek, then turned his head to Nonie. "She'd never stand for it, Nonie."

Following him in, she responded, "No, but it did give me a scare, for a moment." It was true—the others would not stand idly by—unless, they thought it was merely a ploy, and didn't realize that she and Tahriz were making the beast with two backs whenever they had five minutes and a shipping crate to spare.

But Jamie had moved on to a topic of more compelling interest, and had taken Saba's hands to explain in halting Italian that he had spoken to the necromancer, and that they were to be married in the morning. The girl smiled her dazzling smile, and threw her arms around his neck, whilst Nonie tried to find something of interest in the other corner of the room. It didn't help to remember her own wedding, which she'd viewed, at the time, as a small step up from a farce. "You'll need a ring," she reminded him in Gaelic. She rather wished she had a ring, herself.

"Got one," said Jamie with a grin over Saba's shoulder. "Got one in the bazaar, the day after I met her."

"You *are* writing poetry, you nodcock," she observed in mock horror. "Lord."

The couple murmured together in an excited undertone, whilst Nonie tried not to feel like a gooseberry, and wondered if she could pinpoint the moment when Tahriz hit upon his scheme to marry her, willy-nilly. I think that everything shifted between us, the night I confronted him about his multiple non-wives, she thought. Perhaps it is not such a terrible thing to be so outspoken; he may never have felt encouraged to hoodwink me, else.

The atmosphere changed subtly as Jamie withdrew from Saba's embrace, his expression somber. "

have to tell her that I'm to be leaving, right after we are married."

"I'll take a walk, then." With a smile that conveyed her sympathy and encouragement, she slipped out the door, and into the hot Algerian night.

CHAPTER THIRTY-SEVEN

The next day, they were assembled in the necromancer's chambers, Jamil and Tahriz standing by the window and quietly conferring with Jamie and Saba, whilst Nonie was holding her own low-voiced conversation with Fatima. "I've half a mind to push you out the window, I do—best mind yourself."

The smaller woman touched Nonie's arm in distress, her soft eyes pleading. "I am so sorry, Nonie. It was for the greater good."

But Nonie was not to be placated, and tossed her head. "I'll greater-good you one, I will. We are friends, and friends do not dupe each other—it's out the window with you, and a good riddance."

Coming to the realization that Nonie was teasing, Fatima smiled with relief, and then confessed, "I am glad you didn't sail—and Saba is so happy."

This was inarguable; Saba was breathtakingly beautiful in a *takchita* of blue silk, her eyes like stars, as she stole glances at her bridegroom. Nonie was dressed once more in a *kaftan,* and reconciled to reprising her role as the necromancer's latest bride—at least until she was ostensibly made a widow, later this evening. She wasn't clear on the outlines of Tahriz's plan to fake his own murder—no doubt because he didn't quite trust her people not to interfere—and so she'd been forced to take a secondary role, which was a novel situation, but one to which she must become accustomed, if she was to stay on, and help him with his slaves-smuggling. She met his gaze across the room, and felt a slight breathlessness—the man is thinking about the session on the crate, she thought. Shame on him.

With an effort, she pulled her attention back to Fatima, and decided to ask a few questions, being as her better half never wanted to tell her anything. "Captain de Gilles said the girls were on their way to France."

Fatima smoothed her sleeve. "Yes—to France."

Nonie waited, but Fatima offered nothing further, so she prodded, "France seems a strange choice, all things considered. The emperor-who-shall-not-be-named seems bent on stirring things up, yet again."

Fatima hesitated, then offered, "We send them to a convent near Honfleur, on the coast. Then the attempt is made to reunite them with their families. If their families cannot be found, they are housed and educated at the convent."

These are good, good people, Nonie thought, much impressed. And then there will be me, the token sinner, amongst them. "Lord, that's a mighty undertaking. How many have you done?"

Fatima looked up, as Tahriz approached them, and replied a bit sadly, "Many hundreds."

Nonie took her husband's arm with affection, smiling up into his face, and knowing down to her toes that she could never willingly leave him, come what may. "You are a fine man," she pronounced, and privately thought; he's a Knight, and I'm a murderess—we are a strange pairing, indeed.

He tilted his head slightly. "I haven't always treated you well."

But she wouldn't hear of it. "Nonsense; do you think I'd give a moment's admiration to any man who couldn't outthink me at every turn? I would not."

"Rather than outthink you, it seems instead that we have played to a draw."

"I suppose that is true—well then; we are well-matched." With a causal air, she suggested, "Perhaps I should wear a wedding ring, now that I know I'm well and truly shackled."

With an air of contrition, he explained, "Your ring is in Malta, I am afraid. It is an heirloom, several centuries old. I had no idea that I would be needing it."

"Tahriz," she cautioned after a moment's dismayed pause. "You are a madman; your people will take one look at my freckled face, and know me for a sham."

He replied steadily, "No one dare; and if they did, they would have to answer to me."

She looked up into his dark eyes, and relished another novel sensation—that she'd managed to land an honorable man who would defend her from all detractors, whether she deserved it or not. "You are too good to be true."

He lifted her hand, and kissed the knuckles. "I am the lucky one."

"I will see to *that* when we have a few minutes' privacy."

With one of his rare, genuine smiles he replied, "Later—after I am dead."

Laughing, she declared, "Now, there would be some impressive necromancing—"

Unfortunately, Jamil put an end to this promising flirtation by announcing that they were ready to begin. Taking her hand, Tahriz led Nonie over to where Jamie and Saba had assembled before Jamil; Jamie quietly happy, his eyes straying for a moment to meet Nonie's, before they returned to his bride like a lodestar.

Who could have imagined all this? Nonie thought as she clasped Tahriz's hand in the folds of her overdress.

We stumble into this miserable backwater—minding our own business, and hoping to get out as quickly as possible—but instead, we each find something wonderful; something worth changing our lives over. Good on us, Jamie.

"In the name of the Father, the Son, and the Holy Spirit," Jamil began in English, and the others made the Sign of the Cross, Nonie belatedly catching up. He then conducted the ceremony in English and Maltese, while Tahriz listened intently, holding Nonie's hand firmly in his. They are all very religious, she thought, observing them. Which makes sense, if they are willing to risk so much. I'll be lucky if I'm not struck by lightning on the spot, in the midst of such holy company.

Her gaze rested for a moment on Fatima, whose head was bent, contemplating her hands folded before her. Now, there is a nun if I ever saw one, Nonie realized. She must be from the French convent, working from this end—that's why she's allied with the Maltese contingent; and there are obviously sea captains—like de Gilles—who are involved, also. A parallel operation of personnel, who were not so very interested in saving the world from a despot, as they were in saving fragile young lives—one at a time—from the misery that was slavery.

She brought her attention back to the ceremony as Jamie and Saba exchanged their vows, Saba's voice tremulous with emotion, but Jamie's steady and sincere his joy palpable. After the benediction, he kissed hi bride, and the happy couple accepted congratulations, Jamie enveloping Nonie in a fierce embrace that somehow brought to mind everything they had experienced together—the horror, the rootlessness, the life of shadowy service to a country not their own, and through it all, the bond that had never faltered. "*Graim thu,*" he said in her ear.

"*Graim thu,*" she responded, fighting tears.

Tahriz had managed to smuggle in a very fine bottle of wine for the occasion, and they all toasted the newly-minted O'Hays. All too soon, it was time for Jamie to leave for his assignment, and the others moved into the antechamber to give the newlyweds some privacy to say their goodbyes.

Alive to her husband's disposition to meddle, Nonie warned him in a low tone, "Promise you won't be interfering with him; it is important we infiltrate those on the receiving end of the pearls."

Tahriz nodded, thinking. "Will he have any supporters on board?"

"Of course," she assured him. "But there's little danger; he'll bring no attention to himself until they make landfall in France—that's when he'll need to step lively." Privately, she had little doubt that Tahriz would have someone aboard to watch over Saba's new husband—in fact, she was rather counting on it.

He bent his head to hers, and said quietly, "Speaking of which, I would like to send Jamil with you, when you go to warn the Dey. It is important that the Agha do nothing to thwart the plan."

But she couldn't be comfortable with this suggestion, and frowned at him. "I don't know, Tahriz; I've been lately reminded that the last time that I collaborated with someone else, it nearly ended in disaster."

"The Dey knows of Jamil's role with the rescues; it will add credibility to your story. He will answer to you, not me—my promise on it."

Apparently, marriage required compromises. "All right, then. What's the timeline?"

"We will give Mr. O'Hay time to establish his position, and then I will go to board the ship, while you will go to warn the Dey."

She thought it over. "Will you arrange matters so that there are witnesses to your sad demise, or doesn't it matter?"

"I will assess, as the situation unfolds."

This was the type of equivocal answer she herself would have given—no point in relinquishing one's flexibility— and so, she grudgingly accepted it. "How will you stage it so that *Le Capitaine* is the culprit?"

"He'll think I've come to steal the pearls—I will be discovered, and confronted."

She nodded—that should do the trick, and stir up the hornet's nest. "Do you need Jamie to pretend to shoot you? He's a foyster of the first order."

But he declined the offer of assistance. "No—matters have already been arranged, and it would be best to draw down no attention on Mr. O'Hay."

"Good point. Although, Jamie shot me, once," she fondly reminisced. "We'd staged a blackmail feint in Barcelona—I bled buckets all over the curtains, and died in his arms. It was all very touching."

His eyes gleamed with amusement. "Can you ever tell me of it—of the stories you have?"

"Probably not," she admitted. "Although I suppose I could mention that *Le Capitaine*'s eye rests in a pickle jar, on the top shelf at the Cat n' Fiddle."

"Good God," he exclaimed slowly.

"Mostly, you'd be very disappointed in me—there were a lot of dark doings."

But he was unfazed by this admission of the obvious. "No—I could never be disappointed in you. I think you are the most extraordinary woman I have ever met."

The words were palpably sincere, and to reward him, she lifted on tiptoe to kiss his mouth, even though the others could see. "I love you," she said, holding his gaze with her own. "Try not to let that miserable Frenchman put a period to your existence."

"On the contrary; I will see to it that he does." With a nod at Jamil, he squeezed her hands briefly, and took his leave.

Jamie then approached, gathering up Nonie in an easy embrace. "I'll be seeing you."

She clasped his neck in a heartfelt goodbye. "All right, then; have a good voyage, you."

But now that the moment to part was actually upon them, Saba began to weep, and seeing Jamie's stricken face, Nonie ruthlessly pushed him out the door, and shut it behind him.

She then turned to Saba, and asked Fatima to translate, "I know you're grieving, Saba, but you mustn't leave him with such a memory; next time you must try to give him a smile, even if it kills you."

Ashamed, Saba nodded, wiping the tears from her eyes. "You stay here, with Fatima," Nonie directed the girl, "—being as Jamil and I have to put the cat amongst the pigeons."

CHAPTER THIRTY-EIGHT

J amil had entered the Dey's chamber, seeking a private audience for Nonie whilst she waited outside in the hallway with mixed emotions—truly, it was a mournful shame that she'd decided to stand down from her assignment, since it seemed unlikely that a more convenient opportunity to put a period to the Dey's existence would present itself. Ah well; she would turn over a new leaf, and try to avoid cutting a swath of destruction wherever she went, however tempting it might be to revert to old habits.

The doors were opened by a guard, who called her forward to join Jamil. The Dey was seated at his sumptuous dinner—apparently, the man never stopped eating, and small blame to him, since everything always looked delicious.

"Your Excellency," said Nonie, as she bobbed a nervous curtsey. "I am sorry to intrude, but I have dire news from Nadia, and I thought I should not wait for my husband."

Intrigued, the Dey regarded her with his opaque gaze, as he wiped his chin with a silken napkin. "Yes—this man tells me of this. What is it?"

"It's a bit disturbing," she warned him. "Treachery, and double-dealing." Taking a glance from side to side she lowered her voice. "Brace yourself."

All attention, the Dey leaned forward. "Speak, girl—do not be afraid to tell me."

"It's a vision I had as the half-moon was on the set. I saw my husband—your necromancer—carried off by Napoleon's eagle." She raised her hands and gazed into the distance, stricken by the memory. "He was snatched in its talons, and taken away, never to return." Pausing for a moment, she knit her brow. "I saw girls—girls who were weeping for him, and wearing chains."

Alarmed, the Dey sank back in his chair and blew out his cheeks. "You saw this? Then it is as the Agha foretold—it has come to pass."

"Oh," Nonie ventured, surprised by this non-sequitur, and groping slightly. "Yes, the Agha knows of this—or so Nadia told me. She is very unhappy with him, must say."

But the Dey only shook his head. "No—she does not know that the Agha is a loyal friend. Indeed, he told me this very day of the French plot to seize my necromancer." Frowning, he contemplated her with grave disquiet. "The French seek to possess his powers."

"I believe—sir—that it is the Agha, who is conspiring with the French." Nonie spread her hands apologetically. "It seems unlikely that Nadia is mistaken, being as she is in the afterworld, an' all."

The Dey fixed his brooding gaze on her, and considered for a moment, stroking his cheek with a finger. "No—my beloved Nadia is mistaken; the Agha warned me of the plan, and he has promised that he will disrupt it."

Trying to make sense of this alarming revelation, Nonie suggested diffidently, "Perhaps you should be sending someone down to the harbor, then, just to see what's what."

"What's what?" The Dey shot a confused glance at Jamil, who made a translation in Arabic. Watching them, Nonie thought in dismay, I've a bad feeling about this—there was no French plot—was there? Surely not—I'm making the whole thing up. But it seems almost certain there is an Agha plot, and that does not bode well; not at all. And I have that feeling I have when I think I've missed something important; it is almost as though the Agha knew about the necromancer's plan to stage his own death, and is looking to pull a double-cross—

The Dey abruptly rose, and said to her. "Yes—I will go to see 'what is what'. If Nadia is concerned, I must look into it." He rounded the table, and formally took her hand to kiss it. "I thank you."

Lord, she thought, barely refraining from snatching her hand away; he'll be coming after me when I'm a widow—best that I disappear from these parts, quick as a whisker, before I am forced to fight him off.

As the Dey strode from the room, Nonie whirled on Jamil. "I can't like this development—we should warn the necromancer that the Agha is meddling in his plan."

But although Jamil's gaze held a trace of concern, he shook his head. "He is aware that the Agha is an enemy, and he will take all precautions."

Contemplating him for a moment, she decided she couldn't shake her uneasiness, and announced, "Be that as it may, I'm going down there—I'm worried we've a traitor in our midst. You can come or stay, and it doesn't matter to me."

With an apologetic gesture, the man cautioned, "I've been instructed to keep you away from the harbor, ma'am."

She eyed him, not very much surprised. "Well, I've been instructed in turn that you will answer to me."

"In all things but this." He added as an afterthought, "Please."

But before she could decide how best to overpower a priest, the door opened, and Ibram slipped through, glancing up at them, as he quietly closed the door behind them. "Have you had your meeting? Do you need to send any messages?"

In an instant, Nonie's attitude changed, and she approached the table in a desultory fashion, to look over the leftovers. "I do—I'd like to send a message to the necromancer." She turned to smile at him. "Although we may as well eat something—look at this glorious leg o' lamb." With a gleam, she picked up a slice with her fingers, and popped it in her mouth.

Ibram—rather nonplussed—hovered beside her. "Yes, it does look very good."

"You've probably well-tired of eating with the fish-mongers; you must have some," she teased. "I'll not be the only gleaner, here." She partook of another slice, sliding Jamil a mock-guilty glance.

With a small smile, Ibram reached toward the platter, and with a quick movement, Nonie grasped the carving knife from the lamb, and plunged it through Ibram's hand, pinning it to the wooden table.

Horrified, the slave cried out in pain, but Nonie ruthlessly twisted his other arm behind him, and shoved him, face first, into the table. "I was trying to turn over a new leaf, here," she bit out in exasperation as he struggled and gasped. "Lord, you are an annoyance—you will tell me what is afoot, before Jamil blows your brains out, all over the table."

That Jamil was unlikely to comply with this threat went without saying, but the other man willingly stepped forward, and drew his pistol in a menacing manner.

Gasping in agony, Ibram watched the blood flow from his hand, and made no response.

"Shoot him," she commanded coolly, and Jamil cocked the hammer of the pistol.

"No—no!" the young man stammered, frantic. "I don't understand—please—"

"You serve the Agha," she accused. "Don't deny it." Upon seeing him, she'd remembered what had eluded her—every time Ibram appeared on the scene, one of the Agha's men followed shortly thereafter, and always to her disadvantage. Ibram must be the Agha's man, and now the Agha knew of the plot to stage the necromancer's death.

"Miss—oh, miss; please—"

"Twisting his arm to a tortuous angle, she hissed at her most malevolent, "Speak, before I lose my patience."

He closed his eyes, and took a shuddering breath. "The Agha is concerned that the necromancer has too much influence—"

"Yes?" She applied more pressure to his arm, so that he groaned in pain, his face necessarily pressed into the greasy platter of lamb. "So, what is the Agha's plan? Tell me now, or you will lose your hand."

The young man panted in agony, "He will—he will have the Frenchman framed for the necromancer's death—"

This, of course, was in alignment with their own plan, and so Nonie felt the tightening in her breast ease a bit. His next words, however, brought it back again.

"—but the shooter will be the Agha's man, not the necromancer's."

Nonie paused in disbelief—Mother a' mercy, the shooting wouldn't be staged, it would be real, and Tahriz had to be warned—if it wasn't too late already. First things first, though; she couldn't allow Ibram to survive, so as to tell this tale. "Forgive me, Father," she said over her shoulder to Jamil, "I'll be sinning, just now."

But before she could reach for her blade, she heard footsteps approaching from the entryway. "Put your pistol on the table," she commanded Jamil. "Quickly."

Jamil, to his credit, stepped forward immediately, and deposited his pistol onto the table, just as a guard entered the room—pausing to take in the tableau before him with an incredulous expression.

Ibram called out in Arabic, and as he did, Nonie grasped the knife that pinned his hand to the table, and with an expert flick of her wrist, hurled it toward the newcomer, twisting Ibram around before her like a shield. In a reflex action, the guard fired at Ibram, just as Nonie fired Jamil's pistol back at him. As a result, both Ibram and the guard simultaneously collapsed to the floor, dead.

"I'm heading to the harbor," she announced to Jamil, as she stepped over the wreckage. Seizing a pear on her way out, she walked rapidly into the hallway, knowing the gunfire would soon attract others. "You say you're escorting me to safety, and I'll play the damsel—here's your pistol back."

"Yes, ma'am," Jamil replied, accepting his role without demur.

And so, when two guards confronted them in the hallway, she gestured in tearful dismay toward the Dey's chambers, as Jamil made an explanation in Arabic. Alarmed, the men hurried past, and Jamil quickly led her down a stairway, and out to the back alleyway.

It is a shame I'm to give all this up, she thought, as they made a rapid progress toward the harbor; I am so very good at it. Of course, I'd best not tell Tahriz about this little episode, or he'll be up all night, wearing a hair shirt, and praying for my poor misbegotten soul. Reminded, she slowed down to walk abreast of Jamil. "Are you a Hospitaller, too?"

He hesitated. "I'd rather not say, ma'am."

Frustrated, she persisted, "I'm only wanting to know if that husband of mine has taken holy orders."

It was clear that she'd finally shocked poor Jamil, and he stared for a moment. "No—no, of course not."

"For heaven's sake, keep moving," she retorted irritably. "I don't know if all the Knights of Malta are priests, and I was worried about it." She amended, honestly, "Not so very worried, but a little."

"No. Not all Knights are priests." He still sounded a bit shocked that she had entertained such a possibility.

Goaded, she tugged on his sleeve. "Listen, my friend, I've met priests who would sell the Blessed Mother for a tuppence and a half-pint, so don't come over so righteous with me."

"My lord is not one of them," he answered firmly. "You do him a disservice."

"All right—I beg your pardon, then; you'll not mention it?"

"No," he agreed immediately, making it clear he didn't wish to even think of it again.

"You're very disapproving, for an assassin's accomplice," she chided.

There was a pause, while he thought this over. "Perhaps you'll not mention it, in turn?"

"Done," she agreed.

CHAPTER THIRTY-NINE

"Who is supposed to be the shooter?" Nonie asked Jamil, as they crouched to observe the flurry of activity aboard the French frigate. "Whoever he is, he's tainted—he's a turncoat."

They were hidden behind a pile of nets, Nonie debating the best strategy. The light was fading, and at this distance it was difficult to make out the figures on the deck, but she didn't think she recognized Tahriz. He was undoubtedly aboard, nonetheless, even though the fishmongers hadn't spotted him—if he didn't want to be noticed, he wouldn't be.

"I do not know—I am not aware of the particulars," the man admitted. "I am sorry."

"Then I'll just have to get to Tahriz, and warn him. He'll handle it." She turned to ask one of the fishmongers, "Have you heard any shots?"

The man eyed Jamil with misgiving, and Nonie could scarce blame him, being as Jamil was allied with the mark, and the fishmongers were unaware that she was allied with the mark, herself. "Never mind him—tell me," she insisted.

"No," the man replied. "No trouble. Are we expecting trouble?"

"I believe we are," she replied absently, thinking. "Is Jamie aboard?"

The man's gaze slid once again to Jamil. "Yes. And the woman."

She turned to regard him with surprise. "What woman?"

The one from the mark's entourage," the man explained, and then gave her a meaningful look. "The beauty."

Nonie stared at him in astonishment. "Saba? When? Did she come with Jamie?"

"No—later, and alone."

Lord, she thought in exasperation; everyone needs to stay in one place for two minutes at a time, so that I can sort it all out. "Was she being forced against her will, do you think?"

The fishmonger considered, and then shook his head. "It did not seem so—she carried a basket."

"Holy Mother," Nonie breathed in dismay. "*Saba* is the shooter."

"No," Jamil protested immediately. "There has been a mistake."

"Then why is she there?" Try as she might, Nonie was hard-pressed not to agree with Jamil—it was almost inconceivable that Saba would betray Tahriz. She shook her head. "No matter speculating—if she's there, I've got to get on board, and straightaway. We'll need some men in boats, positioned along the perimeter to provide support—make certain everyone is armed, but make no move without my say-so; we need that ship to sail. Quickly, now."

"I will accompany you," Jamil said firmly.

She gave him a wry glance. "Sorry, your holiness, but I'll not be trusting anyone, just now, especially after this Saba wrinkle." Thinking it over, she offered, "Although I'll be looking to offload her, and it may be best if a familiar face was on one of the dory boats." She nodded toward one of the fishmongers. "Bring this one along, and keep a sharp eye—I may have to wiggle the girl out of a porthole, on the sly."

A short time later, she was stepping off the small tender boat to climb the rope ladder onto the French frigate, whilst two of the fishmongers loaded a barrel of brined fish into a cargo net, pretending to be suppliers. She addressed the sailor on the gunwale, who was observing her ascent with no small surprise. "I am here to fetch my friend—the dark-haired woman. Can you show me where she is?"

Alarmingly, the sailor immediately drew a pistol, and stepped back. "Hold," he commanded. "Do not move."

"Oh, dear," exclaimed Nonie in confused dismay, "Silly thing—what has she done, now?" She leaned toward him, and continued in a confiding manner, "She tends to stir up trouble, amongst the men."

The sailor ignored her, and said to another over his shoulder, "Send word—tell *Le Capitaine* another woman boards, seeking the first one."

"*Monsieur*, surely there is no need for your pistol—"

"Silence," the sailor commanded, and gestured in a menacing manner with his weapon.

Subsiding, Nonie struck a cowed and nervous posture until—right on cue—another sailor approached in the welcome form of Jamie. "I'm to take her below."

"Below where?" asked Nonie in a small voice. "There has been a terrible misunderstanding; I am here to fetch my fellow wife, Saba, who I understand is on board—"

"You will see her; the captain believes she conspires with the others to steal our cargo." Making a gesture with his head, Jamie commanded, "Let's go."

Pale and shaken, she hesitated, then clasped her hands and raised her eyes toward the heavens, murmuring prayerfully in Gaelic, "The staged shooter is the Agha's man, and means to kill Tahriz."

"Enough of this nonsense," Jamie interrupted, giving her a small shove. "Walk."

"Please, *monsieur*," she begged, stumbling forward. "I don't understand—please, *please* let me go back—" With great trepidation, she followed Jamie to the companionway stairs, where for a brief few seconds they could not be overheard. "Saba may be the shooter," she murmured bluntly.

"No," he returned under his breath. "She was fashed that she'd cried when I left, and so she crept aboard to say goodbye again. She smuggled in a letter, and a lock of hair, but the Frenchman thinks she sought to smuggle the pearls out." He paused. "First Fatima came to fetch her, and now you."

Nonie made a small sound of annoyance; the sudden congregation of the necromancer's wives would indeed appear suspicious, not to mention the necromancer himself had no business being aboard the French ship, in the first place. The plan was quickly unraveling, unless she could think of a way to exonerate the women, and leave Tahriz on the hook so that he got himself shot. It didn't help matters that she'd unwittingly precipitated this particular crisis by scolding Saba in the first place. I will never learn to hold my tongue, she thought with resignation; Lord.

Jamie prodded her toward the captain's quarters saying in a harsh tone, "We will get to the bottom of this—such thieving will not be tolerated."

Terrified, she bowed her head and murmured a quick prayer in Gaelic. "Anchor chain—get us to the gun deck."

He knocked on the door to the captain's cabin and announced, "The other woman, sir."

The door was opened by another sailor, and Nonie stepped in to observe a tense tableau, with *Le Capitaine* standing beside his map table, as he confronted the necromancer, the air between the two men thick with barely-constrained anger. Saba stood beside Tahriz, pale but composed, with Fatima to his other side. On the small table between them sat the familiar casket containing the pearls, and it seemed evident the angry Frenchman had just accused them of attempted thievery.

"Why, what's amiss?" asked Nonie, her voice trembling, and her surprised gaze upon the participants. "What's happened?"

But the Frenchman indicated with a gesture that she was to be silent, and slowly approached to stand before her, his attitude menacing.

Nonie, however, was never one to be impressed by menacing attitudes, and her gaze fell to the Frenchman's sling. "Oh, *monsieur*—whatever has happened to your poor arm?"

"Your business is with me," the necromancer quickly interrupted in an autocratic tone. "Let the women go— come; you demean yourself."

But the Frenchman continued his fearsome scrutiny of Nonie from his one good eye. He thinks to prod me into gabbling, as though I'm a naughty schoolgirl, she thought. Good luck to him, and it was truly a shame that she was not slated to do him in, as he was one who deserved it more than most.

Finally, he rasped, "What did your master command you to do, here?"

"Husband," she corrected apologetically. "It's free-born, I am."

"Speak," he commanded her in an ominous tone. "Unlike the Dey, I have little patience for your nonsense."

With a fearful glance at the necromancer, Nonie offered in a small voice, "I'd rather not say—it is a private matter—"

Alive to the nuance in her tone, her tormentor rested his gaze upon the others for a thoughtful moment. "You will tell me, or discover whether you are able to swim to shore."

"I've done it before—it is truly not so very far," she assured him. "I imagine it is difficult for you to gauge distances, what with only the one eye."

Angrily, he lowered his face to hers. "You, *madame*, need to watch what you say."

"Yes, *monsieur*, she replied humbly. "I beg your pardon."

"Speak," he commanded, with unmistakable menace.

Swallowing, she confessed in a rush, "I came to fetch Saba—she has an inordinate affection for one of the sailors, and we feared—Fatima and I—that she would disgrace us all."

The Frenchman's surprised gaze shifted over to contemplate Saba, who promptly hung her head in shame. "This is true?" he asked her.

The necromancer, furious, issued a rebuke in Arabic to Saba, but the Frenchman silenced him with a curt gesture, saying with amused scorn, "Come, you will not be the first man to discover he is a cuckold."

"It is none of your affair," the other man ground out. "You forget who I am, and you will pay for this insult."

But clearly, the Frenchman was now enjoying the situation, and circled around the fearful Nonie, who'd ducked her trembling chin so as to avoid his eye. "On the contrary, you forget that this is my ship, and the Dey has no authority here. Now tell me, *madame*, what do you know of this little *affaire de coeur?*

"Say nothing," commanded Tahriz.

The Frenchman drew his sword, and held it to Nonie's throat, whilst Fatima stifled a gasp. "You will speak," he commanded. "I am out of patience."

In a semi-hysterical rush, Nonie offered, "I know she wrote him a letter, and cut off a lock of her hair to give to him." Pleading, she added, "Please, *please* don't hurt me."

With a deliberate movement, *Le Capitaine* walked over to Saba's basket, and pulled it away from her. Lifting the lock of hair, he addressed the necromancer in a sardonic tone. "It appears you have a problem, my friend; perhaps you have taken in another's bastards as your own."

"It is none of your concern." The necromancer's fists were clenched in fury.

The Frenchman smirked. "It is my ship. And I am not convinced that you aren't after my pearls, after all— you knew nothing of the lovers, which is why your other wives came to save her from her folly."

"That is nonsense," said the necromancer with full scorn. However, he made no attempt to explain his presence, and there was a moment of tense silence.

"Shall I detain him, below, sir?" asked Jamie. "I will send the women off."

"No," answered the Frenchman. "Leave him here, and hold the women in the brig against his good behavior, until we are out of the harbor."

As Jamie seized her arm, Nonie struggled against him, hanging on to the door jamb, and pleading with her husband, making her accent as thick as she could, "Nay, 'tis tainted, the shooter is."

"What did she say—*dechue?*" the Frenchman asked Jamie irritably.

"I don't know—I can't understand her." With a yank, Jamie pulled Nonie out the door.

CHAPTER FORTY

The party left the companionway at the gun deck, instead of continuing on down to the brig, and headed toward the anchor chain, which would provide for an easier escape than jumping from a port hole. Looking up, Jamie paused. "Do you hear that?"

Nonie listened to the sudden activity above decks—raised voices, and rapid footsteps. "It may be the Dey," she guessed. "But we've got to stop the tainted shooter; do you think the mark understood me?"

"I'll go make sure, while you off-load them." Jamie's glance rested on Saba.

"I'll have them away in two shakes," she assured him. "If you have a chance, create a diversion until they are out of range."

"Nonie, what is it?" asked Fatima, her smooth brow furrowed, as she looked from one to the other. "What is a 'tainted shooter'?"

"Too hard to explain, Fatima," Nonie replied almost kindly, and then turned to Saba. "Down the anchor chain with you, my friend; now is a good time, while everyone is distracted by whoever is arriving on deck."

Jamie translated, then rested a hand briefly on Saba's arm, before he trotted over to the companionway, checking his pistol as he went. The girl watched him go, and then turned her pale face to Nonie, to speak in her halting Italian, "I am sorry, Nonie."

"Nonsense—it's my own fault for meddling, and that's enough said." Carefully, Nonie poked her head through the cannon gun-port opening that was closest to the anchor chain, and took a quick survey of the immediate area below. "Good. Now, you've got to climb up into the gun-port, here, and leap out to catch the chain. "I've done it before—it's easier than it looks, I promise."

After only a brief hesitation, Saba climbed through the iron-rimmed opening, and then launched herself to grasp the thick chain, wrapping her legs around the links before carefully sliding down toward the water.

Watching her, Nonie called out softly, "Good; now with any luck, there's someone about—ah—there we go." A fishmonger's boat bumped up against the hull between the chain and the ship, the fishmonger maneuvering the oars while Jamil sat in the stern, quietl speaking words of encouragement to Saba in her own language.

"What's the commotion, above?" Nonie called down to them.

"The Dey has arrived, and the Agha, as well."

"Naturally they have. Lord, it's a gathering of black-legs, it is. Hurry then, and get them away whilst everyone's distracted."

The two men stood in the boat, balancing against the rocking of the waves as they reached for the girl, and brought her down safely onto the floorboards. "I'll be needing a pistol," Nonie called down. "Quickly, please."

"You must come with us to shore," Jamil insisted, still standing with his arms raised. "Come, now."

"I will not, and I'll have no more of your mutiny," she replied. "You are an unmanageable henchman, and I'll be complaining to your master at the first opportunity."

"If you please," Jamil amended in a more conciliatory tone.

"No. Take Saba and Fatima straight to shore, and hide them in the safe house until you hear word from me. Now, where is that weapon?" The fishmonger carefully tossed up a pistol, but it fell out of her grasp, and disappeared into the waves. "Bloody hell—my fault. Do you have another?"

Instead, Jamil grasped the chain, then climbed toward her—hand over hand—until he paused to swing his legs so as to gain enough momentum to hook his feet onto the nearest gun port opening, and clamber through it.

Watching this performance without comment, Nonie asked in a dry tone, "Were you not hearing what I just said?"

"I must have misunderstood you," Jamil replied, as he handed her a pistol.

She shook her head in resignation. "All right—we'll argue about it when Fatima is safely off."

The man raised his brows in surprise. "Fatima? Is Fatima on board?"

Whirling, Nonie saw that the other woman had indeed left the gun deck for parts unknown. "Bloody *hell*, was there never such a place for double-dealing backstabbers—if Fatima is the shooter, I will break her in half, and then in half again."

But Jamil would not be shaken by the woman's unexpected disappearance. "Impossible. She will do nothing to hurt our cause."

Exasperated, Nonie tucked the pistol into her undergarment, and pulled the kaftan back down over it. "Well, she's mucking up my cause like nobody's business. We'd best go track her down." With a gesture, she signaled he was to follow, and then ran on light feet over to the companionway, only to be brought up short by the sight of Tahriz and Jamie, rapidly descending the stairway.

"Lord," she teased, happy to see that her husband remained in one piece. "Who's minding the assignment?"

With a quick glance up the stairs, the necromancer took her elbow, and pulled her under the companionway stairs, as Jamie and Jamil ducked under to join them. "The Dey has arrived, and *Le Capitaine* was necessarily required to greet him, so Mr. O'Hay and I came to seek you out."

"Is Saba away?" Jamie asked with some urgency.

"She is indeed; but Fatima has disappeared—I don't suppose you've come across her?"

The necromancer's black brows drew together. "Fatima has left?"

"Could she be tainted?" Nonie hated to ask, but the possibility had to be breached—Fatima was French, after all.

"No." The necromancer shook his head with the same unshakable faith that Jamil had, and Nonie was hard-pressed not to agree with their assessment; a less likely turncoat could hardly be imagined. "She must have gone to find me."

"Yes—she was worried, when I spoke of the tainted shooter." Reminded, Nonie asked, "You know your shooter is tainted, right?"

"No longer a problem." Jamie gave her a look that conveyed a familiar message of satisfaction—and there was nothing quite so satisfactory as giving a turncoat a well-deserved comeuppance.

"You've been busy, the both of you," she noted admiringly. "I'm a piker, by comparison."

They all paused to listen to the sudden, faint sound of voices raised in anger above them—time was short, and it was imperative that the ship sail with Jamie and the pearls, even though events seemed to be conspiring against this outcome. Nonie asked Tahriz, "Can you trust anyone else to kill you properly, or shall we make a new plan?"

"Mr. O'Hay is the new shooter. He will be defending the Frenchman from my attack."

"Well—good plan, but don't forget to remove the ball from the pistol," she advised Jamie. "What is the timeline?"

"You will proceed immediately to shore."

The necromancer's gaze was implacable, and she could only agree; now that he'd been warned, she would only put the assignment at risk, if she stayed. "Believe me, I'm ready. I'll leave the three of you to worry about Fatima, then."

Nodding his head, Tahriz walked over to peer out the gun-port opening, to the water below. "You have men in the water?"

She followed him over, debating whether or not to shed her *kaftan*. "I do—and recall I've swum this swim before. Don't worry about me; I will meet you at the safe house, and good luck to the both of you."

Quickly, she placed a foot on the opening's rim, and prepared to launch herself toward the anchor chain.

hoping another fishmonger's boat would turn up, before she had to swim very far.

"Stop her!" A shout rang out from the companion-way stairs.

"Go—go," urged Tahriz, who turned to block any view of her.

Scrambling through, Nonie gulped in a deep breath, knowing she would have to swim for a distance under-water, so as to hopefully avoid being shot, but just before she leapt out over the vasty deep, she heard the Agha's voice shout, "Don't shoot her—she has the pearls."

CHAPTER FORTY-ONE

Checking herself mid-leap, Nonie turned and clawed for a handhold on the cannon's barrel, grimacing as she knocked her forearms against the cold iron in the process. If they thought she'd stolen the pearls, it meant that the pearls were missing, and if the pearls were missing, that meant their assignment had to be scrubbed. She'd never scrubbed an assignment, and would be *damned* if her very last one ended in such a wretched fashion.

Clutching the cannon and swinging from the side of the ship, Nonie tried to grip the barrel in an awkward embrace whilst stretching her feet in an unsuccessful attempt to get a foothold on the side of the hull

The Agha's men rushed to secure her, and she peered over the cannon to meet Tahriz's unhappy gaze—but he must know that they'd never let her get away in the water; not if they thought she had the pearls. Best drum up a new plan on the fly, which she did better than most.

She cried out in alarm as multiple hands dragged her ignominiously back onto the gun deck, and after she'd gained her feet, she surveyed her bruised and scraped arms, noting that Jamie was no longer amongst the sailors. "Normandy," she said loudly in disgust, and straightened her head dress.

The Agha stood before her, with the necromancer corralled between two guards—it appeared the Agha's men remembered the lightning weapon, and were reluctant to seize him.

Hoping he remembered seeing her use the "safe" signal with Jamie, Nonie placed her right hand on her left shoulder, and met her husband's eyes for a moment. During their Normandy assignment, she and Jamie had needed a diversion and so, very obligingly, Jamie had started ringing the fire bell at the grain silo. Nothing like a healthy dose of fear, to disrupt the proceedings.

Tahriz must have understood her unspoken message, because he said a quiet word in his own language—no doubt directed to Jamil, who stood with arms crossed, watching these developments with a stoic expression.

Frowning at Jamil, the Agha asked an impatient question in Arabic, no doubt wondering why a slave master had found his way onto the Frenchman's ship, and the man began a rambling, defensive explanation which sounded as though—in the international language of foot soldiers everywhere—he was only doing what Tahriz told him to do, and was not to blame for any repercussions.

"The man's a blackguard—always following me around," Nonie interrupted hotly, pulling her arm angrily out of the grip of a guard. "I wouldn't believe a word he says."

"Silence." The Agha turned his gaze from Jamil, and surveyed her for a moment, his expression cold and slightly incredulous. "I have lately heard the most extraordinary rumors about you, madam."

Stung, Nonie retorted, "Well, if it was my landlord, that was a misunderstanding, only. You shouldn't believe everything you're told."

The Agha pressed his fleshy lips into a thin, angry line. "Where are the pearls?"

Her eyes wide, Nonie shrugged her shoulders. "I could ask the same question. I lay claim to the ones Captain Spoor bestowed upon me, and it is the height of unfairness that they were taken away." She paused, thinking about it. "I certainly earned them."

The Agha took a menacing step closer, and made an impatient gesture toward the gun-port. "Then why were you trying to escape?"

Flustered, Nonie ducked her chin slightly, and cast a self-conscious glance toward Tahriz. "I was trying to stow away to France, so as to escape this place and my wretched, wretched, husband—who was forced upon me without so much as a by-your-leave. When he showed up here, I decided to jump." She paused, and leaned forward to add in a scandalized tone, "You have no idea what he makes me do."

There was a pause, whilst the men surrounding her contemplated this revelation in stunned silence. It was a useful tactic; Nonie had discovered early in her career that men's minds—even the best of them—went blank at a sexual reference. They went even blanker at the sight of naked female breasts, but this did not seem the time nor the place.

Recovering, the Agha made an abrupt gesture to his men. "Search her."

"You will not touch my wife," said the necromancer, in no uncertain terms.

"We'll compromise," Nonie suggested, stalling, and wishing Jamie would hurry. "I'll remove my *kaftan*, and you'll see for yourself that I do not have the pearls." With slow, deliberative movements, she bestowed a teasing glance on the guards, and began to untie her fastenings, pulling her overdress over her head, while the men surrounding her watched in abject silence. Unhurried, she began to unhook the *kaftan* itself, her fingers brushing against the pistol hidden in the placket at her waist. Come along, Jamie—no time like the present—

One of the Agha's men tore his gaze from Nonie, and lifted his head. He made a comment in Arabic, just as the smell of something burning could be discerned. With a thunderous report, two of the cannons at the other end of the deck fired, the heavy weapons recoiling with the blast, and smoke filling the narrow confines of the area. With panicked cries, the Agha's men drew their weapons, and closed around the Agha in confusion, whilst Nonie felt Tahriz grasp her around the waist, and propel her toward the stairs under the cover of the smoke.

"Hold," she protested. "Jamie will—"

"If you remain here, I am helpless," he said in her ear. "Come, you must get off."

Lord, she thought; I suppose I must do as he says— he's my husband, after all. "All right, then."

Grasping her hand, he pulled her up the companionway, away from the confused shouts of the Agha's men, only to be met by a throng of French sailors who were rapidly coming the other way down the stairs, to find out why the ship's cannons were firing off.

"There's a fire, down below," Tahriz shouted in French, as he held out an arm to flatten Nonie against the bulkhead. "Man the buckets."

With cries of alarm, the men hurried past them to the gun deck—a fire on board was a grave danger and superseded any paltry consideration of pearls and double-dealings.

"Good one," Nonie panted, as they emerged onto the main deck, where the cries of fire were being echoed back to others.

With a quick glance around them, Tahriz dodged running sailors and led her toward the stern, away from the confusion of the main deck. His gaze ran over her, as he lifted her to the back balustrade. "Can you swim in the *kaftan*?"

"I swim like a seal," she assured him. "Where are the pearls?"

"I know not," he said in a repressive tone, and steadied her on the railing. "Over you go."

"Tahriz," she protested, "if the pearls aren't on board—"

"Not now, Nonie. I don't want to push you, but I will."

"I rather like it when you push me," she teased, but had no further opportunity for ribald comments, as a voice rang out from the quarterdeck above them.

"Stop, or I will shoot her."

Nonie froze where she stood, and met Tahriz's gaze in puzzlement, before they both slowly turned to face Jamie, who stood on the quarterdeck, his pistol aimed at Nonie. A cohort of French sailors backed him up, their own weapons at the ready.

Now, here's a wrinkle, Nonie thought, as she raised her hands, and backed away from the railing. "Perhaps," she suggested, "—perhaps you mean to shoot the necromancer, here."

"Silence," Jamie exhorted, his pistol never wavering. "Now come away from there, or you'll never find yourself in Saragossa again."

Lord, thought Nonie in abject confusion. What's afoot? When cornered, the Saragossa mark had tried to extort his way out of his troubles—little good it had done him; she and Jamie were not extortable. I feel as though I'm shooting at birds in the dark, she thought a bit crossly as she walked slowly toward Jamie. Honestly; why didn't he just pretend to shoot Tahriz into the sea, and be done with it?

She was soon to see the reason, as they made a reluctant procession toward the bow of the ship. The panicked sounds below decks were subsiding, as the sailors realized there was no fire, and instead, Nonie beheld a throng of angry men gathered in the foredeck—the Dey and his entourage on one side, and *Le Capitaine* and his guards on the other, each group shouting heated recriminations at the other. Behind her, she heard Tahriz make a dismayed sound, just before some of the men moved aside, so that she could see what everyone else could see; Fatima, balanced on the narrow bowsprit that extended from the ship's bow over the water, a basket resting on her hip, and a tangle of pearls in one hand outstretched over the churning sea.

"Mother a' mercy," breathed Nonie. "It *is* Saragossa.

CHAPTER FORTY-TWO

"I've found them, sir," Jamie announced to *Le Capitaine*. "The wife was about to leap overboard."

With a furious gesture, the Frenchman ordered, "Bring them forward," then turned to shout to Fatima, "There, you see, *madame*? Behold your husband."

With an effort, Fatima raised her soft voice so that she could be heard over the whipping wind. "He must be allowed to depart on a boat. The Irish wife, also."

Recalculating, Nonie decided that Fatima's plan was not a mortal blow to the assignment; the necromancer could still be killed in some public fashion, and the pearls restored to the Frenchman. All in all, it was not a bad turn of events, considering matters had looked grim, only a short while before. The only rub, of course, was the fate of the diminutive woman perched on the bowsprit, and dangling a handful of pearls over the water. It was difficult to gauge who was more furious with her, the Dey or *Le Capitaine*, and no promise of safe passage would mean a thing to either of them.

With angry strides, the Frenchman approached the necromancer, and raised a pistol to his temple. "Relinquish the pearls, *madame*, or you will watch him die."

With a stealthy movement, Nonie reached within her *kaftan*, to close her hand around her pistol as she met Jamie's eyes, sending a message that it was time to abandon the assignment without a qualm, and to incite a gun battle in the desperate hope that some of them would survive. While they tensed for this inevitability, however, Fatima had other plans. With a calm flick of her wrist, the tangle of pearls she'd held dropped down, and disappeared into the churning waves. With a deliberate motion, she reached into the basket, and drew out another.

"Stop, I command you," shouted *Le Capitaine* as a collective gasp could be heard from the men who watched.

Ignoring him, she dangled the next handful, gleaming in the twilight, over the water.

Cursing, the Frenchman lowered his pistol, and Nonie let out a relieved breath. I don't know why I ever thought Fatima was naïve, or timid, she thought. But one thing I know for certain—I'm not going to allow the likes of her to sacrifice herself to save the likes of me.

With an angry shout, the Agha made his way through the crowd, and into the forefront of the strange stand-off. "What nonsense is this? Shoot her!"

"No—I must have the pearls," ground out the Frenchman. "Stand down, and do as she asks—safe passage for everyone to get off the ship, so that I can set sail and begone from this place."

"Yes—stand down," agreed the Dey, glancing uneasily toward his necromancer. "It has been nothing more than a misunderstanding."

But the Agha was not so willing to concede, and stalked over to confront *Le Capitaine,* his heavy bulk nearly shaking with fury. "No—no, you *fools*—they must all be killed; they are not what they seem." With a trembling arm, the Agha pointed an accusing finger at Nonie. "This woman is a notorious slayer of men."

"Calm yourself," admonished the Dey, with a full measure of icy scorn. "You make yourself foolish."

"I do not care one way or another," responded the French captain, in cutting tones. "Leave me the pearls, and get off my ship."

But Nonie had heard enough, and carefully withdrew her pistol from its hiding place, as she pretended to cower behind her husband. "The Agha knows too much," she murmured, and raised the pistol to prop the barrel on Tahriz's shoulder, so that no one could see what she was about. "Hold still."

"Nonie—no," he said quietly, without looking at her.

"My last one, I promise."

"No, Nonie," he said again, standing completely still.

She hesitated, responding, despite herself, to the moral imperative in his voice. "I'm not like you."

But he only replied steadily, "We are who we wish to be."

She quirked her mouth. "I don't wish to be dead, my friend."

"There are worse things."

Lord, she thought in exasperation; I suppose he truly believes it, and I suppose I must at least make an effort to pretend he's right. "All right; you win—I'll run a diversion, instead." Adjusting her aim, she tilted the pistol so that she could sight it on the block pulley that held the foresail over Fatima's head. Aiming carefully, she squeezed the trigger.

The result was all she could have hoped for; with a crack of splintering wood, the sail fell—billowing out, and then slowly collapsing to the fore deck before the astonished men, who drew back with exclamations of alarm.

Like a hound to the whistle, Jamie reacted by leaping over the canvas sail, so as to seize the loose rigging and swing out over the bowsprit, toward Fatima. To all appearances, the two then engaged in a short struggle and at its conclusion, Jamil wrested the basket from the small woman, and pushed her into the sea below.

As *Le Capitaine* strode over to render his thanks to Jamie, Nonie murmured to Tahriz, "My people will fish her out, never fear."

"Prepare to follow her." He touched her arm, gently.

Uneasy, she glanced over at the congratulatory group that surrounded Jamie. "Do you think Jamie can shoot you before the Agha does? The man is fit to be tied."

"You must go, *namrata*. I will create my own diversion."

"Will it be as good as mine?" she teased, as she backed away toward the water.

He tilted his head slightly. "That was a very good shot."

"Is there anything worth shooting on Malta?"

"Wild boar. It is good sport." His eyes met hers. "I will meet you on shore."

"All right, all right—I'm going. Where's your much-ballyhooed diversion? Best hurry."

That an argument had indeed broken out among the main players seemed evident, and Nonie strained to hear the angry words that were exchanged. "Our one-eyed friend is unhappy he's been shorted on the pearls," she guessed. "One can hardly blame him; Fatima is the prodigal nun, tossing them about like so much fish food."

"Go," said Tahriz urgently, as he met her eyes. "I am going to start a fire, and I'd rather you didn't witness it."

Touched by this consideration, Nonie said no more, clambering over the gunwale just as an ominous crackling sound could be heard, closely followed by a collective gasp—the lightning weapon had been unleashed. Reluctantly, she swung her legs over the side, and took a quick glance over her shoulder to see that the downed foresail was suddenly aflame. Because sail canvas was treated with wax, the inferno was immediate and impressive. Mother a' mercy, she thought as she quickly turned her eyes away. He's going to provoke the Frenchman by burning his ship, then get himself shot by Jamie as a grand finale. I wish I could stay to see it. With an unhappy sigh, she dropped into the sea.

CHAPTER FORTY-THREE

The water was cool, but not a brutal shock, like the water in the English Channel, when one was forced into it by exigent circumstances. Nonie struck out underwater for as long as she could, then surfaced as quietly as possible to take a breath, and regain her bearings in the darkness. The *kaftan* was actually easier to swim in, than the skirts in which she had taken that initial midnight swim; the silk was light, and there were no petticoats to bundle up around her legs. The crests of the waves around her reflected the orange light from the burst of flames on deck, and she quickly averted her gaze to the horizon, hoping that her people had seen her jump. On cue, a man's voice could be heard in the darkness, coming over the water from a point nearby. "There she is—hold right there, ma'am."

Turning toward the voice, Nonie continued to tread water as she watched a fishmonger's boat advance upon her, Saba sitting in the bow, and holding a shaded lantern at arm's length so that he could see Nonie in the dark water.

"You were supposed to take her to shore," Nonie admonished the man, who brought the boat alongside her.

The fishmonger shrugged his shoulders in apology, as he gave Nonie a hand to hoist her into the rocking vessel. "She asked if she could stay to help."

"And she's very pretty," Nonie added, as this was the most significant factor.

"And she's very pretty," he agreed.

"The ship—it is on fire," Saba interrupted in her halting Italian, trying with only moderate success to hide her alarm.

Nonie wrung out the skirt of her soggy *kaftan,* and kept her gaze on her knees. "Yes—don't worry; that was Tahriz's doing, and I'm sure he has everything well in hand. Has someone found poor Fatima? Jamie had to be cruel to be kind, I'm afraid."

The man nodded, his expression impassive in the dim light. "She has been brought to shore, and is safe."

This was a bit unexpected; the fishmongers would have no particular interest in Fatima, and should have waited for Nonie's order. Nevertheless, it was welcome news, and letting out a breath, she lifted her face for a moment, to give Saba a reassuring smile, and say to the fishmonger, "We should hear Jamie shoot the necromancer at any moment, and then he'll need to be fished out, too. Stand by." She was striving mightily not to listen to the alarmed cries of the sailors; the crackling of the flames.

"Where is Jamie? Where is Tahriz?" Saba turned to watch the ship with a worried frown.

In a reassuring gesture, Nonie touched the girl's knee. "Listen for a gunshot; it should be at any moment."

The three of them sat quietly in the darkness, listening to the sounds of panicked, shouting voices echoing over the water as the sailors battled the spreading fire. Finally, Nonie turned to look, her skin suddenly turning clammy, as she viewed the flaming vessel. "I can't see them—get closer," she directed, through a clenched jaw. "Do you have a scope?"

"No, ma'am," the man replied with regret, as he took up the oars. "Should we board for an extraction?"

She turned to look at him, and thought, thank God for the courage of ordinary people. "Yes; if the fire reaches the armory in the hold, there will be an explosion like the crack o' doom, so we must get them off before then—by hook or by crook."

The man nodded, and began to row them toward the ship. There was no longer a need to be quiet, as other small boats in the area were also approaching to offer assistance to any who wished to abandon ship. Confusion reigned, as would-be rescuers called in Arabic to the frantic French sailors.

"I—I don't see them," Saba stammered, her face pale in the reflected light of the flames.

Nonie turned to the fishmonger, as she ruthlessly tied her incorrigible hair into a wet knot at the nape of her neck. "I need to give her some instructions. Do you speak Italian?"

"No," the man admitted. "But I speak Maltese."

Nonie's face jerked up to his, and he met her eyes with a wooden expression. So, she thought—the fishmongers have been infiltrated by the Maltese contingent. Her husband was a wily one, and it appeared the Home Office's spy network was nothing compared to his. It was lucky she and Jamie never told anyone anything ahead of time—mainly because they made it up, as they went along. "I see; could you translate for me, then?"

At the man's nod, she took a shuddering breath, and tried to hold her voice steady. "You'll be stayin' in the boat, Saba, while we go get the two men. Stay back at least fifty yards—there may be an explosion. Watch for us—stay on this side, and wait. Don't allow anyone else to get close enough to see that you are alone. Do you know how to row? We can't have you driftin' out to sea."

Her troubled gaze resting on the fishmonger as he translated, Saba nodded in understanding. She spoke a few words, and the man translated, "She says you are not to worry."

"Never for a moment," Nonie responded grimly, fighting nausea as the acrid smell of the smoke drifted toward them. She glanced up quickly, as they came alongside the ship, close enough to hear the now-roaring flames.

All right, she thought, as she lowered her gaze again; all right—you can do this. Something's amiss, and Tahriz needs to know about the armory—he may not be as familiar with the anatomy of a warship as you are— and you are not going to lose him because you are being *utterly stupid* about something that happened—for the *love of Mike*—a thousand years ago. And Jamie—Lord, poor Jamie is in that inferno—

"I'll be needin' a dry pistol," she said in a brisk tone to the fishmonger, depositing her wet one on the seat beside her with a clunk. "Do you have a spare?"

"I have only the one."

She held out her hand, which was trembling. "Give me yours, then."

After only the barest moment's hesitation, he handed it over, and with a final, tremulous smile at Saba, she turned and quickly mounted the rope ladder to climb aboard, determined to shut out the sounds and smells of the fire, and clenching her jaw so hard that her teeth ached.

The scene on deck was not as chaotic as she'd expected; the disciplined crew was manning a bucket line, and attempting to contain the fire to the bow area, but the roaring flames had already snaked up the foremast to the yardarms, so that the furled sails were ablaze; it was evident that the crew fought a losing battle.

Of Tahriz or Jamie there was no sign, and she quickly looked away from the fire and took a shuddering breath to calm herself; there—you see? It's not the same at all; there is no one screamin' and the lovely, lovely sea is all around you. Take hold of your foolish self, and get your business done; there'll be plenty of time to be as missish as you please, once everyone is safe.

In the general chaos, no one paid the smallest attention to her, and so she said to the fishmonger, "They must be below decks; follow me." But as she walked across the deck to the companionway stairs, she was forced to retreat back to allow *Le Capitaine* to pass, flanked by several of his officers—his face set in grim lines as he barked orders at the sailors; it appeared the good captain was abandoning ship. Even more ominous, Jamie was not sticking to him like a burr, but instead was nowhere in sight.

"Follow him," she instructed the fishmonger in a low voice. "It is very important that we keep track of that one." She waited, not certain—now that she knew hi allegiances—that the man would obey her. But he only nodded, and quietly moved to join the Frenchman's retinue.

With a monumental effort, Nonie turned back to the companionway, feeling the tremendous heat of the approaching flames on the side of her face as she hurried down the stairs. Emerging onto the gun deck, the first thing she noticed were hundreds of loose pearls, scattered across the deck as several men frantically worked to scoop them up into the basket before the fire reached them—that she had come upon the aftermath of a first-class donnybrook appeared evident.

Carefully creeping forward so that she could peer down the cannon line, she beheld an alarming scene; Tahriz stood framed in a gun-port, the unconscious figure of Jamie slung over his shoulder, as he was confronted by the Agha, who was triumphantly wielding a pistol. Jamil stood beside Tahriz, his hands spread in a disarming gesture, but the look in his eye was a familiar one to Nonie—he was going to inch forward, and then lunge for the weapon. Another brave man, she thought distractedly; I need to pull myself together, and pretend to be equally brave for the space of ten minutes at a time.

A loud crash could be heard above decks, and involuntarily, she flinched. Tahriz's gaze flew to her, and with a barely perceptible movement, he tilted his head, directing her to retreat.

In a strange way, it was just what she needed to provoke her into action, and she strode toward them. "Is it *mad*, you are?" she exclaimed, hearing the overloud thread of hysteria in her own voice, but unable to control it. "The ship is afire, and you fools are fightin' like fishwives at Lent."

Startled by her voice, the Agha whirled around to back against the bulkhead, so as to include Nonie within the ambit of the threatening pistol. Warily, he looked behind her, but saw no one else. "What do you do here? Get back."

"God in heaven, you idiots—the ship is going to explode." Distractedly, she ran her hands through her hair, her voice overloud and uneven. "There is—there is black powder, here in the cannons, and in the armory, below decks—"

"Hurry," the Agha barked at the men who were gathering up the pearls.

"It's madder than a March hare, you are," Nonie exclaimed in wonder. "Much good the pearls will do you— the ship's goin' to blow."

"I believe," Jamil offered, addressing the Agha. "I believe the lady herself has several very fine pearls, tied up in her hem." He then met her gaze with a great deal of meaning.

Exasperated, she chided him, "I don't have *time* for that, Jamil." Drawing her weapon, she shot the Agha through the heart, before he'd even had a chance to react.

As the Agha collapsed to the deck, his men leapt to their feet in alarm. "You're next," she threatened, and the men bolted up the stairs, nearly falling over each other in their haste to get away. "It's a single-fire pistol," she called up after them, with all due scorn. "Bloody *idiots.*"

"Come, Nonie." With Jamie's heavy form still prone over his shoulder, Tahriz gently pulled on her arm with his free one. "We'll go, now."

Trembling, she turned to him, and wiped her eyes with the palm of her hand. "I'm sorry I up and killed him. I'm stretched a bit thin."

"No matter," he said in the same gentle tone. "We're all going to jump, now." With Jamil's help, Tahriz, propped Jamie into the gun-port opening, preparing to push him through.

With a mighty effort, Nonie pulled herself together. "No—Saba's waiting in a boat on the port side. I'll—I'll go get her, and we'll come around to pick you up. We can't leave her alone, and we can't swim around to her—not with Jamie out cold."

"Go with her," said Tahriz to Jamil.

Taking a breath, Nonie replied as calmly as she was able. "No—you need Jamil to help keep Jamie afloat. I'll run across, and jump off in two shakes, I promise.

We should be around within twenty minutes, but get as far away from the ship as you can—you'll need to be avoidin' the masts, if it heels over in this direction."

She didn't wait to see if her husband would protest; she'd always relied on her instinct, and her instinct told her it was time for action. Whirling, she sprinted up the companionway stairs.

CHAPTER FORTY-FOUR

The fire had spread so that the heat was oppressive, as Nonie emerged up on deck, the flames crackling overhead, and glowing between the wooden planks under her feet. There was no one in the immediate area, as most of the sailors had already leapt overboard, so she hoisted her *kaftan* and ran lightly across the deck, the heat stinging her bare legs as she tried to spot Saba's dory. On account of the brightness around her, she couldn't see into the darkness, and so she stood for a moment at the rail, hoping she was silhouetted and plainly visible, then made to jump.

"There you are," a voice called to her weakly, from under the shrouds. "God is good."

Nonie looked over to see the Dey, propped up against the railing, a bright bloodstain splayed across one shoulder of his embroidered tunic. "Lord," she exclaimed, trying to process this latest development, while the flames licked closer and closer. "It hardly seems fair; everyone else had a crackin' set-to, as soon as I jumped overboard."

The man frowned, his head nodding forward. "Your husband—is he dead?"

"He's off—and I'll best be off, too." She added as an afterthought, "—bein' as how the ship is afire."

Fixing her with an unfocused gaze, the Dey licked his lips. "He—he betrayed me. May he die a thousand deaths."

"You are a nodcock of the first order," she retorted crossly. "He has been your staunchest ally—not that you deserve him for an instant."

With a frown, the Dey tried to focus on her face. "No—no; he works against me—"

He was interrupted by a blast that shook the deck beneath them, and caused the ship to groan, and then list in an alarming manner.

"There'll be more where that came from," she shouted, and took his arm, pulling him upright with an effort, so that he leaned weakly against the rail, as the deck began to slope the other way, beneath their feet. "Can't wait—let's go." She leapt out as far as she could, yanking his good arm so that he leapt also, just as th force from another deafening blast could be felt behind them.

For the second time in an hour, Nonie plunged into the Bay of Algiers and felt the blessedly cool water close over her head. She enjoyed the relief from the heat for a brief moment, then kicked to the surface to with the wretched Dey in tow—and wasn't it *bloody* ironic that she was slated to save him for Tahriz's sake, instead of just kill the stupid tyrant, which was much more in keeping with her inclination, let alone her assignment.

She grasped his collar, and pulled him away from the groaning ship, now completely engulfed in flames. "I've got you," she gasped. "Try to float—don't fight me."

"No," he whispered, and lay perfectly still, atop the water.

Pausing for a moment, she put her fingers in her mouth to blow two short, shrill whistles, then grabbed the sinking Dey again, and continued pulling him away from the flaming wreckage as best she could. Hopefully, Saba would show up soon—she was fast losing her strength.

"Nonie," Saba called out from the near distance. "*Ancora.*"

Obediently, Nonie gave another quick blast, and then saw the silhouette of the dory boat, with its flickering lantern. "Over here—over here, oh, Saba—well done."

Anne Cleeland

In a moment, Nonie was clinging to the side of the dory alongside the Dey, and trying to catch her breath. It seemed clear they wouldn't be able to manage getting aboard, so they'd have to be content with hanging onto the boat, whilst Saba rowed it around the sinking ship.

As Saba looked at the Dey with wide eyes, Nonie pantomimed. "We have to row around to the other side, Saba—"

Suddenly, the night grew dark, as the burning ship heeled over, and slipped beneath the waves, the flames hissing into submission.

In the dim light of the lantern, Nonie signaled to Saba to keep rowing. "I'll kick, and help out as best I can, Saba, but we've got to hurry—"

A whistle blew out over the water, a long blast, followed by a short one. Stay in place, it meant; help is coming.

Overcome, Nonie bent her head for a moment. It was Jamie. Jamie was all right—she'd not been certain, truth to tell, if he weren't already dead, when she saw Tahriz carrying him. Lifting her head, she blew an answering whistle, then smiled at Saba. "Jamie's comin'." With one hand, she pantomimed, "We'll wait."

Like a deer, Saba raised her head and turned it toward the whistle, alert and unmoving.

Harboring mixed emotions, Nonie hung on to the side of the dory under the starry Algerian sky, and waited for rescue—something entirely unfamiliar to her. "I

378

suppose that tears it," she remarked aloud. "This assignment is officially a disaster—worse than Flanders, and
that's saying something."

"God is good."

Nonie turned to address the Dey, clinging to their
boat, and watching her with a dazed, incredulous expression. "Who shot you? Never say it was the necromancer; I'll not believe it."

"The Agha," the man murmured. "He sought to
seize power."

"No surprise, there, I must say. Why are you so fashed
about the necromancer, then?"

"He—he is a traitor," the Dey answered, with halting
words. "The fire—while the French captain was dealing
with the fire, the Agha ordered his men to shoot me.
They also seized the pearls—" here, the man coughed
weakly. "The necromancer did not come to my aid, but
showed his true loyalty, to the French captain."

Nonie frowned at him for a moment, but then her
brow cleared. "Because he chose to rescue the French
sailor—the one who'd been holding the pearls—and
not you." Small wonder no one understood Tahriz's motives; as far as they knew, Jamie was a Frenchman. She
rested her forehead on the side of the boat for a moment, grateful down to her bones that she had such a
fine, fine husband.

Two short whistles could be heard, and Nonie returned two, gauging they were getting close. "We're

to get out of this with a whole skin, you and me," she remarked to the Dey. "You'll be back to thieving and double-crossing in no time."

"Nadia said it would be so," agreed the Dey in a whisper.

Nonie shifted her grip, and regarded him, quirking her mouth in grim amusement. "Hold a moment; if you are speaking to Nadia all on your own, then what's the point of paying a necromancer?"

It was too dark to see his expression, but the Dey answered softly, "It was only the once. In a dream, Nadia told me that the necromancer's red-headed wife would save my life."

There was a long pause, whilst Nonie gazed upon him in astonishment. "Well, knock me down."

With an excited gesture, Saba pointed, and lifted the lantern, slightly, so that they were more visible. Only a few more minutes, then, and the rescuers would arrive.

In the brighter light, Nonie could see that the Dey's hair was matted with blood, but head wounds always bled a lot—as she knew better than most—and there did not appear to be any fresh bleeding. Grabbing his sleeve, and hoping he stayed conscious, she considered his odd comment about Nadia. I wish Tanny would visit me, she thought; just once—although she'd probably not be best pleased with me, truth to tell. But she'd be astonished to discover I climbed into a burning ship— I'm still rather astonished, myself. I'd tell her what a good man Jamie has become, and I'd tell her of Tahriz and how he saw something in me—something fine, despite everything—

Unable to help it, she began to cry, and pressed her mouth into her elbow, so that Saba wouldn't hear her sob aloud. *I suppose I can't go about killin' people anymore, and must try to be better—Tanny'd be pleased to hear it; she always would say there was never a girl so beloved by the angels, what with so many freckles.* Suddenly struck, she lifted her chin, and said aloud, "My father had a mass of freckles on his face—fancy that; I'd completely forgotten."

"*Che?*" asked Saba, startled.

"Over there—there they are." The other dory boat came alongside, and Tahriz's tall figure bent over Nonie to lift her in, as the fishmongers hauled in the Dey.

As he enveloped her in his arms, an intense feeling of euphoria washed over Nonie—the feeling one experienced when one had cheated death, yet again; only this time it was all wound up in the deep and abiding emotion she felt for the man who now held her. "I saved your stupid Dey."

"Sit here, let me warm you." He bundled her into his lap, and leaned against the bow, out of the wind.

"You are as wet as I am, my friend." Nonetheless, she burrowed into his chest, breathing in the scent of sea water, and sighing in deep contentment. "And you are supposed to be dead, I might add. Let's salvage *something* from this out-and-out disaster."

"Later," he promised. "Are you injured?"

"No—a bit singed, is all." She watched Jamie join Saba in her dory, and assessed him with a critical eye. "How's Jamie?"

"He has a hard head."

"Yes," she agreed fondly. "The Saragossa mark tested it out, once."

His arms tightened around her, as he rested his cheek on the top of her head. "Am I the Algerian mark?"

"The Barbary mark," she corrected. "My only failed assignment, but small blame to me; the information-gatherers misread the situation."

"I can't say that I am sorry."

She smiled to herself, as the two boats made a stealthy progress toward the fishmonger's dock.

CHAPTER FORTY-FIVE

"I still hate this place." Nonie lay with Tahriz on the rooftop of the safe house, idly tracing her fingers on his bare chest, as she gazed up at the stars above them. "Make no mistake." They had graciously agreed to allow Jamie and Saba the privacy of the house, and had retreated for a frenzied session of lovemaking in the open air atop the roof; at present, they were catching their breath before round two would commence.

"It won't be much longer," he soothed, his mouth on her temple. "Between the Congress in Vienna, the Americans and the British Navy, I imagine the slave trade will be curtailed within the year."

She shrugged a shoulder to convey her skepticism. "You are far more optimistic than I, Tahriz. I suppose it comes naturally to the likes of you, while dour pessimism comes more naturally to the likes of me."

He bent an elbow to prop up his head, and replied in a mild tone, "Then we shall see which view will prevail."

Still in a happy haze, as a result of surviving her latest misadventure, she turned to look at him—he was a sight, was her husband; with his lean face, and the dark hair falling across his damp brow. "I hope I don't drive you mad, Tahriz—I'm not very tidy, and I tend to say flippant things when I shouldn't."

But he did not recoil in horror at these revelations, instead merely replying, "And I am too sober, and too staid; no match for you."

Laughing, she pinched at his chin. "Is that what you think?"

He smiled, amused in turn. "It is the truth." With a gentle finger, he traced a ringlet that fell down the side of her face.

She grasped his hand and turned her face to kiss it. "Well, you weren't very sober and staid a few minutes ago—I feared you'd wake the poor neighbors, I did."

He arched a dark brow in acknowledgment. "I cannot resist you."

"No—nor should you; best resign yourself to more of the same."

"Willingly. Which reminds me, I have a gift for you—a wedding gift." Rolling to his side, he searched through their hastily discarded, damp clothing, and pulled out a gleaming strand of pearls, from his sash.

She fingered them in delighted surprise, as they dangled before her. "Lord, Tahriz—you are as light-fingered as Jamie. Are they real ones?"

"They are."

Sitting up, she crossed her legs. "Shall we see if they look paltry against my bare skin?"

"We should." He placed the strand around her neck, bending to bestow a lingering kiss on the area framed by the pearls.

"*Les jeune filles.*" Looking up to him, she confessed, "I couldn't understand why you showed no interest in them—it drove me mad, after all the trouble I'd taken to bait the trap."

"I was too busy trying not to show an interest in you."

She laughed. "You weren't successful, I'm afraid; I knew you were interested from the first—which only served to drive me more mad, since you wouldn't act on it."

To reward this insight, he leaned to kiss her, and then pulled her to lie down beside him again on the pallet. "I could hardly sleep—you filled my mind."

"Of course. You were busy plotting various plots to remove me from the arena."

"Unfair," he protested. "I did marry you."

"Foyster," she accused, "—and with me all unknowin'."

He laughed his rare laugh, pulled her close to his side.

Another ten minutes, she reckoned, gauging his mood; then we'll be havin' at it again, so I should try to get some questions answered, in the meantime. "Where is our Fatima? I should make her go retrieve my poor pearls from the bottom of the sea."

"She is at the palace, nursing the Dey, and starting to show signs of alarm that I am unaccounted for."

"She's the true foyster," Nonie declared in admiration. "I can't hold a candle."

His voice suddenly serious, he said slowly, "I am of two minds, *nomrata*; it is dangerous work that I do."

"Tahriz," she replied ominously, "—don't you *dare* try to keep me away from you."

"You would have to work behind the scenes; you are easily recognized."

She had already come to the same conclusion. "I'm willing to do whatever is necessary, as long as I'm useful." Thinking it over, she added, "And it's just as well that I stay away from the slave market; Jamil is unhappy with me because I thought you a priest."

His hand moved lightly over her breast, and he asked in a mild tone, "You thought me a priest?"

"Well, I was a bit hazy on the whole Knights of Malta thing."

She could hear the amused incredulity in his voice. "Would you have married me, if I were indeed a priest?"

"Lord, yes. It's irredeemable, I am."

Chuckling, he rolled to pin her beneath him. "I am determined to redeem you; prepare yourself." He bent to kiss her with no little heat.

"Ouch," she murmured into his mouth. "Let me move the pearls out of the way."

Sometime later, she was drifting in and out of sleep, when she heard a soft sound from below that sounded like a mourning dove; not that a mourning dove would be calling in the middle of the night, or in the middle of Algiers. She felt Tahriz tense, and whispered, "It's Jamie—do you mind if I speak with him?"

"No—of course not."

She whistled softly in return, and in a small space of time, Jamie came through the rooftop door, not at all discomfited by the sight of Nonie, bare-legged and hastily clothed in Tahriz's rumpled tunic. "Hallo, you," she greeted him. "How's your noggin?"

Obediently, he bent his head forward so that she could inspect the lump, but his gaze rested on Tahriz. "Will you tell me of that lightning weapon—is it related to Volta's work?"

The other man hesitated only for the barest moment. "Yes. It can only be used once, though; I am working on multiple uses."

Fascinated, Jamie approached to sit next to him. "How far a distance?"

"It depends on the conduit; not very far, in most cases."

Jamie considered this for a moment, absently rubbing his neck. "Have you heard they are working on a repeating rifle?"

"Isn't this your wedding night?" Nonie asked in amusement.

With a grin, he confessed, "Saba's asleep. She's worn through, I'm afraid. Fancy—she told me she clambered down the anchor chain, quick as a cat."

"She's a brick," Nonie agreed. "The best of all wives. Saved me and the Dey from a watery grave. Never faltered."

But her words triggered a different reaction from what she'd expected, and he ducked his head. "I wish I could say the same, Nonie. When—when the fire started, I couldn't hold my position, and then I got coshed like a gudgeon."

She had guessed as much; Jamie was not one to be taken advantage of in a fight, and she was surprised to hear that he'd needed rescuing. They'd confronted a fire only the one time in Flanders, and had promptly retreated in disarray. Since retreat was not an option this time, each had suffered for it.

Laying a gentle hand on his arm, she leaned in and whispered, "You must tell Saba, Jamie—she will hel share the burden, and then it doesn't seem quite so unbearable. Tanny worked so hard to heal us; we owe it to her. And tell Saba of Rorie, and Dennie, and little Nell—"

"Nonie—stop." He shook his head, his voice hoarse.

Her own voice breaking, she continued, "They deserve to be spoken of, Jamie—" unable to go on, she pressed her face against his shoulder, as he put his arms around her for a long moment, the bond between them poignant, and bittersweet.

"I'll need my orders," Jamie said softly. "Being as how the assignment is in a shambles."

It was just the touch she needed, and she began to laugh, and he laughed in response, while Tahriz smiled along with them, relieved that her sadness had passed. "We can attempt a reboot—shadow *Le Capitaine*, who must be desperate for treasure at this juncture, and feed him something else, to serve as a consolation prize. Fortunately, he'll need a few days to reorganize, so perhaps all is not lost, if we can put together an alternative plan."

He nodded. "Does Saba still go to London?"

She turned to include Tahriz in the conversation. "Do you think Saba is safer in London, or on Malta?"

He tilted his head slightly, considering. "Probably Malta. The coming months should see activity toward the north, and there is no telling how far north; it may reach into England."

"Lord, he's well-informed," Jamie commented in Gaelic.

"Yes—no other mark could hold a candle."

Jamie gave her a look. "Perhaps we shouldn't call him 'the mark' anymore."

"Tahriz," she corrected, a bit self-consciously. "I'll be staying with Tahriz, to see if there is any hope to be had for me; but rest assured, we'll bundle Saba off to Malta, guarded to the teeth."

He met her gaze thoughtfully. "And what am I to tell them, when I report back alone?"

"Tell them you don't know where I am."

He made a wry mouth. "They'll not believe it, Nonie."

She sighed with resigned exasperation. "All right then, tell them I'm freeing the slaves, like a bloody Moses, and if they want me back, they'd best send someone with a decent fleet to annihilate Algiers."

Grinning, he teased, "Next you'll be going back to church."

"Can you imagine? They'd make me stand by the altar in sackcloth, as a cautionary tale. Tahriz would be mortified."

He ducked his chin for a moment. "Shall I stay with you?"

She had known he would ask—she knew him better than anyone; anyone who was still alive, that was. "No; they need you—I feel badly enough, bowing out. But I suppose you should try not to be killing anyone—anyone who doesn't truly deserve it, I suppose. The Maltese contingent frowns on it."

Inviting her to share in the irony, he observed, "And now we're part of the Maltese contingent."

"We are indeed. A bit different than the English contingent, but I suppose we'll adjust."

He looked out over the surrounding rooftops, a trace of bitterness in his voice. "The English contingent did us no favors."

Suddenly serious, she put a hand on his arm. "I don't know, Jamie; we were bent on destruction, you and I—how long would we have lasted? And thanks to the English contingent, instead we wound up in gaol, and met that man without a name, and went adventuring all over the world until we finally ended up here, where we met two people who love us, despite it all. It's enough to make one believe in—well, believe in *something*. It's such a tall tale, no one would believe it, even at the Cat n' Fiddle."

"All right." He drew her toward him, to kiss her forehead. "You are the best and the greatest. Try not to get yourself killed."

"You neither; we will meet up on Malta, when all is said and done, and take an inventory of Saba's fine dowry."

"I'll bring a trophy back from France; what would you like?"

She twinkled at him. "A lock o' hair—from the worthy Tauris, himself." Tauris being Napoleon's favorite horse.

"Done." After clasping Tahriz's hand, Jamie left to return to his sleeping bride.

With a happy sigh, Nonie settled in beside her husband again, and gazed up at the sky. "You'll have someone watching him, I suppose. I know you've already infiltrated the fishmongers, wretched man."

He did not disclaim, and was unrepentant. "The side with the best information will always prevail."

Shaking her head, she turned to meet his gaze. "I disagree, my friend. The side with the most money always wins. Which is why we're working so hard to make certain that the emperor's next go-round is a short-lived affair."

He tilted his head slightly. "I bow to your wisdom."

She eyed him. "I am always suspicious when you concede something."

"Don't be—before I met you, I had no idea how much I didn't know."

Wickedly, she teased, "And there's plenty more to come, staid-and-sober. Brace yourself."

"Willingly," he agreed, and kissed her soundly.

Made in United States
North Haven, CT
27 August 2022

23355637R00243